BALLS IN PLAY

Book Three from Stories in Glass

Paul S. Moore

Cover design copyright © 2020 by Niki Lenhart
nikilen-designs.com

Published by Water Dragon Publishing
waterdragonpublishing.com

ISBN 978-1-953469-69-4 (Trade Paperback)

FIRST EDITION

10 9 8 7 6 5 4 3 2

1

BILL ELLIOT'S STUDIO
APRIL 4, 2025

T HE MARBLE FLOOR IN BILL'S OLD STUDIO shined so brightly it was hard to remember it was once a bloody field of bagels and cantaloupes. Po made a few changes to the room, but she kept much of it just as it was on the night Bobby disappeared.

The panel on the wall was still dented, the wiring still exposed. The computer and vaporizer were still operational. Overhead, Icarus and the fliers of myth and fiction still spun slowly every time the air conditioner blew fresh air into the room.

On the desk, a single figurine of a glass angel replaced Bill's usual assortment of curios and artifacts. The caterer's cart was gone. The plug-in boards were packed away. Under the desk, Bill's refrigerator and Fax were unplugged.

Po came to the studio once a week, mopped the marble floor and climbed atop the desk to keep Bobby's art project free of dust. Every time she came to clean, she checked Bill's computer for email, always deleting, deleting, deleting. On April 3, 2025, she opened an email with the heading, *About Bobby*.

On this morning, one day after opening the email, Po wasn't in the room alone. The glass angel was joined on the desktop by a blue marble. Otis Beckley sat on the couch with his glow-in-the-dark shoes perched atop a footrest.

Po sat in Bill's chair. She barely took her eyes off the orb on the desk while recordings from the moon, and the narration at Harbinger played, It was dusk when the recording finished and Po announced she was going to call out for pizza.

"Hayak is with Roberta in St. Louis," she said. "Roberta is starting her freshman year at Washington University. They'll be back tomorrow. I'll order a medium. Is green pepper and onion okay?"

Otis recognized the bland manner in Po's voice. She was functioning in one zone, but thinking in another. "Perfect," he said, and waited for Po to place the order.

"It won't take long. They're right across the street, where the laundry used to be. Let's wait at the gate. We can discuss the future over pizza in the courtyard"

*　　　*　　　*

The big oak still towered over the park bench. "It's survived some big blows over the last twenty years," Po said. "Hurricanes have moved north with the climate change. We still call them Nor'easters."

Both of them sat on the bench without attempting small talk. After the silent interlude, Po broke the ice for discussing the issues surrounding Bobby's return. "It was right here, under the tree, where Robert first told me his name. I was so confused that night. I was worried about our baby."

"How is Roberta? What does she know about her father?" Otis was eager to learn how Bobby's return would affect the family.

Po pointed to the marble. "Is that thing recording?"

"It doesn't have to," Otis answered. He touched the marble and laid it at his feet. "Let's just talk."

"We home-schooled her," Po said proudly. "Hayak and I wanted to keep her protected, but she isn't one to allow herself to be sheltered. She signed herself up for softball and soccer in the public leagues when she was eight years old. I became a soccer mom.

"When she started making friends her own age, I pushed our talk about her father deeper into the future. Roberta was eleven years old when we told her everything. We had to. Things piled up. The laundry man told her she looked like her father. Her soccer coach asked her why her dad stopped doing his radio show. She collected our DNA and sent away for three DNA tests.

"One day, when I thought she was busy with Hayak in the basement, she popped in on me while I was dusting the studio and asked, 'Is this where my real father worked?' She set the DNA results on the desk and sat down in the big chair, next to the Bible. We told her everything, even played Asitr's radio appearance. Everything we knew at the time."

Otis groaned. "It must have been devastating."

"You don't know Roberta, Mr. Beckley." Po reached for Otis's hand and squeezed. "She asked us if we still believed her father would return. She wanted to know which of the books in the library he read. 'Not Bill, but my daddy,' she said. 'If he comes back, I want to know him a little.'

"The next day, she found his parents' burial plots on a grave-search website. 'I had to look,' she said. 'Sometimes people like to stand in front of a headstone to tell the dead they forgive them. They're buried next to each other. Weird, huh?'

"We haven't spoken about him since." Po craned her neck to look past the gate. "False alarm," she said. "The pizza guy wears shoes like yours, but that isn't him."

Otis watched the shoes as they made their way across the dark sidewalk in front of the gate. "Looks like glow worms playing leapfrog," he chuckled.

With the night deepening in the weak glow of a dim quarter moon, Po seemed to melt away in the shadows of the oak. Otis heard her breathing, but her facial features disappeared. He could see her profile. He heard her shiver. "Are you okay?" he asked her after a pause.

"I hope she can stay on course," Po sighed. "Her future's bright."

"How well does she get along with Hayak? Does she treat him like a father? I mean, does she respect him?"

Po laughed at the question. "They're buddies," she said. "They have a two-person ham radio club. They have a mail order import business together. Neither of them can carry a tune, but they go to karaoke on Friday nights. They're going to miss each other when she goes off to college."

"Wash U?" When he asked the question, headlights from the street flashed through the courtyard, and Otis glimpsed the smile on Po's face.

"Roberta had killer SATs," she said. "She chose Washington University for their accelerated political science program and sent them an essay on the role of mass media in crushing dialogue about new ideas and isms. She'll start there in the fall. Full ride. She and Hayak are touring the campus right now. She called yesterday and told me she discovered provel cheese and toasted ravioli."

Po stood up when she noticed the pizza guy crossing the street. "I'm her mom, but Hayak's a good buddy. I don't know how she'll react to a long-lost father with the mind of a child coming back into her life at this moment."

Otis stood up and reached for his ETM, but Po stopped him. "My treat Mr. Beckley, I'm done talking about Roberta for the moment. Over pizza, maybe you can tell me how you plan on getting rid of that devil in my basement before they get back from St. Louis."

2

EVICTING THE DEVIL

"IT'S POSSIBLE, OFFICER, that people haven't been so excited over a few sparks since Ben Franklin flew his kite." The electrician lifted his toolbox into the back of his van, while eyeing the parking ticket in the policeman's hand.

"People get excited when they lose their electricity, Mr. ..." The officer looked at his ticket.

"Chee." The electrician took the ticket from the officer's hand.

"This little reminder is just a warning. Obey the street signs. Just six feet forward, you would have been legal."

Mr. Chee lifted the last box off the pavement and wrapped it in a tarp. "I don't want to hear that squirrel rattling the box all the way to the park," he said. "After all the trouble he's caused, I'd sooner fly him straight to hell."

After wrapping the violently rattling box, and closing the door on the van, Chee tipped his hat to Po. "Thank you for the business, madam. We're never far away; we just can't always come when called."

"Bless you," Po said, "So happy to get rid of that big devil before something really bad happened."

On the passenger side of the van, Chee's assistant waved through the window.

"Thank you, too, Mr. Clary."

As the van pulled away from the curb, the officer asked, "You've used them before?"

"They were highly recommended."

"I thought I knew all the electricians operating around here." The policeman read the logo aloud as the van turned the corner:

Ol' Friend Chee.
I Ain't Lyin' When Sparks are Flyin' Call on Me

"To hear your neighbors tell it, sparks were shootin' to the moon around here this morning. I think they're more panicked than that squirrel in the transformer."

"Well it's all better now," Po said. "Thanks for your help." She turned to look at the bench under the oak tree and gave Otis a thumb up.

Under the tree, Otis smiled and lifted his marble off the bench. "One more stop," he said to himself. "Then vacation."

3

CLOUD SURFING

O TIS RELAXED IN THE COCKPIT and enjoyed his ride into a valley of puffed clouds. He surfed a white highway, hovering on the blue side of the cloud cover, cruising between titanic, cotton-like columns of cumulus. It was a good Thursday for a Sunday drive through the pillars of Valhalla.

Approaching the Andes, the cotton clouds wisped into thinning puffs of wet vapor, and Otis sat up straight, alerted by fleeting glimpses of the green beneath the *shem*. He knew he was getting close to his destination when his flying machine dove below the cover and skimmed above the trees along the banks of a stream in the Peruvian Amazon.

Otis knew he was hovering over Eden. He saw the bald knob below him. Scattered pieces of a helicopter skeleton stood out atop the rocky surface of the knob. A circle of limestone made a giant 'O' around where he hung in the air. A halo of green topped the cliffs.

Otis squinted through the cockpit window. Without further prompting, his flying machine slowly circumnavigated Eden. A closer look at the vines proved them to be poison ivy. He spotted a suit of armor, fifteenth-century Portuguese, lying in the vines outside the ring. On its inner side, he spied two skeletons, spottily covered in rotted, but modern, textile.

At the edge of the cliff, outside of Eden, two women washed clothes in the stream. Neither of them seemed to notice the shadow pass over them.

Inside the ring, Otis took a gliding tour of the former Savant home. He peered down the hole that was once a spring and decided to land.

His hike from the spring to the bald knob rewarded him with souvenirs: the metal form for an old army-issue Castro cap lying next to the bleached skeleton of a monkey. At the helicopter carcass, he collected shell casings from a 9mm pistol, a few Panamanian coins, and a headpiece of red feathers.

After kicking around in the bushes at the edge of the site, Otis found a mound of gravel. He dug through it with a stick until he unearthed a stitched corner from a piece of clothing he believed to be a seersucker robe.

While examining the helicopter remains, he fingered two small punctures in the gas tank and came to conclusions: The Weareus have a new chief, and all the pieces of a helicopter that can fit through Quetzacatls' door.

Otis shielded his eyes from the sun, scanned the ridge of the cliff where the two bodies in modern clothing reposed, and added another conclusion: Sam and Shori won a battle for the bird, but lost the war by attempting to climb out of Eden.

After returning to the *Shem*, Otis opened his vacation brochure and studied the layout of the resort. A mix of iconic Hollywood structures provided quirky accommodations for adventurous tourists willing to forego the pampered life for a few days of immersion into a familiar, but mysterious, world.

For all but the first week of each month, activities like movie night, weaving classes, fishing expeditions, and hiding games replaced the usual routine of the modern world.

For the homesick, the brochure suggested a night spent in a replica of the bar in the movie, *Casablanca*.

Huana's World
*Satellite TV *Not available in Rainy Season*
*Island-Brewed liquor *We Dare You*
Rickshaw Transport Back to Your Room is Available.

Otis knew he would be arriving early, after the *ayahuasca* ceremony, but before the first week's tourists.

Perfect, he thought. *A chance to speak with Huana before the other guests arrived.*

He climbed into the cockpit and shut his eyes. The *Shem* veered left and climbed upward, leveling off after heading east. Ahead, a rainbow bridged the dark blanket of green from horizon to horizon.

"Dorothy's rainbow," he gushed to his flying machine. "What did she leave behind for me to see on the island?"

4

BOBBY'S ROOM WITH A VIEW

DR. MILTON NEEDED A NEW PROCEDURE. His method of listening before analyzing wasn't going to work on a silent patient. He started his treatment program as soon as Bobby was lifted onto the bed in his room.

Jarvis threw open the window curtains and removed the blinds. Together, they unhooked the monitoring equipment, muscled the bed to the window, and worked the controls to elevate the patient's head, making it easy to view the meadow below.

"Keep an eye on the meadow, Bobby," the doctor suggested. "Try to understand what the changes mean for you. There's no skipping over childhood."

Predictably, Bobby didn't respond.

"We won't speak much, just yet, I'm leaving on a trip Friday, but I'll have news for you when I return. If you want to talk before then, Jarvis Douglas is the man for that."

Jarvis pushed a cart to the bedside with a water pitcher and glass. "You could start by giving me a heads-up about needing help to the restroom and such. I can bring you a bedpan, if your muscles ain't ready for walkin', but I'm not keen on surprises."

Bobby gave no indication he'd heard either of the men, but when Dr. Milton came by the room on Thursday, Jarvis told him the patient had been incontinent overnight, but cleaned himself up and removed his own soiled bedding. Afterward, he returned to his silent protest.

While Jarvis took his lunch break, the doctor observed Bobby from a chair set away from the window. In his notes, he wrote:

Patient follows with his eyes, the mowing, tilling, and measuring Mr. Fosdick is doing in the meadow.

When Jarvis returned, Dr. Milton had suggestions. 'When his meal gets here, don't try to feed him. Leave it in reach. Announce you'll be leaving him alone for half-hour periods. Do that several times a day. Make notations on his chart if he uses those opportunities to use the bathroom, or if he feeds himself while you're out of the room. Reinforce with the rest of the staff that they aren't to initiate conversation with him."

On Friday afternoon, after the budget meeting, Dr. Milton stopped by the meadow to let Fosdick know he could expect delivery of the fencing. "I want you to supervise the construction, but the fencing company will do the work."

The doctor rushed to his buggy and made two calls while riding to his waiting automobile. The first was to Jarvis. The news was good. Bobby ate and drank sparingly. The sound of a flushing toilet made Jarvis happy when he heard it from his chair in the hallway. "So far, so good," he reported. "Have a good trip."

The second call was to his wife. "I'm taking a self-driving Uber," he said. "I'll be on time."

*   *   *

Otis circled the island three times before he accepted that he was in the right place. The northern end of the island didn't have the features he expected. No heliport. No large beds of pineapple. Clusters of small homes, interspersed under cover of old jungle growth, bordered windmills facing east. Solar panels on the roofs of the houses surprised him.

On the southern shore, the town plaza had grown larger than Dorothy described. The ocean was close enough to the guesthouse to fit the brochure description as ocean-view lodging.

Skimming the trails, Otis found the warehouse, the tree house, and, at the end of the stream splitting the island, a peculiar structure built on stilts. Closer inspection jogged his memory. Atop the stilts was a replica of the schoolhouse from the show, *Little House on the Prairie.*

Pass after pass over the island led to a dilemma. The *Shem* was stealthy when it flew. On the ground, it was as easy to see as a statue. Otis came up with a plan after investigating the warehouse.

Where there was once a short trail leading from the boat dock, a swamp blocked travel. The larger trails leading to the old *agllawasi* area and the tree house were nearly overgrown. The warehouse roof was in a state of disrepair. Some steel panels were missing. A spire of vines in the back of the building gave evidence the tower was still there.

Otis guided the *Shem* into the palmetto field at the back of the warehouse and nestled it against the wall. When he landed, he popped the cockpit, stepped onto the craft, and reached for the tower. From the tower to the roof, then a leap to the ground, and Otis stood on the sand of the island.

Immediately after the thud of his feet finalized the transfer, Otis realized his mistake. "*Sheeshka Mushka,*" he cursed. "I left the marble in the *Shem!*"

Effort wasn't the problem. Otis tried hard to get back to the *Shem.* He first attempted to cut through the warehouse. When he threw open the door, rats skittered out of the light. The stacks of boxes between the door and window and the secret room threw enough shade against the wall that visibility was next to nil. Something ran across his shoe and brushed against his pant leg, but he persisted, groping the wall with his hands, searching for a device to open the hidden door. A noise from behind the wall stopped him. He put his ear to the wood for a better listen. A deep growl sent him rushing toward the light and out of the warehouse.

At the back side of the building, Otis discovered the same barriers Lockjaw had found: impenetrable palmetto and shrouds of vines. He didn't waste effort with an attempt to fight his way through to the *Shem*. Instead, he wasted effort on attempts to climb trees with branches overhanging the roof.

Sweaty and drained of energy, he decided to find his way to the main square, have an island-brewed beverage, and use his five days of reservations to procure a ladder. Huana, he decided, wouldn't need to hear his story on the marble to be helpful, but revealing the *Shem* was a serious violation of his usage agreement.

Relief was the overwhelming feeling that dominated Otis's mind when he stepped into the clearing and spotted the guest house. A man with a shovel walked toward him from the blacksmith's station, and a huddle of people at the cooking fire looked at him curiously, not vacantly. He took it as an encouraging sign.

When he regained consciousness in the *Casablanca* bar room, he recalled the reason for his headache. He was too slow to duck a well-aimed shovel.

*   *   *

For Dr. Milton, Saturday morning in the Big Apple was all about waking up late, luxuriating in the old familiar smell of Mom's French Toast and bacon.

Saturday afternoon was all about butting heads with Po.

"We're talking family here, Doctor, that's a trump card." Po presented her position firmly. "When Hayak and Roberta return, I'm going to tell them everything. It's the way we do it. We have room for Robert. He needs to know he's among loved ones. Roberta will want it that way, and Hayak will understand. Robert will trust my decision."

Dr. Milton eased into his argument gently. "Can we talk about this on the way to Bill's studio? I'd like to see Bobby's artwork."

On the way, he offered his diagnosis. "Robert is tangled up with multiple disorders: severe infantile regression, detachment issues after suffering from a psychotic break, and PTSD. The good news is also the bad news. Robert wants badly to be a father to his child. His need is strong enough to keep him fighting."

"And the bad news?" Po asked.

The bad side of that is the predictable failure outcome. Robert doesn't need to be set up to fail at the one thing that keeps him hopeful."

Po slowed her pace down the hallway, almost stopping. "Do you have a prognosis?"

"My prognosis is dependent on course of treatment." Dr. Milton stopped walking and waited for Po to turn toward him. When eye contact was achieved, he spelled his professional opinion out for her. "If Robert is immediately reunited with family, my prognosis is further regression and possible suicide. On the other hand, self-healing the scars from his psychotic break is unpredictable, and may be enhanced if reunited immediately."

Po hung her head and squeezed her eyes while considering the doctor's words. With his words weighed, she continued her slow pace down the hall. "So we can agree that an immediate reunion could give some instant relief from obsessing over bad memories?"

"It's the only potential positive in the instant reunification scenario."

"What are you suggesting then?" Po's voice cracked.

"With Robert under psychiatric care for a period of a year or more, the prognosis is positive for measurable maturity growth and self-image. Positive experiences should facilitate masking bad memories and lessen the tendency to obsess over them.

The hallway stroll ended at the door to Bill's studio. Po reached for the lock with key in hand, but she froze when Dr. Milton spoke his next words.

"I would like your support for my treatment plan, but I'm prepared to take it to the courts if I have to. I have the power word to be successful."

"'Power word'?" Po placed the key into the lock and turned the doorknob.

"Suicidal. The use of that word makes my legal position assured. Your petition for guardianship over a John Doe, with no connection other than paternity, doesn't make for ..." Dr. Milton reached toward the hand that held the key. "Your hand is shaking. Will you listen?"

"I am listening." Po pushed the door open, ignoring Milton's offer of consolation. "If I interfere, Robert and Roberta will suffer. You're very cruel."

"I believe there is something here bigger than family values." The doctor placed his hands in the prayer position, touched them to his lips and continued. "I have a personal opinion about what Otis and Asitr call a chain. I don't think the protection of Heaven failed because Asitr didn't eat raw garlic. I believe Bobby has yet to play his role in the chain."

Po's mouth worked like she had words waiting to emerge from her dry throat, but she deleted each one before they could scrape their way past her lips.

"I'm a link in the chain." The doctor said, suddenly. "My contribution may last only a few days, maybe a year, but the chain is still connecting. Asitr kept the links hooking up for more than seventy lives. Lockjaw bridged Asitr and Dorothy in just one lifetime. Otis may have a purpose, still, whatever it may be, but Robert is yet to play his role. He wants to play his role. If you shelter him now, he won't get the chance. Snap, clink, boom. The chain is broken. But, that's only my personal opinion," he said, slowly. "My professional opinion is what's important for the courts." Dr. Milton faced Po and spoke sternly. "In court, I'll fight with my professional voice, but you should know, the steel of my resolve is in my personal belief."

Po sidestepped, letting Dr. Milton enter the room first. "Quite a ceiling," she said, after flipping the lights.

The doctor stopped in the doorway and stared at the dangling fliers.

Po turned down the thermostat to force the air conditioner to blow. "Family knows best." she repeated mournfully, as if she knew her straw wasn't enough to float her hopes.

Above them, the ceiling came to life as cool air blew through the vents. "Do you see what he's done?" Dr. Milton spun under the display, head bent back, hands in pockets. "Kid stuff, kid stuff, kid stuff, then, oh no, it's Icarus. Poor Icarus, the cursed son. This is Bobby's voice, wrapped in art. Help me free him."

"You make it sound complicated." Po sat behind the desk. "It's simple: we'll love him, no matter what."

"Good, it's settled," Dr. Milton said. "We'll review the arrangement in one year."

"Wait. What's settled?" Po recoiled. "What did we agree to?"

"We agreed you would trust me with Bobby for one year. I agreed to return him to you as a young man."

"But, I'll have to keep Roberta and Hayak in the dark?" Po fidgeted with her fingers, looking uncomfortable in her chair.

"You can tell Hayak, if you trust him with the secret. We'll stay in touch."

5

FOREVER YOUNG

THAT EVENING, AFTER THE VALET DROVE THE CHEVY AWAY, Aileen Milton fixed her hair before going into the theater and told her husband, "I think I'm in love with our new car. On the way back, can we avoid the interstates? I want to take our time."

"We have the time, the right car for touring, and good weather ahead. I'll leave right now if you want to skip this musical."

"And miss the twelfth revival of *Peter Pan*? What do you have against kids staying kids forever?"

"The singing, Dear. Let's leave it at that. I'm in vacation mode."

6

I TRY TO BE CLEAR

OTIS OPENED HIS EYES to the sight of spinning ceiling fans, fuzzy in thinking and vision. Breathing in the odor of stale beer and cigarettes had the effect of smelling salts. He pulled himself up into a seated position when movement turned his attention to a woman leaning against a long, curved bar, cigarette in one hand, highball glass in the other.

"So, Dude, why are you here?" The woman sloshed her drink in a circle and watched the ice spin while waiting for an answer

Otis pulled himself up into a sitting position and glanced around the room before he answered. A middle-aged man, possibly a bartender, stared at him from behind the bar, his chin resting on his hands. A man in the doorway stared as well, his weight resting against the handle of the shovel that gave Otis his headache.

Something was off in the décor. The painted piano sat in the right spot. The curved bar and hookahs added legitimacy, and the ceiling fans looked right. The big-screen TV and wall hangings were out of place. The room itself was too small to replicate *Rick's Café Americain.*

Otis pulled his body onto a chair and moaned, "Why am I here? The question is getting old. Why greet me with a shovel to the face? I came to talk."

"To me? You want to talk to me?" The woman tossed her head back and poured the drink down her throat, catching an ice cube with the last drops. She bit down, and the sound of ice being crushed mingled with her words. "Hit me again with the ginger ale, Mr. Velas. Yes to the *Brain slap*; no to the ice."

Otis responded energetically to the bartender's name. "Velas! From movie night and ... and ..." His voice trailed off into uncomfortable silence. He rubbed his face before continuing. "Dorothy mentioned you. She says you came to the guesthouse when Mr. Wally ... You saw Dorothy on the day ..."

Velas stiffened, his mouth working into a sneer. "That was not me, *brujo*."

"I understand. Dorothy told me what happened." Otis extended an arm to the woman at the bar and turned his palm upward. "And you," he said, "Huana. I'm happy to know you survived the war. We need to talk."

On the last bar stool, behind the final curve of the counter top, in the shadow of a decorative pillar where Hollywood movie actors sat in secrecy while they monitored the comings and goings through the front door of the fictional Casablanca gin joint, a light flared. Otis turned his attention to the corner in time to see a silhouette appear in the light of an inhaled cigarette.

"You have me confused with my sister," a voice from the shadow said. "Caspi's the pretty one."

A face moved slowly into the light, a cigarette dangling from the lips and an eye patch over the left eye being the features that first stood out. A young woman in red sweatpants and a yellow T-shirt hopped off the bar stool and walked toward Otis. A large scar at the corner of her mouth and the offset slant of a poorly repaired broken nose made the threat of the large butcher knife in her hand feel very viable. "I'm Huana," she said coldly. "Would you prefer your tombstone to read Dead Bitch, or do you want to give me your name?"

"Otis Beckley. I'm Otis Beckley, I have reservations."

Velas answered, "We don't have a Beckley coming."

"I'm listed as Milton. His secretary was going to call."

Caspi laughed. "That information would be handled on the mainland, at the dock. You're two days early. How did you get here without taking the boat?"

"I'm a friend of Mr. Lockjaw. I came to talk."

"Did you know Willa? Was she your friend?" Huana ran her finger over the blade of the knife. "Where did you beach your boat, Mr. Beckley/Milton?"

"I don't have a boat."

"Yep. He's one of them," Velas drawled. "Want me to set up for video or just dump him in the swamp?

Huana walked to Velas and set the knife on the bar. "Set up the video equipment," she said. "Splice the acetaminophen discussion from Mr. Wally's flash drive onto the execution video and upload it from Sam's laptop. They'll get the message."

"Otis slumped in his chair. Mention of an execution video sent his mind scrambling to find a new approach. "Test me. I can tell you things the X-Club doesn't know. Your last words to Dorothy: 'Fist pump, Dude. I'll see you at the spring.'

"I know you helped bury the shiny beast near the helicopter crash. I can show you which of the wall hangings in the bar were made by Dorothy. I think I'm here to finish her work."

Like a projector freezing on a frame, the silence in the room seemed to wrap around the frozen movement. The people around Otis held tight to their place in the room and gave no indication they even breathed. The stillness lingered until the ash from Huana's cigarette fell to the floor and she asked, "What was my intelligence report on the day we knew we were at war?"

Otis searched his memory. "I don't have the mind of a Savant, so pardon me if I don't get it word for word, but you reported that Lock and Willa were dead, you wet your pants, Caspi was going to be raped, Dorothy was going to be dissected like a frog, and everyone was going to die. Close enough?"

Caspi and Velas looked toward Huana. Otis glanced toward the door and noticed the man with the shovel leaning toward her as well. It was clear that only Huana knew if he'd given the right answer. Smiling in relief, he felt confident enough to add a phrase Huana would be familiar with. "I try to be clear."

7

GOOD NEWS / BAD NEWS

A S SOON AS JARVIS DOUGLAS LEFT the office of the angry Dr. Abrams, he called Dr. Milton. It was noon in New York; late morning in Lawrence.

Dr. Milton took the call and excused himself from the good-bye hugs at his mother's front door.

Behind him, Doris presented Aileen with her old riding scarf for the ride back to Kansas.

"I'm glad I got one more trip down memory lane before you drove the old jalopy away," she said. "It's been awhile since I've been in the back seat." After a beat, she blushed. "Oh! I didn't mean it that way."

The two girls' laughter tapered off into smiles and they hugged. "I love the old thing. It will be well cared for," Aileen promised.

"Henry? Or the car?" Doris asked, mischievously.

Both women turned to look at Dr. Milton, on the lawn, phone to his ear. His face said the call brought good news. "Throw that damned phone out the window as soon as you hit the open road," Doris whispered. "You're on vacation."

"Finally," Aileen sighed. "Something always seems to … uh oh."

The big happy grin on the doctor's face wrinkled into a look of concern, then a scowl. "You tell that pompous son of a bitch he doesn't have access to my patient. No, wait." Dr. Milton pulled the phone to his chest and closed his eyes. His body heaved after one long inhalation and, when he reopened his eyes, he gave the two women in the doorway a long look of helpless resignation.

"Tell Dr. Abrams I'm flying in tonight. Put a quarantine sign on the door if you have to, I don't want him near Bobby. Tell Bobby I'm coming back early with good news and some presents. Yes. Thanks, Jarvis … Tell Abrams to trust me."

If you were a stranger, and no student of body language, the silent scene in Doris Milton's front yard wouldn't need interpretation. Both women wore the same pose: each put a hand to her hip, cocked her head to one side, and glowered with the power of dark magic eye beams. Only the differences in ages separated the messages. The older woman was saying: *You've been a very bad boy*. The younger woman had a simpler message: *Asshole*.

The intrepid doctor plowed ahead. "I need to book a flight out of town today, and I need to find a sporting goods store on the way to the airport." It wasn't until he wilted under their gaze that he hung his head and added in a sheepish voice, "Aw, c'mon. One year. I have to. Trust me?"

8

PETRIFYING THE *SHEM*

O TIS WAS SHOWN TO THE GUESTHOUSE. The steps to the porch still squeaked, igniting his memory of Dorothy's island tales. Standing in the doorway, he turned around to take in the view. The blacksmith station, the water tower, the big house where the *ayahuasca* ceremonies were held slipped easily into the mental slots where Otis imagined Lockjaw's last days. He glanced at the floor by the door frame and imagined Willa, pulling herself tight against the wall to escape Waldo's view. The table where the three of them had dined and made plans together was just as he imagined. The French press coffee maker sat next to the stove.

As if Huana understood his immersion in putting the scene into focus, she waited before interrupting his thoughts. "This is the palm plant where Dorothy snooped with her ears."

Otis turned to look and huffed a laugh. "Right next to the lounger?"

"She was really good at the hiding game." Huana walked to the closet and opened the door. "Best seat in the house for watching nightmares," she said, and shut the door again softly, as if not to disturb the ghosts. "We don't rent this place out to tourists, but we let them gather on the porch for movie night."

"May I?" Otis put a hand on a chair next to the table. "I want to know what happened after Sam and Shori left on the helicopter."

Huana chose a chair across from Otis and motioned for him to sit, then turned to the porch and motioned for Caspi and Velas to join them.

Velas inserted a dart into a long tube and tapped it against his palm. "I'll stand," he said humorlessly and leaned against the wall.

"I gotta go feed my badger," Caspi said, and bounced down the stairs, missing the squeaky spots.

"A badger?" Otis asked the question reflexively, out of surprise.

"We were going to build a zoo. That was before we realized the island was sinking. Caspi thinks it's Dorothy's head spirit, but she doesn't remember the real Dorothy. We're going to send it back to New York before we move."

"New York?"

Huana tilted her head and curled one side of her lip while reaching a finger underneath her eye patch to scratch. "Yeah, New York. We do business with a family there. We send fish, and they find stuff. Caspi got a little ahead of herself with the badger."

"I'm not even gonna try," Otis moaned. "I think I understand how Lock felt the whole time he was on this island. Confusion reigns. How about you tell me how you won the war?"

"You first, Mr. Beckley/Milton. How do you know things only Dorothy could have told you?"

"… told you after she was dead," Velas added pointedly, disdain dripping from his voice.

Otis squirmed in his chair and shut his eyes. "I don't know how to explain this. I have to go get a recording device, but I have to go alone … and I need a ladder."

"I told you he was one of them," Velas said. "Don't let him get away."

"Where do you need to go and why do you need a ladder?"

Huana stared at Otis with her one good eye and held a palm out toward Velas, as if to tell him to wait. The fingers of her other hand tapped on the table, getting louder and heavier with each moment no explanation came to her questions.

"The warehouse," Otis said suddenly. "Trust me?"

A dart thudded into the table, missing Otis's hand by six inches.

"Oops," Velas said. "I was trying to get a little closer."

Otis watched him reload and turned to Huana. Her fingers once again drummed on the table. Her eye, unflinching in its steady stare, broke him down.

"I have a marble," he said. I got it from an angel on the moon. Dorothy was with me. You can hear her voice. It records everything. If you let me get it, I'll play it for you."

"Tell me where it is, we'll go with you." Huana's eye bore, unblinking, and her fingers continued to drum.

"It's not … it's not that easy," Otis stammered. Another dart thudded two inches from his fidgeting fingers. "I have a pact, a user agreement. I came here in a flying vehicle. If I let anyone see it, it won't work anymore."

A sharp pain in the neck caused Otis to slap his hand against the side of his face, but the area was already numb. Huana barked sharply at Velas, while the curare spread rapidly down Otis's body and he began to slump.

"Dude!" she said angrily, "What up with that? I wasn't done with him."

Otis slumped off his chair and hit the floor, aware of the sound of his own heartbeat and the words being spoken in the room.

It didn't take long for Otis to realize that breathing had stopped and struggle was impossible. He knew enough about curare to know he would live, when Velas strapped a breathing device to his face and pumped air in and out of his lungs.

"The *brujo* thinks we're idiots. We'll get better answers when we bring him back," he said.

Hours of helplessness and awareness passed, before his body recovered. Of all the talk he heard in that time, two things affected him the most.

Huana remarked that he was lying on a rug that covered the blood stain from Willa's kill shot. While Willa's horror came without hope for dignity or life, it did end quickly with the squeeze of Sam's finger on the trigger. He realized Huana and Velas, standing over his body, were justified in their suspicion of him. His earlier calculations about these survivors' emotions had none of the accuracy of his calculations with numbers.

The other powerful realization came when Caspi came back from feeding her badger. Now he understood the low growl he'd heard coming from the secret room.

"There's a weird sculpture behind the warehouse," she said. "It looks like Flash Gordon's spaceship."

Now, he knew he needed to come up with a new dialogue, but his mind kept short circuiting over an intruding question.

"How do I get the marble out of a petrified *shem*?"

9

PLAY BALL!

D R. MILTON KNEW HE WAS PLANNING to break his own personal protocols against revolutionary acts, but those protocols were in place for a reason. Long ago, he realized futile acts of rage against the machine were counterproductive. Production in his chosen field, in his estimation, was measured by staying true to one unwavering personal principle: *One man. One mind.*

In Milton's professional opinion, his master, who believed himself to be his mentor, Dr. Abrams, would not be swayed by the argument, *Do no harm.* Pompous, empty platitudes may be the armored hide of his institution's administrator, but at his core, love of money ruled his spirit, shouted sweet nothings to his id, blinded his ego, and strangled his super ego. Buried so deep in Abrams's psyche that he couldn't see it in the shattered shards of shade in his mind, was his fatal mental illness. Long ago, Abrams's defect grabbed him by his man parts, and kicked his spirit to the nether regions of unreachable mania. It was the disease that made him successful in the short life.

Perhaps, a week ago, Dr. Milton would have folded his tent and said, "Next patient, please." That was before he realized he was a link in a chain made in Heaven. On the flight back to Lawrence, the doctor struggled to find a plan with a chance of success. He should have relaxed and enjoyed the ride. Help was coming because of a traditional gathering in the rec room of the Sylvan building, and from the mind of a man Milton was helping to heal.

Because the well-appointed private rooms of the Sylvan building were the most therapeutic areas for the celebrities, pro athletes, and market makers of Wall Street who sought refuge at the institution, the tiny rec room was hardly ever utilized. Organized activities, like bingo and aerobics, never took place.

On April 7, 2025, residents and staff were enjoying an exception to that norm. They gathered for a party. A seafood buffet, with a salad and sushi bar, along with the traditional hot dogs, peanuts, and Cracker Jack, were provided for the celebration of baseball's opening day.

Liquor and drugs were forbidden. It was a hard and fast rule, punishable by *permanent* expulsion from the institution. When, in the past, this rule was ignored, Dr. Abrams showed he was serious about the ban. Along with expulsion, permanent until new financial arrangements could be made, he added a clause in the user agreement. Liquor and drug use in the rec. room would be considered a negation of privacy guarantees, and the names of the violators would be published

With the exception of the recording industry and Hollywood tribes in the Sylvan cocoon, the privacy-stripping threat was effective. Those fading celebrities, like Ms. Hoopla earlier in the week, used the publicity as career therapy. For the rest of the residents, they restricted drug usage to their private rooms, using their lawyers to mule their favorite recreational choices into the building.

In short, the Sylvan was the monetary center of off-the-books profit for the entire institute. It was Dr. Abrams's pet project, and he wasn't going to fool around with a John Doe occupying a profitable space.

When Nurse Rishard contacted him with information that Dr. Milton had altered his budget to squeeze out an indoor swimming pool in favor of building a baseball field in the meadow, he was angry. Further news about a John Doe in the Hoopla room made him furious. He cut his working vacation short in order to come home and lay down the law to his suddenly independent underling.

On April 6, while Dr. Milton was still in the air, on his way to protect his patient, all of Abrams's issues were resolved in a meeting with Jarvis Douglas and a celebrity resident named Freddy McPheeters.

The resolution of issues didn't prohibit the central characters from becoming grist for the mill of Sylvan gossip. So, before the first pitch was thrown out, on April 7, conversation in the recreation room batted back and forth between two different topics.

Everyone wanted to know who the new patient was in Hoopla's room. It was mysterious. The TV, wet bar, entertainment center, canopied bed, and fish tanks were all removed. Medical monitoring equipment replaced them. A man was wheeled in, seemingly comatose, in a standard medical bed. Nobody recognized him. The conclusion of the group was, "He's replaced *Da Bum* as the most reclusive man in the building."

Da Bum was the second topic of pregame conversation.

Da Bum began life in the town of Malden, Missouri. He became famous among his school mates in third grade for being the only kid outside of sixth grader Bruce Fore capable of hitting a softball all the way from home plate to the teeter totters. Legend said he once plunked one off the jungle gym, but it was a playground myth, started after he graduated to junior high.

The first time Freddy hit the concrete between the ball field and the playground on the other side, he got a name change. Before that majestic moment, he was Freddy McPheeters. By the time he stepped on home plate, he was *Big Dog*.

To Cub Scout pack 346, in Sikeston, Missouri, he was *Freddy Krueger,* after launching one over the fence and bouncing it off Elm Street — the road that paralleled right field. After he broke the window of a parked car to win the tournament finale, he became *The Nightmare on Elm Street.*

In junior high, he reverted to *Big Dog,* after growing to six feet tall and adding muscle to his big-boned frame.

In high school, Coach insisted on the nickname *Backdraft,* after his catcher repeatedly had to rearrange his mask after reflexively jerking his head away from Freddy's long, quick, powerful swing.

In American Legion ball, he picked up the name *Bomber.* For a while, it stuck.

In 2023, at the age of eighteen, he signed a contract with the Mexican expansion team, *The Baja Bombers.* From there, it was all downhill for both the team and Freddy.

Even though, like most other pro stadium locations in the league, tax dollars built the facility, and ticket prices excluded the majority of the tax payers, the owner boasted, "I built this beautifullest in the world arena and made Mexico pay for it."

Although many of the wealthy Americans who retired to Baja praised the owner's business acumen for the massive profit he made in the bankruptcy, the facility celebrated the old American past-time for one very brief and controversial year. As usual, the victim was blamed for the failure.

Freddy McPheeters was the victim.

Freddy barely got his cleats wet in low A-ball when ownership chose to make him the face of the franchise. "We're *The Bombers,* he's *The Bomber.* He will take us to the World Series in the first year. I know it. You know it. Everyone knows it. What more can you ask?"

Scouts and experts tried to provide answers to the question. "Footwork," they said.

"I've already fixed that problem," the boss replied. "Dance instructors are on the way." It was part of the master plan for making baseball fun again. Choreographed celebrations were requirements in Freddie's trend setting half-billion-dollar, four-year contract.

"Repetition with quality pitchers," the experts added.

"Wrong. So wrong. So, so wrong. So very wrong. Our world-class batting cage throws fast. Very fast. Nobody can believe how fast," the owner tweeted.

"Work on shortening the swing," the experts insisted.

"I know more about baseball than the professionals do. Sad. Very sad." It became apparent the boss couldn't be swayed from promoting the green teenager.

"Kiss Abner Doubleday's dead wrinkled ass," his three-time World Series winning manager told him.

"You're fired," came the predictable response. Professional wrestling promoter Vladmir "The Cossak Impaler" Bendovrankov, replaced him.

In the boss's tweets, the record low turnout for games had nothing to do with his touting of the all-North American player team, the all-Mexican ground crew, dressed in serapes, or the failure to show off the Mexican hat-dance routine that had been choreographed for each home run the boss promised. "*The Bomber* will mash, like nobody you've ever seen," he tweeted after a dry April.

In July, when the bat boy never had occasion to drop the golden sombrero on top of home plate, and the mariachi band never had occasion to take the field for the home-run celebration, the Twitter community was treated with Freddy's new nicknames. *The Bomber,* became *The Bummer*, then finally, in September, *Da Bum.*

Freddy offered to donate his after-tax salary to a project for funding the building and maintenance of ball fields, where uniforms, fees, and structured scheduling didn't override the sandlot chemistry of childhood.

The boss's response, via news conference, was, "I'm suing for every penny."

Freddy's response wasn't original. "Kiss Abner Doubleday's dead wrinkled ass," he said.

The next day, he checked himself in to Harbinger, with symptoms of a nervous breakdown.

"Don't let an emperor with no clothes get to you," Dr. Milton told him.

"I don't givea damn about that empty suit," Freddy responded. "I'm crushed by my loss of love for the game."

Freddy took his final step back to love for the game when he recognized the diamond pattern Fosdick was making in the meadow and he asked, "What's up?"

Fosdick pointed to the man at the window on the third floor and said, "Doc thinks the kid needs to play ball."

For Freddy, the idea was a hit. It felt like an off-the-wall idea. A double. He slid into third base when he got the details from Jarvis.

Freddy McPheeters stole home when he and Jarvis met with Dr. Abrams and promised to build a swimming pool and finance the Hoopla room for one year if he didn't interfere with Dr. Milton's project.

"Don't tell the kid who I am," Freddy told Milton when he arrived. "I don't need to do no Mexican hat dance. Let's just play ball."

10

FISHY BUSINESS

NOBODY EVER DOUBTED PO'S ABILITY TO ORGANIZE. On April 6th, she had her hands full. Hayak and Roberta had just returned from their visit to St. Louis. Plans and connections were securely in place for a transition between a campus visit for two and a vacation for three.

Bags were packed, passports were updated, and a mix-up with fish orders was resolved. Even though Hayak kept the location for their vacation a secret, she felt ready.

It's tropical," he told her. "Expect a beach and unusual accommodations."

Only the organization of secrets was left unsettled in her mind. She waited by the gate, under her oak tree, for her loved ones to arrive home. Worries over Hayak's secret beach adventure didn't concern her thoughts beyond the little chill she felt to hear the refrain, "It's tropical." The same two words Lockjaw heard before grabbing his prepacked bags for an adventure to a lost world in the Amazon.

Po brushed those chills aside and mentally rehearsed how she would tell Hayak that Bobby was back, he couldn't be contacted for a year, and Roberta couldn't be told.

Having to conjure trips down memory lane from another period of her life was intrusive and difficult. Thoughts crowded together; past and present felt like equal parts of déjà vu. Po felt like the nervous woman at the window, watching ant-men, putting clues together, and worrying about her baby. A car pulled up to the gate, and she pushed it all to the back of her mind. Two-thirds of her family was home.

Roberta bounded through the gate and hugged her mom. "I already made friends," she bubbled. "They call me Berti. They'll be back after the summer break. I met one of my professors. He's a schmuck, but it'll be okay."

"Tell your mother what your professor said about your plan for the inter-collegiate *Ideas Conference*," Hayak interjected.

"He said I could never get more than three people together who could accept a political landscape without demolicans and republicrats. He thinks everyone's stuck on believing in that wasted-vote phobia. I told him I thought we were better than that. I said the popular belief is that it's stupid to waste your vote, but I believed it was the definition of insanity to keep doing the same things over and over and expecting a different outcome."

"She told him she'd rather be stupid than crazy," Hayak deadpanned, with a smile.

Willa shivered, recalling the same sentiment in Lockjaw's rant to Po. "And, how did he respond?" she asked.

"He said I was ahead of schedule. I was just starting my freshman year and already I was hopelessly sophomoric. I told you he was a schmuck, but that's okay. I don't expect the elite to come up with new ideas, but their education infrastructure could become useful."

"Roberta?"

"Yes, Mom?"

"Can we talk about this tomorrow, when we're on the beach and you've calmed down? I have a headache."

"Sure, mom, I know I'm all hyper. It's just so cool. I'll make dinner and you relax."

After Roberta went into the house, Hayak hugged Po and whispered in her ear, "What's wrong?"

"Everything's just ..." She hugged him tight without finishing. "I talked to your people in Panama about a mix-up with the Corvina orders. Is Caspi a common name? I feel like Lockjaw is trying to tell me something, like what he said on the radio about Asitr's story. It all starts at one source, breaks apart into little channels and rejoins to spill into a dark hole of uncertainty. Anyway, she asked if you found a home for her badger. It's all just *bump, bump, bump.*"

Hayak put his hand to Po's head to check for fever. "Should we cancel the trip?"

"Absolutely not," Po said with resolve. "We'll talk this out on the beach."

11

TRUST ISSUES

OTIS WALKED IN CIRCLES AROUND THE TABLE in the guest house, enjoying the use of his legs after two decades in a box and several hours of curare.

"That's how I got here," he said after he stopped walking. "It's the short version, but it's all true."

Huana leaned forward and set her glass of iced tea on the table. "Sit down and relax, Mr. Otis." She looked over her shoulder at Velas and back to Otis. "Velas will put his darts away."

"Then you believe me." Otis said the words with conviction, and he sat across from Huana, ready to discuss his agenda. "Can we discuss the *quipus*? I'd like to see all of Dorothy's patches from the looms."

"There's something better," Huana said. "Velas, do you have Dorothy's papers in the order she stacked them?"

"I can rearrange them quickly."

"Bring them here and you can show Mr. Otis what you've found."

Huana waited for the squeak on the stairs, and then she drained the iced tea from her glass. "There goes the best engineer you'll ever know," she said, pointing a thumb toward the door behind her. "Don't underestimate him, dude. He's bad-ass."

"I won't," Otis said, rubbing a hand across the pinhole in his neck. "Is he the brains behind all the construction on the island?"

"He knows how to get things done. Caspi runs the island business. I run the school. For now, our campfire is the governing body."

"For now?"

"After we weaned ourselves from Mr. Wally's *ayahuasca* additives, we got in touch with our spirits again. We had a baby boom. On top of that, our world got smaller. We have to look ahead before we're trapped in place and stuck in a rut. I have a mandate to act as the military leader and head the search for a new home. After the move, we're going to need a new government structure."

Huana wiped the water off her glass with her hands and dried them on her sweatpants. "I'm uncomfortable telling you about our ideas for the future. Our top priority is getting off our island and disappearing to somewhere safe. Our second priority is to figure out the *quipu* mysteries. We have to leave the X-Club in the dark about both."

"I'm happy you trust me to help with the *quipus*." Otis grinned.

"Dude, don't make me say things that will make Confucius beat me with a stick. *Quipus* are the second priority. I don't trust you. I want your help."

In spite of the eye patch, Huana's famous stare had lost none of its ability to unnerve. Otis stiffened in his chair, but responded confidently. "I didn't come back from the moon to fail. We need each other."

"Our war isn't over. It's too early to trust."

"Your enemy knows how you saved the island and sent Mr. Wally to his private hell. I don't. Will you share with me?" Otis went to the fridge and removed a bottle of water. "May I?"

For the first time since he met Huana, she laughed, and Otis could picture the giggling girl that Dorothy had bonded with. "I'll tell you my war stories, but you may want to wait before you drink that water, Mr. Otis."

Otis paused before twisting the cap. "Trust," he said, raising the bottle in a toast. "Go ahead, I'm listening. I know you sabotaged Sam's helicopter. How did you deal with Waldo Kurtwood?"

"He did it to himself." Huana's lip quivered and she gasped a sudden breath. Her lips pulled tight to her teeth before she opened her mouth to take a long, purposeful breath. "I thought she would send those monsters to hell." She spat the words like her anger was fresh. "We both did our duty, but she didn't live to see the tribe come back to life."

"She's happy now, Huana. I don't know what goes on in Heaven, but I'd say she's proud of you." Otis took another drink from the bottle and watched Huana's body relax as her tensions eased.

With a quietness in her tone, Huana began to recite the events that followed her last contact with Dorothy. She focused her eye on the empty glass in front of her and started speaking so softly that Otis leaned forward to hear.

"I went to the warehouse to dump Mr. Wally's drugs out. I didn't know which ones would kill my tribe, so my plan was to pour them all out on the floor. On the way, I couldn't stop thinking I should go back and try to save Dorothy. At the dock where the *Wally K* was tied, I stopped like I'd run into a wall.

"Big shiny shoes, funny-looking things, weird-colored things, where scattered around. A bright green pile of hair was bobbing in the waves. I thought, maybe this is important intelligence for the war. When I looked in the boat, I saw the big plastic bag, and I knew it was Willa.

"I wanted to do something, but I couldn't. I couldn't cry, or scream, or think. That's when I asked myself, *What would Dorothy do?*

"She would be smart, not dump all the poison out and let them know to get more. I ran to the warehouse and gathered the empty water bottles. As fast as I could, I filled the bottles with all of Mr. Wally's poisons. Then, I screwed the caps on real tight and placed the bottles in the refrigerator."

Otis brought his water bottle up to his lips, furtively sniffing the liquid before taking another drink.

'I put all the little empty vials in the pillowcase and ran to the river, where I washed them out and refilled them with water. I almost didn't get back in time

"I was still putting the vials into the fridge when I heard the warehouse door close. When the secret door opened, I was behind the curtain, shivering and panting.

"I was heard. The refrigerator door opened and Mr. Wally asked, 'Should I get us both a bottle?'

"I ran through the curtain, toward the door, but he grabbed my arm and spun me into the wall. He kicked me in the face when I fell to the floor. He kicked so hard it made me dizzy.

"The face of a different Mr. Wally pushed close to mine. It was scratched-up and swollen. One eye was red where it should be white. A napkin was taped over one cheek. 'Hu haw-w-w,' he whispered, creepy-like, while he hovered over me, moving his head like a snake scanning a rat, his body still, his head dipping and tilting back and forth. 'You're a young thing' he said. 'Too young to die, but what can I do?'

"He kicked me again. 'We should get along better. You have a certain animal attraction.' He put his foot on my neck and unscrewed the cap from his water bottle. 'You don't know where I could find the *Silver Book*, do you?' He answered his own question after taking a long drink. 'Of course you don't.'

"Suddenly, he stepped away from me and stumbled. He fell on his back and slapped at his injured eye until he went stiff and still.

"I thought he was dead. On the way back to the guest house, I heard Sam's helicopter leave. I thought the war was over."

"But it isn't, is it?" Otis took another drink from his water bottle and leaned his chair back on two legs. "Wally might have scarred your face and taken one of your eyes, but if you saw him now, you would know you got the best of it."

Huana jerked her head and narrowed her eye, looking at Otis like she was surprised and insulted. "Dude, for real, what up with that stupid stuff? Mr. Wally is a punk. Caspi's badger gave me this face job a year ago."

"Caspi's badger?"

"Sometime you're an innocent victim. Next time you're just kind of asking for it. On *ayahuasca* night, Caspi told me she thought the badger was Dorothy's head spirit and I got all mushy and stupid. I didn't follow the rules of the ceremony. I went to the warehouse and tried to give the badger a hug. Badgers don't do hugs."

Otis put his chair back on its four legs and stared, open mouthed, until he could think of something to say. "Well, I guess I don't know how a mind reacts to some things. You must have gotten to a hospital really fast."

"We have a good Shaman. She's training more of us." After an uncomfortable pause, Huana added, "I didn't ask the shaman to help Mr. Wally. When we found out he was alive, I tied him up in the secret room and left him alone with the rats. They chewed his ankles and died by the dozens. Mr. Wally was better than peanut butter.

"I was happy to let him die, until we found out from his computer how to talk to the X-Club. We told them he knew how to find the *Silver Book*. They gave us papers that say we own our island, and we gave them Mr. Wally. From what you tell me, his people aren't doing him much good either."

"They just want to ..." The squeaking stair interrupted. When Velas walked through the door carrying a stack of papers, Huana finished. "They only want to know about the *Silver Book*."

"Silver, silver, silver. Hu haw silver. Why don't they want to know about the blue?" Velas grumbled, as he plopped his stack of papers on the table. "The *Blue Codex* is what Dorothy was interested in."

"The *Blue Codex*?" Otis reached for the stack, but Huana slapped his hand and he pulled it back.

"Don't look so puzzled until you know what's puzzling you, Dude. Let Velas tell you what he knows."

Velas didn't wait. "We showed the Caral *quipu* photos from Wally's computer to *quipucamayacs* from many tribes. All of them said the same thing. They can read numbers and resources for trading, but those things are scattered randomly on the *quipu*. They say it is incoherent rambling and accidental *knotsense*.

"You should know that what we are calling a *book* is actually translated as a *codex* — or book of science. The *quipu* mentions a silver and blue codex. Most codex were burned by the Spanish and Portuguese during their *conquistador* invasions. They said the science in them was heretical.

"Dorothy found organization in the chaos of the *quipu*. We don't know how she found it. We don't know what she found. This is her work." Velas patted the stack of papers. "She told Huana to save these, in this order, moments before she went to war for us. They are important enough to protect with our life. They are important enough to make you cold and dead — or worse. We have darts tipped in the Mr. Wally poisons. That will be for you if you have fooled us."

Huana stood and placed her chair under the table. "I have work to do at the school. Guests are coming tomorrow, and, Mr. Otis? We are good at the hiding game. Don't think I'm leaving you alone with Velas and the papers."

On the way out, Huana hopped from side to side on the stairs, avoiding the squeaks.

12

IF YOU BUILD IT …

AFTER THE SURPRISE OF A PLEASANT MEETING with Dr. Abrams, Dr. Milton whistled happy tunes. It was almost noon and the air felt almost warm. Redbuds and dogwoods were in bloom. Jonquils were giving way to freshly budding rows of tulips along the walkway to the Sylvan Building. Across the street, on the small bench half-way between home plate and first base, Freddy McPheeters sat, bouncing a tennis ball and catching it in his glove, waiting for someone to show up and play.

As the buggy carrying Dr. Milton came to a stop in front of the building, a sudden gust of wind briefly conjured a dust devil behind the pitcher's mound. It was opening day for sandlot fun at Harbinger Institute.

Inside the building, in the rec room, the national anthem boomed from the big-screen television as Dr. Milton pressed the elevator button for the third floor. By the time he entered Bobby's room, the rec room gathering was discussing the lineup for the day's festivities. To the delight of both the home crowd and the fans of the visiting team, both pitcher and leadoff hitter had signed just in time. With the extra years and millions agreed to, the first pitch, thrown with serious intent, was on the way.

The batter would decide how opening day would begin. A crack of the bat, a whiff of air, a called ball, a called strike, even a hit-by-pitch, were possibilities. Anything could happen. The crowd would cheer, no matter what the first pitch brought. It was game-on.

On the third floor, Bobby McKinney stood at his window, watching the lonely man below bounce his fuzzy green ball. When Dr. Milton walked into the room, bat, glove, and bag of balls in hand, negotiations began. The contract was agreed to. Six months of childhood, followed by an unspecified time of adult therapy, culminating in Bobby's induction into the hall of fatherhood.

While changing from his hospital gown into street clothes, Bobby told the doctor he accepted that Po had married another man. He told him he was happy for her. He added, "I appreciate that you understand how I don't want my child to think of me as her crazy little brother. I'm going to make this work."

*   *   *

On the field, Bobby approached Freddy. In unison, they nodded to the other and said, "Hey."

"Wanna play?" Freddy asked.

"Yeah, sure," Bobby answered. "Play what?"

"I don't know. Catch? Or we can practice grounders. If you let one get by, it's a base hit. Catch it and it's an out. Three outs, then you bat."

"No fair if you hit it too far away to catch."

Freddy walked into the field and placed his glove between second and third base. "You have to hit it between second base and the glove, or it's an out."

"Okay, but we do *handsies* to decide who goes first."

"Fine, but no *bottle caps.*

"Okay, but no fair spreading your fingers."

"Who do you think I am, O.J.?"

"You're funny. I'm Bobby."

"Freddy."

Freddy McPheeters tossed the bat straight up and Bobby McKinney caught it above the pine tar line, and then, taking turns, they placed one hand above the other until there was no place left to hold on to.

"You bat first," Bobby said, and he ran out on the field.

With fresh chalk to mark the foul lines, and rules to judge what's fair between them, Freddy tossed his first pitch up in the air and hit a hopper to Bobby. He muffed it, trying to catch it as he retreated. What else would you expect from his first grounder? Both players laughed.

"You have to charge the ball," Freddy advised.

It was game-on.

13

THE BLUE CODEX

T HE FIRST DISAPPOINTMENT FOR OTIS in his discussions with Velas
was the answer to his request for access to the golden beast.
"It can't be done," Velas answered. "We melted it."

"Explain that, please?" Otis flushed at the thought of losing the
record on the bull's face. It was like smashing half the Rosetta stone.

"We needed money. After gold was discovered on our lands
in Peru, we learned the value to those who want to own it. We
made gold bars out of the beast and sought out partners who
would trade with us. Caspi used the ham radio in the warehouse
and found someone in New York."

Velas pulled a coin from his pocket and placed it on the table.
On its face, a pineapple, bathed in beams of light from a
rising/setting sun, floated above the date: 2007. On the reverse, a
fat-headed corvina leaped over the word *ESPIRITU*.

"We sell the coins as commemorative, limited edition rarities.
Our new business partners told us. 'For the gold bars, you could get
a fine fishing vessel and have money left over. If you made coins,
you could have a fishing vessel, windmills for electricity, equipment

to package the fish, and material for permanent housing. Still, after you accomplished all of that, you would have money left over.'

"We called a campfire. Caspi told us she had read these words: *If you give a man a fish, he will eat for a day. If you teach a man to fish, he will eat for the rest of his life.* She suggested it would be wise to partner with people who teach us to see the advantages in selling a man his fish, 'They are telling us we can sell a man his fish and we will eat and profit for the rest of our lives.'

"It was an easy decision to multiply the value of the gold, and use the wealth to secure our long road into the future.'

"But Velas, I don't think we can decipher these *quipus* without the beast."

"See what Dorothy has done, then wring your hands and wail, if you must." Velas pushed the top layer of papers across the table to Otis and crossed his arms. "This is her list of sounds, written in English. The sounds are written in order of their appearance on each *quipu* strand. Above each column is a symbol. Sometimes it is a circle, like the bead on the brow of the beast. Sometime it's the number that correlates to a strand on the Caral *quipu*. From this, we can make sounds, but we don't know the words, or why they are organized in this way. Can you help?"

Otis read slowly, mumbling unintelligibly. "Not English ... not ..." Suddenly, he stopped and grabbed Velas's hand, squeezing hard. "We're going to need coffee. Listen to this."

> *Pachacamac, Our pact is an eternal chain.*
> *Inevitable is reversible.*
> *We have obtained the light.*
> *We hold the star map.*
> *Pachacamac, we preserve the secrets of earth and time in*
>   *your silver book.*

Velas gathered the bundle and stood up. "We need to go to my home in the restricted zone. Soon, our guests arrive. If alertness is what you need, my wife will brew *yerba mate* for us."

Both men smiled across the table. Velas asked, "What have we found?"

I don't know," Otis answered, "but I believe we have obtained the light."

14

A SMALL, SMALL WORLD

T HE ASMUDI FAMILY VACATION STARTED with a bumpy ride on a shuttle that doubled as a fishing boat. The smell indicated that it had recently held a good catch of premium corvina — the best fish for gourmet fish tacos. As the advertising on the frozen packets said:

True Panamanian Corvina
Cosmpolitan Seasoning meets wild-caught flavor

The harvesting, cleaning, seasoning, flash freezing, and packaging were handled on the northern end of what was still called Sam's Island. The shipping arrangements and international sales were handled by Hayak and Roberta Asmudi from their computer in New York. Nearness to the Panama Canal guaranteed international markets.

As the guests on board stepped on to the island for their week of whimsical, unpampered adventure, Po was noticeably distracted, even withdrawn. After she and her family settled into their Swiss

Family tree-house accommodations she studied the map of the island features and chose a spot to confide in her husband.

"What do you want to see first, Roberta?" she asked. "I want to hike upriver with Hayak and get over my seasickness before I do the beach. I'm not ready to yuk it up with the other tourists yet."

"That sounds fun. I'll go ... oh, I see. Seasick, huh? Roberta blushed and giggled. "Okay, kids, get over your motion sickness. I'm going to the beach. First I'm going to stop by the Café and see if I can find Humphrey Bogart."

Hayak looked up from unpacking his travel bag, "You're not twenty-one yet, little girl."

"In Panama, I think the drinking age is thirteen," Roberta teased. "But I'm a lady and I'll wait until after dinner to get snockered."

Po watched her daughter pulley herself down to the ground on the bamboo elevator and shouted, "Do you have your map?"

"Right here," she answered, waving the map over her head.

"Don't wander into the off-limits zone."

Roberta was out of sight without responding. Po tried to peek through the canopy of trees to the ground to check her direction on the trail, but it was impossible. The banyan tree and the palms underneath were too thick.

"Not to worry for her." Hayak stepped behind Po and pulled her into him, kissing her neck. "Look. Is different world from up here. A gorgeous view. Sure you want to hike up a river right now?"

"I want to hike upriver until we find a flat rock in the middle of the stream."

"How you know a flat rock is in the middle of stream?" Hayak backed away and retrieved an island map from the bed. "I see a river and the head spring."

"Maybe it's not there." Po began pulling the rope to bring the elevator back up to the treehouse. "If it is, we'll talk."

15

THERE'S NO COMMISSIONER IN SANDLOT

JARVIS STOOD, WITH HIS HANDS BEHIND HIS BACK, and rocked on the balls and heels of his feet while Dr. Abrams ranted.

Dr. Milton sat silently in the corner of the room. The only thing that differentiated his usual listening posture from his current pose was the pencil, tapping against his notepad.

"One day! One day!" Dr. Abrams screamed at the aide. "In just one day, we have violence. You stand and watch. What were you thinking?"

"Well, Dr. Abrams, I was thinking, looky here, now that's the reason we use those tennis balls and padded bats. It wasn't like they was fixin' to jump-savage and spray lead."

"I'm not interested in ethnocentric bias in the characterization, Mr. Douglas. I want you to justify why you didn't intervene."

Jarvis bristled noticeably at the doctor's comment. "I'm no spokesman for savages, ain't no voting bloc, don't belong to no racial think-alike club, and I'm not to be talked down to, Doctor. I'm sayin' the bloody nose was good ol' fashion therapy for ...

'scuse me if this phrase ain't in your 'lighthouses of luminous learning', but *attitude adjustment* is what it was."

Dr. Milton unfurled from his chair and stepped between the red-faced Dr. Abrams and the tight-jawed aide. "Maybe we should ask Jarvis how it happened. I'm interested in how the incident was resolved."

Abrams sat in his chair and crossed his legs. He placed a finger to the side of his chin and swiveled a quarter turn, putting Jarvis under his gaze at the corner of his eyes. "Don't presume I'm culturally ignorant, Mr. Douglas. I'm hep to what you're telling me."

Dr. Milton rolled his eyes and went back to his corner chair. "Maybe you should tell us what happened, Jarvis. Start at the beginning. Facts first, conclusions second."

Jarvis took a breath and folded his arms across his chest before beginning. "It started when some of the residents from the rec room went outside to catch a smoke. Some of them crossed over to watch Bobby and Mr. McPheeters. Soon as they got there, Mr. McPheeters invited them to play. They was five of 'em on the field after Dixon, Shackelford, and Barron stayed. They figured a way to play *Indian Ball* — rotatin' the teams so everyone got to pitch and hit.

"Those that went back inside told the rest of the folks in the rec room 'bout the game. That led to some new figurin' since now, they had eight men on the field. Mr. McPheeters suggested he and Bobby could take turns on pickin' teams. That's how it started."

"So, someone didn't like the teams?" Dr. Abrams asked. "Is that what you're saying? This is a predictable reaction to chaos ordering. As the authority figure, Mr. Jarvis, you should have organized the team makeup and avoided the intrusion of a non-authorized figure into the decision-making process."

"Done what?" Jarvis pleaded to Dr. Milton with a look of exasperation, but he continued. "This is sandlot. There ain't no commissioner in sandlot."

Doctor Milton put the dialogue back on course by asking, "Was it the team makeup that led to the bloody nose, Jarvis?"

"No. It was Dixon. You know Mr. Dixon, he plays a lawyer on TV and took that to the field. Got puffy 'bout procedure He wanted everybody to vote on captains, nominatin' himself for the job."

"Mr. Dixon was the resident who got the bloody nose. Am I right?" Dr. Abrams shuffled through the nurse's report and verified the name. "Who took offense at Mr. Dixon's recommendation?"

"Nobody, sir. They went in a circle, and, one-at-a-time, they voted. Mr. McPheeters and Bobby got elected. It was the cheatin' and trash talk getting' off the rails what done it."

Abrams shook his head and rose from his chair, put one hand on his hip, and slapped at his desktop. "Bullying is the bastard brother of hate-speech, Mr. Douglas. I won't tolerate it. As the authority figure on-scene, you should have stopped the game."

"It was one guy acting out. The fellows handled it just fine."

Dr. Abrams threw up his hands and let shrillness creep into his voice. "If nothing happened, how did Mr. Dixon get his nose bloodied?"

"Well, sir, it was a chain of events, startin' with balls and strikes. You see, Mr. McPheeters was pitchin' to Bobby. Dixon, he was callin' balls and strikes, 'cause that's the way they settled the rules. Next batter up was the umpire, usin' the honor system, 'cause in Indian ball ..."

"Could you use a more sensitive term than 'Indian ball'? Mind what you say. Perhaps, 'Indigenous Native-American ball'."

"I'll just say they played a game without full teams, and that led to rules like, no base runners, one infielder, a pitcher, and two outfielders. The battin' team called they own balls and strikes, like I said, on the honor system.

"At about the seventh inning, Mr. Dixon, he lost his concept of the honor system. With the bases loaded, in a close game, and two outs, Bobby whiffed, but Dixon called a foul tip.

"On the pitchin' rubber, Freddy disputed the call. Bobby pronounced himself out, sayin' he missed it by a foot.

"Now, this is when Dixon, he starts in with the trash-talk. He's callin' Freddy a washed-out bum, and he's callin' Bobby, *The Comatose Kid.*

Dr. Abrams held his hand out to motion for Jarvis to stop talking. "So Mr. Dixon was assaulted for name-calling?"

"No, sir. It wasn't like that. Freddy's team trotted in from the field, and Bobby's team started headin' out. That is, everyone but Dixon.

"Mr. Dixon, he was all in a frenzy 'bout him bein' the umpire and all. He grabbed onto Bobby's arm and told him to get back in the box or he would eject him from the game.

Bobby, he kinda stiffens up for a bit, then he starts laughin' real loud. 'You're going to put me back in the box? You don't know how funny that is,' he says.

"Dixon, he don't like it when Bobby pulls away from him to take the field. He calls out, 'Hey, Comatose Boy!' When Bobby turns back to him, Dixon bounces a tennis ball off that big scar on Bobby's forehead and catches the rebound.

"Bobby kind of freezes again and this time he don't laugh, but he says real serious like, 'Reel it back in, dipnot.'

"Dixon, he don't stop and think for a second. He says, 'Get in the box, Freaky Boy, or go home,' and he tosses the ball at Bobby's head one more time.

"The rest of the story is, Bobby caught the ball with one hand and put the other hand into a fist that landed square on Mr. Dixon's nose. People got between them and, after some intervention, there was apologies, a handshake, and the game went on."

Dr. Abrams stared at his shoes and pursed his lips, taking his time in thinking the story over. "Did Dixon call his lawyer?" he asked after staring at Dr. Milton.

"No, sir," Milton answered. I've discussed the incident with both parties. Dixon is more embarrassed than anything. He requested more anger-management counseling."

"That's good. That's good," Abrams gushed, "Sign him up. How did Bobby react?"

"Very positively. I believe he's successfully managed several rites of passage in just one day of games. Jarvis should be commended for his attention to treatment plans."

Dr. Abrams frowned. "Hmm," he drawled, "I suppose. But, Jarvis, one reminder: Mind what you say."

"I'm doing that right now, sir."

16

FLIP FLAP FLOP

T HE YERBA MATE WORE OFF. The coffee wore off. The fat candles on the patio table had burned deep enough into their center, the light was muted, and it was difficult to see. After finding it impossible to keep his stacks of papers in order, Otis finally admitted he was done for the night.

Velas was already asleep, head on his arms, arms on the table. A plate of fish and manioc scraps lay on the floor next to his chair.

Otis didn't remember anyone bringing food to him, but he also had a plate at his feet, untouched.

"A night for the ages," he said to the cat sleeping in a window box full of mosquito repelling catnip. "I don't see the sun coming up, but I know it will be soon. I want you to be the first to know. I've unlocked the strange language that puzzled Dorothy. I understand the symbols etched into gold, I've deciphered the circles on the brow of the beast, and I understand the crude schematic of the three-layered balls. How's that for one night's work?"

As if the cat understood the importance of Otis's musing, it suddenly looked up, wide-eyed toward the sound of the voice. Otis reached toward the cat, to pet it, and it began to purr.

"I know," Otis whispered, while stroking its black fur, "I could never have put it together without Dorothy's work. I'm happy, too. Now, what are we going to do with it? Another thing to consider: why am I talking to a cat?"

The black cat rolled over and twitched his tail, then jumped to the floor and satiated his catnip munchies by chomping at the fish on the plate.

Otis satisfied his need to close his eyes and fell almost instantly into sleep. When he woke up, his head was on the table, stuck to a sheet of paper with four parallel lines drawn on either side of the infinity symbol. Embarrassed, he wiped the drool from his cheek and dragged his shirt sleeve across the nearly dried pool atop the symbol.

Velas stared at him from across the table. "You had a long and chatty night, Mr. Otis. First time drinking the *yerba*? Maybe this afternoon you can calm down and tell me what you found. I got lost at the *flip, flap, flop* references. I understand it has something to do with trigonometry and the rotation of triangular tips in a trinary number system. I get the concept of adding a maybe to the binary nature of computers, I even followed solving of event ordering metastability to bypass the alternate logic issues in optic relay, but the cold fusion additive for a continuum in a master-slave ordering of events went way over my head. The *flip, flap, flop* didn't register. Can you explain it all in engineering-friendly terms?"

"Did you say it was afternoon?" Otis looked at the position of the sun in the sky and winced. "Here's the rub, old boy. I need to clean up, reorganize, and start slow. I know the blue codex has a recipe for making more marbles. I have a prototype, but we can't make a duplicate. If we get together over drinks at the café, I think I can spell it out for you. I haven't been drunk in over two decades. Now, I have something to celebrate and something to cry about. As long as it's not Chicha, I'm ready."

Velas wrinkled his nose. "Chicha? We haven't done that Quecha brew since Sam left. Once we got our spirits back, we didn't have enough virgin spit to fill a shot glass."

17

FLAT ROCK TIME MACHINE

WHEN PO AND HAYAK STEPPED OFF THE BAMBOO ELEVATOR at the tree house, she slipped headphones over Hayak's ears and handed him a CD player.

"Don't get this wet in the river," she said, "I only brought one."

Hayak smiled. "Romantic music?"

"Not hardly," Po responded. "This is something I recorded in the radio office, while you and Roberta were in St. Louis. Otis Beckley played this on …"

"Otis Beckley?"

"He's back. I saw him four days ago. He came by the house with a …"

"Otis?" Hayak pulled the headphones off his ears and stammered. "Where he has been? How about Bill? Robert? Did you talk to Lock?"

"There's too much news, dear. That's why you need to listen." Po took the headphones from Hayak's hands and returned them to his ears. "I recorded this while it was being played for me from a blue marble. We should go somewhere more private."

"A blue marble? This I can only disbelieve if I see it being heard. You might as well tell me you talked to the man in the moon."

"You're very close." Po took Hayak by the hand and pointed toward the path to the schoolhouse. "We'll walk upriver from where it meets the ocean."

Hayak shot glances at Po multiple times while he walked and listened, but he didn't speak. When they reached the schoolhouse, he glanced at the stilted structure only briefly before stepping into the water and heading upstream.

Po followed behind, as if being trolled in his wake. When Hayak stood still for extended periods, she swam against the gentle current, refreshing herself for the conversation that was sure to come.

After the hike began feeling more like a trek, they found the rock where tiny waves broke over a barrier and splashed upward as if an invisible fish repeatedly jumped from the same location. When they approached, they saw the rock was an inch below the surface. Along with the rising waters around the island, the river had also gained depth.

Po pulled herself up onto the round button of stone and spoke for the first time since the hike began. "This was Lockjaw and his lady's sanctuary."

Hayak gave no indication he heard Po. He walked to the shore and sat down in shallow water.

The swaying palms, the dappled light, the gentle chill of water, and the warm massage of tropical breezes took Po away from worry. While Hayak listened intently, she looked for Lock and Willa's ghosts dancing among the reflections swirling in the water around her feet. She was open to the magic of the river and confident she was sharing her news with the perfect mate.

Who else but someone from Asitr's inner circle could ever believe the story from the marble?

When the recording was finished, Hayak placed his headphones and the CD player on the bank, then swam over to the rock. He pulled himself up, next to Po, and held her hand.

"These are things very big and important," he started. "Some, too big for me. I 'll start with what is important to me in my own short life and move to what I like and don't like, so you know.

"First, I need ask. Are you my wife, or is Robert here to claim you?"

Po pulled away and emphasized sternly, "You insult me to ask."

"That is something I like." Hayak smiled. "I insult myself to ask."

"Another thing I like. There are no more Baals in the world. Only their bloody culture lingers. To know the last of them was trapped in our basement is for last laughs.

"A thing I don't like is what has taken his place. Satan is now the devil among us, and he is no stupid Foop. In the halls of Babylon, Asitr hear him tell his plan, but to hear is not to resist. To warn is to be laughed at. What to do?"

Hayak paused, his wrinkled brow showed he was thinking. "I like that Heaven has fixed their broken angel.

"I like that Otis is returned. I hope he takes revenge on this X-Club. I know the man, Sam, who flew the big helicopter. I hope he is rotted in Eden.

"I mystify myself with thoughts, amazed at how this island is a bridge. To think, Lockjaw was here. I do business with these people. Dorothy and Willa find openings to secrets on this very island. We are here with Roberta. This doesn't feel like a last chapter."

"No, dear," Po interjected. "It feels like a channel in Lockjaw's description of Asitr's story. I think we're going to join with other channels, and become one stream, heading into an uncertain ending at a hole in the side of a stone wall."

"Yes," Hayak said the word with trepidation. "A wall. Where the future is written in stone. That is something I don't know to like or not to like. So much will be bad, and so much the better. I can't understand."

Hayak's words were spoken so softly, and the meaning held so much room between dark tragedy and hopeful joyousness, conversation ended, until he spoke one more word: "Roberta."

Po squeezed Hayak's hand and again, there was long silence. She broke the sound of gurgling water with an introduction to her agreement with Dr. Milton. "There's another conversation I need to tell you about. I had a visit with Robert's doctor — a man named Milton. I made him a promise. This is something you won't like."

By the time the couple resolved to keep Po's promises to Dr. Milton, lunchtime had passed. Hungry, they planned to find Roberta and dine at *Rick's Café.*

18

KIDS THESE DAYS

ROBERTA SPENT THE MORNING at the swimming beach getting to know one of the families of tourists who signed up for four days in *The Great Escape* barracks.

"It's ghastly," the mother whined. "It's just like in the movie."

"It has air conditioning," the father said tiredly, like he'd heard the same complaints all morning.

"There's no video games or TV," the oldest son added.

"And no swimming pool," the youngest complained. "It's gross." The mother jumped back in. "No flush toilets."

In unison, the three whiners piled on, "It's like a prison."

"It's everything they advertised," the father said weakly. "We thought they were joking."

"I thought it looked like fun," Roberta laughed. "Did you try to find a way to escape?" she asked. "That looked like the best part."

"And get shot with laser guns?" The oldest looked at Roberta like she was crazy. "After dinner you have to stay in your barracks or get shot. They lock the gate, and there's no TV."

"Or video games," whined the youngest.

"Or flush toilets," Mom reminded.

"If I signed up to stay there, I'd look for the escape tunnel." Roberta made another attempt to cheer the kids up. "If you escape, you can ride motor scooters at the off-road park. Doesn't that sound fun?"

"Ride to where? There's no video games anywhere. We already asked."

"And we can't watch cartoons at the restaurant, or get ice cream cones, or candy. I know, we asked."

"They do have a flush toilet at the cafe."

"I think the beach is nice," Father said, hopefully. "I love the hammocks."

"Where are you staying? Mother asked Roberta.

"We're in the Swiss Family tree house. It's beautiful."

"God, what a nightmare." The mother rolled her eyes and fanned herself. "I'm afraid of heights."

"Well, we said we wanted some adventure." Father slumped and drew circles in the sand with his foot.

"Adventure, yes, but adventure with ..."

"I know ... flush toilets." Roberta finished the mother's sentence and tossed her towel over her shoulder. "I'm going to hike the beach. You guys enjoy yourselves."

"Sure, dear, maybe we can get together at dinner and talk some more?"

"I would be afraid to." Roberta looked at the children in mock horror. "There are Nazi spies everywhere."

19

NEVER A GOOD IDEA

OTIS HAD GIFTED HIS MIDNIGHT SNACK TO THE CAT. Between *yerba*, and immersion in Dorothy's papers, he hadn't given food a second thought.

He slept through lunch, but he didn't wake up hungry. As the only restaurant on the island, *Rick's Café* should have appealed to him for the food alone, but he was stuck on the idea of getting drunk.

On the way to the café, Velas suggested they stop at the warehouse to get the marble. Otis insisted, "Tonight, I party. Tomorrow I'll save the world."

Patiently, Velas reminded Otis that he shouldn't drink on an empty stomach. "Especially," he warned, "If you plan to indulge on a grand scale. The allure is understandable, but the planning is a flawed construct."

It wasn't helpful that the pair arrived at the café between meals. Velas did manage to get Otis to sample the beans and rice, and Otis scooped a bowl of chocolate pudding, left over from the lunch-time salad bar, but, really ... pudding and beans.

"What's your poison?" the barman asked.

"I don't know what I like yet," Otis answered. Bring me anything blue and tropical."

"We have a few to choose from. There's the ..."

"I'll try them all, but don't bring them all at once. I don't want the ice to melt."

The barman eyed Velas, but got only a shrug. Returning the gesture, he asked Otis, "Are you sure, sir?"

"I'm on vacation, I've got myself an impossible purpose, and I have twenty birthdays to celebrate. Bring me those puppies, and let's party."

"And, what for you, Mr. Velas?"

"Coffee ... and have a rickshaw ready. We'll be leaving before the guests arrive for dinner."

20

SPILLING THE BEANS

WHEN PO AND HAYAK REACHED THE SCHOOLHOUSE, they stopped on the path. The sound of Roberta's voice caused them to look toward the school. She and Huana were on the upper platform. Roberta waved and skittered down the winding stairs.

"I hope Huana hasn't spilled the beans," Po moaned.

Roberta was cheerful. "Have fun?" she asked, "You've been upriver all day?"

Without waiting for an answer, she reached for the headphones around Hayak's neck. "Who you listening to?"

Po reacted with a sudden, reflexive jump, but Hayak answered calmly. "Nobody. Not since I took it for a swim. Poof! What you do today?"

"I talked to the family from the boat, with the loud kids. I stumbled on that couple we guessed were newlyweds. Not much of a conversation there. I told them to carry on. They did. I'm still guessing they're newlyweds. The school was the best part. They have a one-eyed schoolteacher; I like her."

"Slow down, girl," Hayak chuckled, while removing the batteries from the CD player. "Did you eat lunch?"

"No, I was having too much fun at the schoolhouse."

Po put her arm around Roberta and squeezed her close. "Good," she said, "We're going to go to the café early. We're famished."

On the way up the path to the tree house, Roberta rambled excitedly about the school. "It has a sign by the stairs that says *Dorothy's School of Higher Learning.* The young ones were leaving when I got there. I asked them why their school had that name. A boy said, 'Because it's up on stilts.' Then this teeny little girl, she says, 'Because it's like Baba Yaga's house, only it stands on wood, not chicken legs.'

"The teacher tousled the little girl's hair and tells me her name is Baba and she's into a Baba Yaga phase, then she prompts her to tell me her poem. Listen to this:

Baba Yaga was so misunderstood
Her chicken legs hopped all over the woods
Her methods were stilted
Her intentions were good
They called her ugly but she helped best she could
She felt like a refugee

"Isn't that adorable? Her teacher, Huana, she says the little girl is training to be a healing shaman."

By the time the three of them reached the tree house, Roberta told her parents about the next class that showed up at the school. "They're having a contest. Did you know the island is sinking? Anyway, the older kids are divided into four groups. Each group studies at the computer classroom in the restricted zone. They're looking for a place to move the whole tribe. Today, one of the groups got together at the schoolhouse to plan their presentation. When all four groups are ready, they're going to present their ideas to a campfire assembly. Pretty cool, huh? Pickin' the brains of the young folks. Sounds like my plan for the inter-collegiate conference. I really like the teacher."

"Roberta, you get first dibs on shower, but hurry up. Try to keep mouth closed, so you don't drown," Hayak said, cheerfully. "I want to get to the café early."

While Roberta showered, Po and Hayak agreed it would be wise to speak to Huana and Caspi before either of them mentioned Lockjaw's name.

After the three of them had their turns luxuriating in the soothing outdoor shower, they were all relaxed. Roberta was calmer. Po turned the conversation to school plans and empty-nest worries.

It wasn't until they approached the café, and two excited children wearing laser tag vests ran up to them, that conversation, again, took a turn to vacation on the island.

"We found the secret tunnel," the younger shouted.

"And some secret rooms," the older one crowed. "I found forged documents that give us access to the motor scooters."

"They found a secret room with a flush toilet," the mother said, putting her hand in the air for a high-five.

Before formal introductions could be made, a disturbance at the entrance to Rick's Café caught their attention.

A man was being poured into a rickshaw, waving at the bartender in the doorway, slurring, "Thansh for the parrtry, we're off like lil Bobby McKinney, chazing a codex. Giddit? Chazing a codex." He raised his hand to high-five Velas, but rolled away from him suddenly, to spill his beans, pudding, and blue liqueurs.

With her face locked down tight with suspicion and anger, Roberta turned to her parents and demanded, "What the hell is going on?"

21

APRIL SHOWERS

AFTER THREE DAYS OF SANDLOT, Bobby was grateful for the two days of rain. The morning after day one, he woke up to the surprise of aching, stiff muscles. On day two, it was worse. He felt like he'd been beaten up by professionals.

"How do kids do it?" he asked Freddy. "I've never been this sore."

"We get over it in about thirty seconds, old timer." Freddy mussed Bobby's graying hair and laughed. "Just wait until we actually run the bases."

On day three, Bobby actually got to enjoy the thrill of base-running. The alcohol rehab unit on campus allowed a mixed group of men and women to join the fun. Fourteen players equaled two teams of seven. The batting team supplied the pitcher and catcher.

Bobby woke up in spastic pain. Along with the muscle soreness, he had a couple bouts of sciatic pain, profuse sweating, and a headache. He felt like every nerve, from core to extremities, was punishing his attempts to get out of bed. On that first day of rain, Bobby took his breakfast in bed and, gratefully, he watched a steady progression of gray clouds bombard and puddle the infield.

After the second day of spring rain, Bobby was bored of watching puddles turn to streams. He lost his fascination with pondering the big questions like: Where do the frogs go when the field is dry? Where do the frogs come from? Why do they leave their homes, just because it rained? Do real adults sit around thinking about the wandering habits of frogs? What is a *real* adult?

Bobby suddenly noticed a pattern. *This is starting to feel like life in the box.*

Stiff-legged, he walked to the hallway and opened the door, relieved to see Jarvis, sitting in his chair, headphones on, and a newspaper folded in his lap.

"Jarvis? I'd like to go down to the rec room," he said.

"Why's that?" Jarvis took the headphones off his ears, and the tinkling sound of music, played too loudly, caused Bobby to pause before answering. "I'm evolving into an amphibian."

"That's as good a reason as any, I s'pose," Jarvis replied, straight-faced. "But I need to call Dr. Milton. He don't think bein' 'round a TV set will be good for you."

22

AFTER THE STORMS PASS

T HEY SAY PANAMA HAS TWO SEASONS. The traditional tourist season sees six months of mostly dry and sunny weather. In the middle of March, the second season begins. Rain falls for two hours in the late afternoon or evening. The intensity varies, the accompaniment of wind and lightning is unpredictable, but the rain and the duration is a safe bet.

On the Caribbean side, there are never any hurricanes, but strong winds, lightning, and booming shouts of angry thunder can sweep in fast enough to scare the off-season tourists out of their sandals and into the safety of the nearest building.

That is exactly how Po, Hayak, Roberta, and Velas achieved privacy for their contentious barrage of mistrusting questions and accusations, while standing in the rain at the center of the village square.

Like the way-too-familiar thunder-babble of voices offering lightning bolts of abstract conclusions, conjured from a dark cloud of alternative facts, shouted in shrill tones of how-dare-you-speak-when-I'm-interrupting-you cable news mayhem, argument was drowned in a torrent of words.

Roberta latched on to two specific words, a name: *Otis Beckley*. On the strength of understanding who the nearly unconscious man in the rickshaw was, she peeled away from the storm and, nearly unnoticed, began pulling the rickshaw toward the path to the tree house.

As the rickshaw bounced past the three angry people in the rain, they stopped their storm of words in mid-sentence.

"I didn't find you. You found ..." Hayak let the thought die.

"I didn't hide what I didn't ..." Po trailed off.

"Your eugenics club makes coincidence too ..." Velas reeled in his accusation and raised his hand like a lightning rod topped with a fist.

At the signal, two hiders scurried into the clearing, tubes loaded with darts.

In a delayed reaction to the fuzzy images of the faces he rolled past, Otis broke the sudden silence.

"Po. Hike. Watcha do comin' ta my birthdray portry?"

He raised his arm, forefinger pointed skyward, then let it fall slowly to his side. By the time it landed on the seat of the rickshaw, he was fully unconscious.

Hayak trotted to Roberta's side.

Po called her name.

Velas dropped his arm, barking a command. "Let them go."

Roberta lumbered forward, ignoring the men with the deadly tubes, Hayak's presence at her side, her mother's call, the lightning, the rain, and the thunder.

"Do you deliver to the tree house?" she shouted.

After a confused pause, Velas asked, "What do you want?"

"Chicken or pizza. I don't care." Roberta answered over her shoulder.

Hayak grabbed one arm of the rickshaw and Roberta shifted to the other. Together the haul was easier.

"Make that three Large. One green pepper and onion. One pepperoni. One mushroom. Add a couple chicken dinners, and if you see Huana, tell her we need to talk." Po rushed to catch up.

In the morning, Otis woke up to a circle of faces, each of them holding a cup of coffee to their lips. Po, Roberta, Hayak, Caspi, Huana, and Velas were waiting for coincidences to add up into something believable. The man with the first hangover of his life was expected to make the pieces fit. Hot coffee and cold pizza were just what the shaman ordered.

23

CRIBBAGE AND KINGS

T HERE'S TRUTH LURKING INSIDE STEREOTYPES. One stereotype about men is the notion that they don't get together to chat about feelings. They do chat about feelings, but they get together for some other reason, then, while engaged in that other reason, they chat about feelings. The stereotype fit, when it came to games of cribbage between Jarvis and Bobby.

Television news had a depressing effect on Bobby. Dr. Milton told him about the need to learn different definitions for words he thought he understood, but nothing could have prepared him for what he experienced by flipping between the cable mouthpiece for the republicrats and the bullhorn for demolicans. The clear and present danger of disguising propaganda inside a shell of selective information seemed obvious to him, but he was insecure in trusting his own judgment.

Over a rainy-day game of cribbage, Bobby broached his worries to Jarvis, using a riddle to start the conversation. "When does one-half and one-half not equal a whole?"

"Hmm ... I got a pair for two, a pair for four and a Jack-queen-king for seven." Jarvis moved his peg seven spaces and addressed the riddle. "When is half and half not a whole? Lessee ... When you puts it in your coffee."

"That's pretty good. It's your crib, but let me ask again. When is one-half and one-half not ..."

"Oh, okay, I got it. You talkin' numbers. Lessee ..." Jarvis leaned back into his chair. "When you holdin' one- half a sandwich and the other half is in your belly. Right? I got one my granddaughter tol' me. When is a car not a car?"

"I heard that one when I was a kid, Jarvis. Cut?"

"No, I need to change my luck. So, what's the answer?"

"When it turns into a driveway. I'm tryin' to make an observation here, you're not cooperating. Let me ask again. When is one-half ...?"

"I done answered you twice. Tell me what is the answer."

"The question popped up when I was flippin' the channels back and forth to catch the news. The answer is ... fifteen for two. The answer is one half-truth, plus one half-truth doesn't add up to one truth. Thirty-one for two. So much for your luck changing."

"I see. You wasn't tryin' to be funny. You was tryin' to be profound. I coulda tol' you there ain't no truth in them places. Might as well listen to radio signals from two alien planets ... pair for two. Nothin' funny there. You listen long 'nuff and you'll start hatin' ..."

"Three fours for six, and ..." Bobby moved his peg six spaces and raised his hands above his head. "Game."

Jarvis tossed his cards face up on the table and cursed. "Damn. A twelve-point hand gone to hell. Thought you was a dead man. Rematch?"

Bobby gathered the deck and began shuffling, but his distant stare let Jarvis know he didn't have his mind on playing another game.

"Listen here," Jarvis said, "It ain't pretty out there. We got computer algorithms censoring what we say on the internet. We have enough people trained to hate each other they vote in blocs. We got less understanding of history's lessons than a house cat and no more feelin' for the next guy than Punch and Judy puppets. Why we don't cut them puppet master strings is beyond thinkin' 'bout. It makes me crazy all the more 'cause I can't blame myself and somebody's to blame. I meet folks one at a time and avoid them when they's in their tribes. I keep my people close and I pray, *Thy kingdom come. Thy will be done,* 'cause we sure done showed our will brings hell. This world you want to get back to is a fever blister waitin' to bust open. I don't say that with happy happy in my heart, and I don't mean to scare you, but I'd hate to see you leave here with an oblivious stare like a cow in line at the slaughter house. Eyes open, man, and courage. That's what I want for you."

A long silence, averted glances, and racing thoughts followed the unexpected diatribe.

Jarvis shut his eyes tight and put folded hands to his lips. Through his fingers, he added, "I don't think what I said is part of Dr. Milton's treatment plan for you."

"I wonder which channel my daughter listens to." Bobby's hand began to shake and his lip quivered. "It isn't really that bad, is it?"

Jarvis struggled against a lump in his throat. He felt his eyes begin to tear up. "I forgot I cared, Bobby. Thank you. Maybe I have some ethno-centric bias. If you can't take it, they got drugs that make you stop caring." Jarvis wiped dampness from the corner of his eye and grinned. "I must have gotten some female hormones mixed in with my vitamins this morning. Just 'tween the two of us, this conversation never happened. We the kings of cool, right?"

Bobby held his hand out in front of him, palm down, and watched it shake. "Kings of cool, Jarvis. I can't wait a whole year before I get out of here, and I can't leave until I have a steady hand."

24

THE BROKEN LINK

O TIS NIBBLED COLD PIZZA, but left his hot coffee untouched until it reached tropical-morning-air temperature. He was shushed when he first tried to speak, and questions were directed to Po and Hayak. Slowly, nibble by nibble, he found the ability to listen to the others without eye-scorching pain. Although he had his eyes tightly closed through most of the what-did-you-know-and-when-did-you-know-it round of suspicious questions by the islanders, he was aware that one other person voluntarily remained silent.

Roberta leaned against the railing of the outdoor sitting area with folded arms and angry facial features. She maintained her pose through the accusations of X-Club plotting, and the increasingly thin explanations of coincidence, supernatural interference, and the ever-popular, *I'm okay, you're insane,* rationale.

Huana was the toughest, most skeptical of the inquisitors. It was she who had memories unclouded by Waldo's soma juice. She was the one who felt the losses of Lock, Willa, and her beloved friend Dorothy. In her mind, they were real memories, not just tales told to her

72

awakening tribe. As the leader in charge of tribal security, frustrated by the lack of answers resolving her paranoia, she reached a decision.

"Surrender all your electronic devices. I'll call for the boat to come get you. Guards will ..."

Otis stood too quickly. He sat back down and massaged his temples while he interrupted Huana. "Please, just get me a ladder and we can go to the warehouse. Most of this can be cleared up. We should listen to the recordings on the marble."

Velas put a hand on Huana's shoulder and spoke reassuringly. "If this will show us what to do with Dorothy's work, we must listen. We don't reject the supernatural. Let's see what the marble has to say."

"Will the marble tell us what to do with Dorothy's work?" Huana's focused gaze in Otis's direction didn't relieve the pressure he felt from Roberta's continuous stare.

Addressing Roberta first, Otis answered, "The marble will tell us painful things about Bobby. He's lost a battle with reality. Roberta shouldn't be here to listen."

Roberta pulled from the rail and stood straight, but Otis turned his attention to Huana's question before she could speak. "The marble will leave no doubt about the supernatural nature of what's brought us together, but Dorothy's work leaves no doubt that we aren't the ones to finish the work. The task is impossible. I can't build the device the *quipus* describe."

"Perhaps you can't, but maybe an engineer can." Velas spread his arms and continued. "Maybe we should trust each other."

Hayak turned his face back and forth between Huana and Otis, aiming his comments mainly to them. "I am no shrinker of Lilies," he began. "When you live a life smuggling in Armenia, you are face to face with the oligarchical slavery of the Russians, the hatred of the Turks and the bloody way things are done in the land of Baal. I know a thing about people who can be given trust. This little girl over here ..." Hayak gestured toward Roberta. "This girl was in the womb, learning about angels and devils, thriving on the nerve endings of my Po, while she fought through blind sides and woman-only hysterical hormones to make a so-full-of-himself smarty man wet his DVDs."

Po touched Hayak's arm and whispered, "That's BVDs, hon."

"Never the mind. PVC, SUV, whatever, you would wet them all." Hayak walked to the drawer in the patio hutch and removed the CD player, popped the back open, and loaded the batteries. "Here is what is on the marble. You should hear what Bobby's doctor has to say, as well. When you listen, trust and apologize. My girl could eat your soiled underpants for breakfast."

Roberta wasn't the only one in the crowd to make a face at the comment.

"Maybe I should say so differently," Hayak recovered as his face reddened. "My Roberta knows nothing, but when she hears all, she will be no Otis Beckley. You, Otis Beckley, are a chain breaker."

25

HI, I'M BOB

D R. MILTON JOINED BOBBY AT THE WINDOW in his room and, for a while, they watched the game below. After an inning-ending fly ball, the doctor got down to business.

"You asked to see me. Is there a problem?"

Bobby exhaled, leaving a patch of s moisture on the pane. As he rubbed the fogged surface with the edge of his robe, he exposed scabbing on his forearm.

"Oh. Your arm is scraped up," Milton observed. "Is that why you're not playing today?"

"No," Bobby answered while walking to the chair at the foot of the bed.

Milton filled the silence with a comment. "Jarvis says we had to buy a lot of tennis balls this week."

"Yeah," Bobby answered. "Freddy kept busting them to pieces, but he's got that under control. He says he's learning to be a contact hitter, saving the all-in swings for when the game is on the line."

Dr. Milton continued the small talk, waiting for Bobby to let him know why he asked to see him.

"How'd you get that scrape?"

Bobby raised his forearm toward his face and examined the scabs. "I got this the day the field dried out."

"How'd it happen?"

"The surface on the base paths dried to a hard crust. Before we played, Freddy and I shuffled around the bases, breaking up the crust, but all we did was make dirt clods." Bobby lowered his arm and laughed. "I learned three lessons that day."

Dr. Milton turned from the window, toward Bobby, and folded his arms, waiting to hear the lessons learned.

Bobby rubbed his forearm and explained. "After the field dried, I was over my muscle soreness and feeling good. In the games before the rain, running felt clumsy. I was slow. On the day after the rains, I had a little muscle memory. Running felt effortless. In the last inning of a 30-9 game, I rounded first base flush with delusions of new-found athleticism. I was feeling good about my chances to hustle a single into a double. While sliding into the waiting glove, I learned that slow and clumsy, even if done effortlessly, is still slow and clumsy."

"The score was 30-9?"

"Yup. Freddy drove that next lesson home by repeating his new attitude. He brushed the pellets out of my scrapes and told me to save the big swings for when the game is on the line."

"What was your third lesson?"

"People respect stupidity. I got a new name and a lot of back-slapping for taking one for the team."

"A new name?"

"Call me 'Bob'. It just happened. Everyone calls me *Bob*. I like it. *Bobby* has so much baggage. *Robert* is not me. I'm Bob."

"I think that's good. It shows insight into your journey. Is this what you wanted to talk to me about?" Dr. Milton pulled the chair away from the desk and turned it toward Bob, a pleased, half-smile on his face.

As he sank into his listening position, his patient returned to the window.

"We're getting some of the staff on their lunch breaks. They watch the games." Bob leaned against the window sill and delayed before broaching the issue on his mind. "I want to go to the picture show and see some movies. I want to go to a mall and walk around. I want to see what life is like, not have it explained to me. Can you arrange that?"

"When I think you're ready, that's a wonderful idea." Dr. Milton nodded his head and smiled in Bob's direction. "When I think you're ready."

"I was thinking, if Jarvis or Freddy went with me, I'm ready now."

"You think so?" Milton stood up and paced, rubbing his chin as he thought. "Why Freddy?"

"He's my friend."

"You were a dead spirit, in a box, a little more than a week ago. You were abused and isolated before that. You were betrayed by the parents you trusted, even before that. What makes you think you're ready to step out and tell the world, 'Hi, I'm Bob.'? People are empowered to trash-talk on the streets. They're angry. The wrong slogan on your T-shirt, the wrong glance, the wrong word can set someone off. It's not sandlot out there. It's not one punch, and then shake hands. Are you ready for that?"

"If Freddy's with me, I'll keep in mind not to swing hard, unless the game is on the line." Bob turned his back to the window and exhaled, loudly. "Besides, I need to know the world my daughter lives in, before we meet."

"I'll talk with Freddy and get back to you. In the meantime, I have a favor to ask."

"A favor?"

"I saw the mobile Bobby made for Bill. I want you to make another one. I want it to be from Bob to Dr. Milton. Put your heart into it." The doctor crossed the room and patted Bob's chest, over his heart. "Tell me who you are."

"I'll need Plasticene clay."

"Okay. Next rainy day, I'll arrange for a self-driver. You and Jarvis can go to the craft store and pick out what you need." Dr. Milton looked at his wristwatch and headed for the door. "We are done here, right? I have a meeting in my office in twenty minutes."

"I'm good, I need to throw on some clothes and get to the field in time to play a couple innings."

26

ELEMENTAL PROGRESSIONS

MOVIE NIGHT WAS AWKWARD, for those who attended. The rain cooperated — in that it gave enough warning to move the event indoors, ahead of the downpour. The newlyweds showed up, but left early, holding hands and laughing while dashing through the rain. They missed out on the dramatic final scene.

Otis, Velas, and Hayak skipped the entire movie. They were huddled over blueprints of their own making, back-engineered from documents Dorothy pulled from *quipus*. While Po, Roberta, children and tourists screamed and threw popcorn, the trio debated.

When debate was over at the tree house, agreement came easily. After all, most of what the three needed to make their miracle machine, was already available to them.

The autoclave used to pressure- steam the fish was suitable for cleansing the materials required. Two such machines were already in use on the island.

Otis believed no device on earth could manufacture the extreme pressure required to elementally reduce two ingredients into a malleable form, as required by the *quipu* recipe. He had been gone awhile, and unaware of the paths where science continued to march.

Velas informed him of a prototype, hand-held device developed at Harvard University. "It is," he said, "capable of applying pressure at thirty-five times the force at the center of the earth. It was invented to test the theory that hydrogen could be manufactured from molecules and liquified. It could also be used for the process described on the *quipu*."

To obtain the device, Hayak volunteered, "For this, I will call my brother, Van. We will be both thief and smuggler."

Otis had one more hurdle he believed was too high to clear. "The first element needing compression," he said, "is under our feet. Sand will yield the silicone. The second element is not available."

"Explain this," Hayak challenged.

"The *quipu* gives the atomic weight and elemental ratio," Otis answered. "The problem is: no element of the specific atomic weight is on the charts.

Velas put forth a suggestion to break off and analyze a piece of the *shem*.

Hayak excitedly agreed to the idea. "I have access to a mass spectrometer, chromatograph thinga-mabobs, CHNX and CHNS fraction combustion doohickeys, and mass-atom quantifiers and qualifiers. They just sit there, reminding me I don't know why I bought them."

Together, Otis and Velas asked, "Where did you ... why did you ..."

"CSI's widow sold them to me after her husband died. He used them to analyze the yellow paint in the Illinois cave. I don't understand the manuals, so they sit in a closet."

Otis recovered from his surprise and quickly threw cold water on the idea of testing the *shem*. "I have a pact with angels of the Lord. I won't allow it to be damaged."

"Relax," Velas said. "We can use the Harvard device to experiment with known elements. Changing the elemental structure will alter the atomic weight. We're not this close and yet so far. Our most difficult problem will be in constructing a facility to manufacture the new orb."

"Why is that?" asked Otis.

"Housing for the process must stabilize fluctuations in naturally occurring magnetic pulses. Additionally, a ground for the safe dissipation of expended electricity and a conduit for transferring the electrical energy to the ground are mandatory. Any suggestions?" He asked. "I'm not visualizing how we can do that."

"Would a ten-by-ten room, surrounded on all six sides with four solid feet of pure gold do the trick?" Otis asked the question while staring at Hayak.

"Only if we could find a power source big enough to initiate the process," Velas answered, "and small enough to fit inside the room."

"I have the room," answered Hayak.

"My marble will provide the energy," Otis said, with confidence.

In the absence of any other obstacles, and chock-full of excitement over the clanking of pieces coming together, it was unanimous. The plan was a go.

Before the girls returned from movie night, the boys were drinking *yerba* and patting each other on the back for being such brilliant recipients of the forerunners of science, like Lavoisier, Dumas, Dorothy, and Baal Zebub.

When Po and Roberta returned, Hayak greeted them at the elevator. "How was the movie?" he asked.

"Not good, it was a western," Po answered. "It ended with the American brats and their parents screaming, 'Kill the savages! Hang the scalpers!' Dishes were broken."

Roberta chimed in. "The island kids yelled back, 'John Wayne is a draft dodger,' and 'Get off our land.' Caspi had to turn the movie off. The family is leaving tomorrow. I'm going with them."

"You what?" Hayak appeared thunder struck. "You take sides with ugly Americans?"

"No," Po sighed. "She has her mind made up to talk with Dr. Milton. She won't wait."

Roberta was quick to change the subject. "So, did you guys get anything accomplished?"

27

LET SLEEPING BADGERS LIE

I N DOCTOR MILTON'S ESTIMATION, Bob was compressing rehabilitation time from the original twelve-month plan into a period of time less than a single season of baseball. He explained the rapid progress to Roberta as, "He's his own best therapist."

Dr. Milton admitted he felt a vicarious thrill from Roberta's close association with the drama in Panama. He said his role in *the chain* was near its end, but the infectious excitement of being involved was going to be hard to leave behind.

For her part, Roberta's comfort level with him began when Po reviewed their meeting in New York. "Because we trust you, and because you should know what my father will be liberated into, I'll tell you everything I know."

The relationship between Doctor Milton and Roberta was strong at its core. They both were invested in seeing a good outcome, but less than an hour after Roberta boarded the boat for her journey to Harbinger, everything she knew became untrustworthy.

The plan for building the blue codex device became profoundly challenged by a crippling complication. Afterward, the information Dr. Milton received from Roberta grew increasingly incomplete. Eventually, what she was told, and what she passed along to Dr. Milton, was nothing short of false.

After Roberta's boat left the dock, Otis, Velas, and Huana procured a ladder and set out to retrieve the all-important marble from the *shem*. Before the party reached the building, two wild-eyed hiders approached, shouting for them to stay put while they retrieved a gun. One of the men ran past them, leaving his partner to explain.

"We didn't see need to interfere," the man said, while shifting from foot to foot and talking rapidly. "We thought, once see rats, they run away."

Velas placed his hands on the man's shoulders, in effect, pinning him in place. While the maneuver stopped his shuffling feet, the excited man began to moan and wring his hands. His eyes darted from face to face, then he cast them toward the ground, clearly uncomfortable with eye contact.

"Take a breath," Velas told him. "Is there something I can do?"

The question had a calming effect. Hyper movement turned to slow rocking, and the hider let one word out very slowly. "N-o-o-o."

"What happened?" Huana asked firmly.

"Is blood. Blood and stink. Nothing could save them."

"Someone went into the warehouse," Velas prompted. "What happened, next?"

"It was newlyweds. We think, ha, they will not stay, but they did. Aras and I, we looked through window. They opened secret door, like they knew what to do. I didn't know what to do, so we waited. The badger, he waited too. It was one minute, then screaming."

"God have mercy. The newlyweds. That explains my wet floor, last night." Huana darted up the path to the warehouse.

"Is too late!"

The shrill certainty in the voice made Huana stop running. She marched back to the group and pierced the hider with her one-eyed stare. "You're sure?"

"Is quiet, now. Door is locked, maybe blocked. Blood. Lots of blood. It runs under secret door. And stink. So much stink."

Huana turned to Otis and explained, "When a badger wants to intimidate a larger foe, he distends his anus. A pouch releases a suffocating odor. Bees fly away. Lions run away. I almost fainted on the night he attacked me."

As if in a trance, the hider whispered, "She say, 'Look under the bed.' He say, 'Get back.' She scream, 'Grab him.' He scream loud. She scream loud, then both of them … then only one is screaming … and then nobody scream, but badger growl and snort, like when he eat."

"We'll wait for the gun," Huana said. Looking at Otis, she rolled her eye and added, "This is my army."

"We should send for the shaman," Velas said. "We should hurry to the warehouse. Maybe there is something we can do."

"If they are alive, I will kill them myself. Who, but us, knows about the secret door? Only the X-Club." Huana turned her eye on Otis. With only a glance, Otis knew she was daring him to disagree. "As long as they know where we are," she said, "we aren't safe. As long as they think we know how to find *The Silver Book* they will not give us peace. If they learn we know nothing about that book, all of us are dead."

Velas hugged Huana and her expression shifted, from grim, into the forced smile of skeptical hopefulness "Peace will come when we make our machine and find a place to hide. Come, let's investigate this accident and see that blue marble."

Caspi and Aras arrived at the warehouse with a shotgun. A tearful Caspi refused to give Velas the weapon. "I will undo my mistake."

Caspi blasted the lock, and the door swung inward. The recoil caused her to stumble backward, off-balance. The barrel of the shotgun pointed toward the ceiling. Her knees buckled, and she struggled to stand straight against the stack of boxes at her back.

A collective gasp came from the group. They held their noses tight and screamed together, "Shoot! Shoot!"

The badger scrambled across the threshold, his front paws turned inward, as if his legs were attached at the wrong angle. This was his species' odd display, a pose, when they are on the attack. More easily recognizable as a sign of bad intent, he churned forward with his mouth open, snarfing as he galumphed down the single step in his dash toward Caspi. Uneven rows of teeth, all of them angled in different directions, perfect for the job of ripping and tearing, flashed in the narrow beams of sunlight penetrating the dark of the room. The animal didn't pause. Even when Caspi dropped the barrel and jabbed, like she was trying to spear the beast, he moved forward and clamped his bone-breaking jaws down on the business end of the shotgun and shook his head fiercely.

Huana rushed forward. Velas fired an impotent dart toward the thick fur and rhino-tough skin, but, with a sudden wail, Caspi pulled the trigger. The blast echoed, and the snarling ceased.

"My poor baby!" Caspi cried out, giving the memory of the smell, sight, and sounds of the carnage a surreal punctuation.

In the horrible quiet of the aftermath, Huana stepped over the animal and pulled a cell phone from a puddle of human blood in the secret room. She wiped it on her sweatpants. A blue light penetrated the dark liquid.

"Read it." she said, before handing the device to Velas.

Velas read the text silently, then he glanced around the room. His eyes stopped when he made eye contact with Otis. "Huana was right," he said, and then he read.

> Searching for files, but check this out.
> This looks like Buck Rogers' sp

The message ended. The last photo taken by the phone was the *shem*, gray and stone-like, as seen through the dirty glass of the windowpane above the air conditioner.

"What's the area code?" Huana asked.

"Laurel Canyon," Velas answered. "To *SilverKnight.*"

Otis walked out into the sunlight and stood, bent over, with his hands on his knees, staring at his bloody shoes, until the squeak of a wheelbarrow interrupted his thoughts. He watched Salas roll the bodies of the newlyweds past him, heading for the swamp by the old dock. Caspi followed, her badger wrapped in a sheet from the bed. Her path turned toward the river. When both processions rounded their turn in the path and disappeared from view, he shivered, and walked tiredly to the ladder.

Velas picked up the back end of the ladder, and they proceeded to the side of the building and climbed to the roof.

After transferring from the ladder, to the roof, and onto the *shem*, Otis dropped to his knees and leaned out over the stubby wing, this time throwing up without benefit of alcohol poisoning.

"I can't get to the marble," Otis told Velas, dejectedly, after wiping his mouth.

Velas rubbed his hands over the surface of the craft, tapping his knuckles on the bump that should have been the cockpit. After failing to find a crack between cockpit and fuselage, he concurred. "It's one solid piece of stone. How are we going to build the device without the marble?"

"How are we going to open the door to the golden room?" Otis added.

"Is everything alright up there?" Huana called.

"No!" the two men answered in unison.

From that moment, all correspondence with Roberta, so she wouldn't worry, was wrapped in the candy-coated message, "Everything is going well."

28

SIX WEEKS OF MAYDAY

O TIS WAS SICK OVER THE LOSS OF HIS NEW TOYS, but he was appalled by the bickering that followed the badger debacle. Frustrations bubbled up in discussions at the tree house.

Hayak let Huana know he believed she was cold-blooded, to allow the unceremonious dumping of the newlyweds into the swamp. "You have more feeling for the animal than for the human."

"Think of them as bloody Turks," Huana retorted. Her rejoinder gave Hayak an explanation he could understand.

Caspi upset Huana by informing her where she had buried the badger. "I think he deserves to join the others at the head spring," she said.

"That's too much honor," Huana said angrily. "Hallowed ground is no place for a pet cemetery."

Po was out of touch with the entire conversation. She said darkly, "We're all going to be drowned in the hole where this flow is taking us."

Velas added an engineering perspective to the gloom. "We're trying to build our house from the roof to the foundation."

Gloom, silent and heavy, lay on top of the people gathered together, and Otis could not lift so weighty a feeling with encouragement. What he said was aimed at shaming them all. "Bobby's been through worse," he said, "more than once."

Caspi addressed the gathering. "If you follow me to the head spring, we will say better words."

The procession walked the bank until they arrived at the bubbling swell of water, where Caspi pointed to a grassy area in front of three stones.

"This," she said, sweeping a hand in the direction of the stones, "is hallowed ground."

Caspi knelt by the first stone and laid her hands on its surface. "Beneath this rock, there is no body, only a guitar. It's all we have left of the man who lost hope, and then found the thread, the end of a chain, he believed was gone with his Grampy."

Reaching her hand toward the next stone, Caspi continued. "Under this stone lies the body of Miss Willa, a woman of learning and need. Fearful but strong, brought together by magic, she bonded with Mr. Lockjaw. Because she knew evil and loved good, she died without knowing how strong was the weld she added to the chain."

Huana stepped forward and placed her hand on the third stone. "Dorothy," she said. "God's child. Wise, simple, trusting, loving. Her spirit knew to love everyone. And she knew when to be a badger to the wicked."

Placing one hand on Dorothy's stone and another on the disturbed soil of the recently dug grave, Caspi pleaded with Huana, "May I love my pet? Don't begrudge him peace in his final burrow. Does it harm you if I give him to Dorothy in respect? There is room for him in my heart. Need he be in yours? My love for him can't spoil our common ground. Respect my belief."

A small stone was placed over the disturbed soil. Nothing was fundamentally changed. Skepticism became pandemic, but Otis stayed on the island to work with Velas. Po and Hayak returned to New York and gathered machinery. Huana continued to oversee the search project with the children. Caspi oversaw the downsizing of the tourist business and expansion of the business of fishing. All of this movement, on an island reaching the end of its history, went on unimpeded by a small marker acknowledging a moment of disruptive history.

The next day, when Po and Hayak boarded the ship to return home, Po hugged the sisters, telling them, "Us old badgers will stay relentless, but we should avoid sharing our setbacks with Bobby and Roberta."

The revision of history began.

All through the month of May, nobody celebrated, but nobody flagged.

29

THE MERRY MONTH OF MAY

AT HARBINGER, THE NUMBER OF BALL PLAYERS waxed and waned unpredictably. New patients approached with the standard, "Hi, can I play?" Charter members dropped out. Some came and went as the mood struck them.

The most constant group to show up every day was the staff members on break. Fearless built a small bleacher for them on which to sit and eat lunch.

Among the regular players, Bob and Freddy were the most dependable. The only day they missed was Tuesday — arts and crafts day.

Because it became a tradition for the two of them to pick sides, they almost never chatted while sitting on the bench. It was on Tuesdays when they talked life, background, future plans, and, for Freddy, the girl in the bleachers with the almond eyes and intense focus on the game.

"I wonder where she works," Freddy asked every week. "Do you think she would disrespect me more for being *Da Bum,* or for being in the nut house?"

Bob's answer varied. The first time Freddy asked the question, he told him, "Go ahead and ask her. She would probably like to hear a new pickup-line."

The next week, he answered, "Seriously, guy, she's a fan of the game. Talk to her about the game, until she gets to know you. Then ask her what she disrespects about you."

On the third Tuesday of arts and crafts, Bob said, "Rip a good swing that tears apart a tennis ball, then pose like the Hulk and growl, *oof, grunt, oof, grunt.* Chicks can't resist that."

On the last Tuesday in May, everything came together. Bob finished his mobile project and carried it to Dr. Milton's office. His secretary promised she would put it on his desk where he would be sure to see it after he returned from his rounds.

The doctor hung the mobile over his desk and sat, studying the art, until, finally, he read the message in the new Icarus.

A yellow-orange sun, surrounded by long, graceful coronas, glared hot at the top of the sculpture. Beneath the sun, Icarus, with one wing burned black and the other not fully feathered, stared into the fiery orb with a look of determination. One hand wrapped around a flaming corona; the other was thrust toward the sun's face, his fingers clenched in a fist. On his back, a parachute pack hung unopened. There were no pigs, fish, or flying monkeys. Just one man, determined but cautious, challenging a powerful symbol of an unbeatable foe. The face on the surface of the angry sun was unmistakable. Bob had captured his own image well.

Dr. Milton clapped his hands together and made two phone calls. The first was to Bob's room. "I can have a car ready today if you like. You and Freddy can pick up movie passes from my secretary. Make sure you get back here by nine."

The second call was to a girl with almond eyes. "Your father is going to the Cinema 24 today. I think he's about to liberate himself."

At the cinema, speaking over the blare of ear-busting car crashes, Freddy returned to his favorite Tuesday topic. "God, I can't believe it. I saw her when I was getting popcorn. My girl from the bleachers is here. Should I talk to her?"

Bob didn't come up with a smart-ass answer for his friend. Freddy was hushed by a woman sitting directly behind them — a girl with pretty almond eyes. Freddy shifted his big frame down into the seat and tried to make himself invisible.

After the movie let out, he told Bob, "She probably thinks I'm goofy."

"Well?" Bob answered, leaving the answer hanging. "Let's pick a restaurant. If she shows up there, tell her you're not goofy. That'll set her straight."

Freddy fumed. "I'd rather be Goofy than Alvin the Chipmunk," he said, then immediately turned red with embarrassment and regret.

"Who wouldn't?" Bob answered with a laugh. "Chicks love a man with big feet."

*   *   *

When Bob returned from his excursion, Jarvis greeted him with a question. "Good movie?"

"No. Good time," he answered. "No angry people. I walked around like a free man."

*   *   *

When Roberta called home that evening, she gave a glowing account of her father's progress, and predicted he would be home much sooner than expected.

On the other end of the line, Po reported good news. This time, it was genuine.

"Hayak was going through the papers that came with CSI's machines. Some of his work was tucked away in the pages of a manual. Are you sitting down? The yellow paint in the Illinois cave is a match for the material we need to finish the recipe. Pray for more good luck."

"Wow. Just like that. Don't get greedy, Mom. Everything is falling right into our laps as it is."

30

THE WHITE BUS TOUR

VELAS TOOK ADVANTAGE OF HAYAK'S SMUGGLING SKILLS and followed his advice. He entered the USA, with dozens of other men, in a white bus.

Hayak provided minimal papers. Velas provided the words sure to get him an invitation to cross the border: "I agree to the wages. I will pick strawberries and oranges for ninety days, then find my way back home."

Velas intended to honor his promise to return home. He lied about picking the red and orange fruits. He came to assist in the harvesting and testing of yellow paint.

On the long bus ride from Nogales, Mexico to Lake Wales, Florida, Velas received an education in the ecology of corporate agrarian economy. He wasn't sure if the overseer for the workers openly mocked the arrangement, or if he was giving a welcoming speech.

"Your sponsor welcomes you. They pay your wages. Under the *Temporary Worker Entry Reform Program,* hereafter referred to as TWERP, a portion of your salary will be deducted to help defray sponsor expenses incurred in transportation to the job-site, drug testing, housing rebates, and food vouchers. After termination, the federal government will assume the responsibilities for assistance in housing, medical care, and education. If you are joined by family members, food vouchers must be updated. Because a web of governmental offices facilitate these benefits, it is imperative paperwork must be properly filled out. If you need help with understanding these documents, assistance will be provided by the TWERP liaison officer at the hiring site. If you don't understand these instructions, ask someone on your bus with skills in the English language. Thank you and welcome to America."

"What is he saying?" Velas asked the man sitting next to him.

The man pulled his hat down over his head, folded his arms, and closed his eyes, preparing to sleep. "What he's not saying is, when the papers expire, taxpayers continue to pay for *cheap* orange juice. If you break the law, you can be deported. If you behave, you become a shadow-American. Stockholders make money. Politicians blame the victims, bill the uninvested, and sell daisy-chain reams of 'reform' laws. He's saying it's a mess, man, but take it while you can."

When Velas arrived at the juicing facility outside of town, he stood in a long line. Other buses were unloading, and it was one man at a time, entering a double-wide trailer on the parking lot, giving a name to a man at the door.

After his name was scratched from the list, Velas opened his mouth to allow a man to flatten his tongue with a thin wooden paddle and go through the motions of staring down his throat.

At his next station in line, he entered a room where a man with a clipboard, standing next to a table full of bottles, asked, "Name?"

"Guapo Legumbres," Velas answered sheepishly.

A woman peeled a stick-on label, applied it to a bottle, and handed it to Velas. Taking the bottle in hand, Velas confirmed it was properly labeled with his false identity.

"Over there." The woman with the labels pointed to an open door.

Inside the room, Velas took his cue from the other men. He lowered his sweatpants, peed into his bottle, capped it, and followed, in line, to a table by the back door. After placing his sample with the others on the table, he followed the line out the door and onto the parking lot.

Hayak was parked nearby. When he opened the passenger door, Velas left the line and climbed into the car.

"How'd it go?" Hayak asked him.

"Couldn't you have just picked me up across the river in Texas?"

"If so, no papers for you. Now, for ninety days, is okay. Put seat belt on. It's the law. They enforce it." Hayak demonstrated the seat belt and pulled out of the parking space.

Velas began pressing buttons on his door panel until he found the right button to open his window. "Why the funny name? Is this American humor?"

Hayak laughed. "I give you a name with no warrants attached. Relax, is a long way to Illinois. I show you Memphis. The Beale Street blues, The King's house, Lorraine Motel, Danny Thomas hospital — is all of America in one place."

"No orange pickers?"

"Same thing, different crops. Is on the way."

"I want to get our business finished and go home."

"Yeah, business. How is Otis doing?"

"He says he understands the symbolism of the Caral balls. One marble, inside another, inside another. Three devices, one machine. We worked out plans for their crucibles. All we need is the paint material ... and the marble."

"I mean, how is Otis doing?"

"He talks to angels every day, still, no marble. I don't think they are listening."

31

UNDER THE JUNE-SWOON MOON

"ALL THOSE SONGS," Freddy drawled, "I never really heard them before."

"Songs?" Bob was barely listening, focused on the stubborn clay dust he was trying to wipe off his shoes before entering The Sylvan.

"June swoon used to mean a slump on the field after April and May." Freddy laughed. "Hell, I had a June swoon for six months running."

"And, now?" Bob swiped at the stains on his blue jeans.

"June. Swoon. Moon. I hear the message. I'm a goofy sap for those almond eyes. I finally worked up the nerve to talk to her."

Bob stood up straight, "I don't think I have enough experience in these things to get sappy about rhymes. What did you guys talk about?"

"I asked her if she wanted to play, where she worked, what's your name ... that stuff." Freddy held the door open for Bob, and they walked together to the elevator.

"What's her name?"

"Berti. She changed the subject without answering the other two questions."

"Ah, a mystery woman," Bob slapped Freddy on the back. "More challenging than those groupies you had on the way up? What did she want to talk about?"

Freddy reached for the elevator button, but paused before pressing. "My swing. I think she fixed my swing."

"How'd she do that?"

"She said I swung from the shoulders when I wanted to mash the ball, but I barreled the ball up when I swung from the wrists. She suggested I move my hips toward the pitch, then start the arm motion from the shoulders to the hands, and then snap the wrist when it all comes together with the ball in your wheelhouse. I can visualize it. It showed promise today. With more repetition ... I think I'll be ready to try the Bigs again." Freddy smiled confidently. "She's a gem."

"You're goofy over this girl because she's a good coach?" Bob watched the lights above the door as the descent ended at the lobby.

When the doors opened, two men stepped out; giving no indication they noticed Bob or Freddy.

"Should I notify the Canyon, Mr. Knight?" The younger man asked while tapping on his phone.

"ASAP," was the brusque answer.

Stepping onto the elevator, Freddy hit the button for his residence on the second floor and another for Bob's third floor box seat. "She seems interested in my sandlot project. She thinks the cultural differences in communities will be the biggest hindrance."

"How's that?" Bob asked.

"Different vandalism expectations, cultural popularity levels for the game, youth violence statistics, etc. How to build safe places, avoid red-lining. How to let the grass-root communities embrace the idea and, the way she put it, 'get them to see the fields as neutral sites, like the indigenous tribes treated places of natural beauty.' She has my head spinning in new directions."

"I think I like this girl."

"Me too," Freddy stepped off the elevator and added, "If I could get her under the moon, I'd swoon, 'cause, I ain't had no lovin' since January, February, July, or June."

32

AYAHUASCA JUNE

OTIS BECKLEY HAD REASONS TO NEVER CONSIDER the idea of participating in an *ayahuasca* ceremony. He brushed those reasons away. They were irrelevant melodrama, he told himself, ashes in the dustbin of the past, disturbances in the present, stowaway moments, without room for storage, on his trip into the future. Instead of reviewing those irrelevancies, he researched the literature of the scientific community and came away convinced he would give it a try.

"I'd like to take part in the *ayahuasca* ceremony," he told the shaman in charge of the event. "I want to experience the voice of my head spirit."

"Your head spirit is only a guide to what you bury inside you and the illustrator for why you are small and the world is large, within and without. He is not the host with a lamp shade on his head at a party."

The shaman studied Otis's face while he silently pondered a response to the shaman's message. When the delay went too long, the shaman startled Otis by thrusting his hands, fingers spread wide, near his face, waving them in front of his eyes while singing a medley of snippets from familiar tunes.

"Incense, peppermint, strawberry fields, in the sky with diamonds, eight miles high ..."

Otis grinned uncomfortably, but turned his head away from the shaman's waving hands and put his own hand out to protest the bizarre eruption. The shaman ended his theater of exaggerated freakiness and began to mimic *The Twilight Zone* theme, all the while taking on a mime pose of a man leaning against a mantlepiece, removing a pipe from his mouth.

"Do do do do, do do do do, dooo, dododado."

At the end of the parody, he spoke in a lecturing Rod Serling tone. "Day after day, alone on a hill, a man, with a foolish grin, is keeping perfectly still. Are you sure you want to know him ... *dododado* ... in *The Twilight Zone*?"

"I, I know what I'm getting into," Otis answered uncomfortably. "I've done my research."

"What have you learned?"

"The *ayahuasca* vine, alone, has no psychedelic effect. The experience is unlocked by a secondary choice of a benign catalyst that allows the psychoactive ingredient to penetrate the stomach lining and enter the bloodstream. From the bloodstream, it travels to the neocortex of the brain and hyper excites the region where the weighing of choices and finalizing of decision-making occurs. Secondarily, it excites the amygdala area, where childhood memories are stored."

"We think of it as stirring the spirits who remember our ancestors and clarify our thoughts, but let's not play word games." The shaman cocked his head and squinted into Otis's eyes. "What are you attempting to clarify and why revisit the voice of your ancestors?"

"I have reasons of my own. I want to share them with my head spirit."

"Your head spirit has his own thoughts. He doesn't care to be your plaything. Look hard into your memories before you open the door for your ... before you unlock your amygdala. If you lock before the leap, you will have fewer surprises."

"Then I have your permission?"

"Wait until July. When Velas returns, ask him to sponsor you. In the meantime, quit begging after the servants of your spirit for a return of your blue toy, and allow yourself to think of it as something you don't own."

"It is something only I can control."

"Really? Evidence indicates otherwise."

33

THE CLOWN HAS LEFT THE CIRCUS

THEY SAY THE EVENTS IN A DREAM play out as if they were unfolding in real time. Measured by the electrical impulses in the dream center of the brain, scientists claim the duration of each dream is measured in fleeting seconds. Perhaps memory-floods operate in the same way.

Po answered the phone as she turned on the street to her house. She was coming home from grocery shopping, stocked up with what she hoped would please her house guest for the week. Hayak and Velas were returning from their cave trip and should arrive sometime that day.

The call was from Roberta. She had nothing to update on her father's progress. "I think he's plateaued at normal," she said. "Have Dad and Velas shown up yet?"

"I'm not sure. I'm pulling into the driveway now." Po hit the remote and the eighteenth-century iron gates swung open.

"How's the weather?" Roberta asked, but she didn't wait for an answer. "I'll wait for you to open the garage door. Tell me if his car is in the garage." Waiting without talking wasn't one of Roberta's trademarks. "It's starting to heat up here. I wish there was shade at the diamond. The marigolds along the walkway to the Sylvan are starting to bloom. They seem to grow brighter at dusk. I miss the tulips ..."

Memory time fell over Po while she raised her remote to open the garage door The cobblestone of the driveway, the massive doors of the old carriage house that framed the new, modern doors, and the mention of tulips joined to put Po on pause. She was transported by memories to her early days as secretary to Bill Elliott.

Long ago, the garage at Bill's compound used to be a functioning carriage house, with a stable, blacksmith station, and indoor parking for a variety of wagons and carriages. The outer architecture had the elegant look of a livery, built for the pleasure of a royal household. Two side-by-side doors, a story-and-a-half tall, each as wide as the doors of a two-engine fire house, gave Po the impression its builders knew how to elevate a functional utility into a statement of grandiose proportion.

An old lithograph of the building hung in Bill's library. On the print, both giant doors stood open. A two-horse team, frozen in high-stepping showiness, as they exited onto the cobblestone, was the focus of the print. The artist's view, with the iron gate at his back, captured the horses as they pranced toward the street. Behind the covered carriage they pulled, inside the building, a blacksmith held his hammer over an anvil. A young boy manned the bellows. A foppishly dressed man with African features held a horse in permanent stillness, while another young child, seemingly a twin of the bellows operator, scrubbed the horse with a long-handled mop.

The sense of motion in the depiction of the horses, details of the carriage, the background figures in the shadow of the carriage house, the cobblestone drive, and even the tulips alongside the driveway, were the work of a master artist.

It had been a long time since Po thought about the lithograph. She had once been so obsessed with the artistry she took it outside, into the light, and counted the bricks in front of the doors to verify the artist's documentation of detail. She had been interrupted by Bill while counting the tulips along the driveway and matching their location with the blooming bulbs adorning the scene on the very spring morning of her curiosity.

Bill interrupted her thoughts with a question for which the answer was obvious. "The work of a genius?"

"It's not signed," Po remembered saying. "How long do tulips live?"

"I never counted the years," he answered. "They're only important for a week at a time, once a year. That is, if you mean that in terms of the bloom. Once, they were, pound for pound, more valuable than gold. This carriage house, the main house, the guest house, the servants' quarters, even Hershey, Pennsylvania, and the city of Winter Haven, Florida ... I could go on. They owe their existence to tulips and the foolishness of tulip fancy."

Po, lost in memories and inattentive to Roberta's words over the phone, whispered the words, "tulip fancy."

"What? 'Tulip fancy'?" Roberta stopped mid-sentence in her monologue and waited for an answer.

The question jarred Po from her thoughts, and she reached for the remote to open the modern garage doors, surprised the device was in her hand, and the door was rising.

"Mom? Still there?"

"Yes. I was just thinking about the tulips. So the marigolds are nice?"

"Is that all you have to say? What about the boy I met? No comment?"

"The boy. What boy? Where did you meet him? Who is he?"

"I met him here, at Harbinger. He's Father's best friend. Were you listening?"

"I'm sorry, I was distracted. He works at Harbinger?"

"He's a patient. He's different."

"Isn't that kind of a given? Seeing how he's a patient in a mental asylum?"

"Mom, he's not crazy, he's got his reasons for being here. I can tell you all about it."

"Tell me all about it at home, young lady. We have lots of things to talk about. I need you here, before we get washed away through a hole in a wall."

"Mom? There's something you're not telling me. You're not okay."

"No. Something is wrong. I ..."

A tap on the passenger side window startled Po, and she jumped at the sound. It was Hayak, bending to the window, smiling. Behind him stood Velas.

Po held one finger up to ask Hayak to wait a moment then moved her hand to the steering wheel, softly touching the indicator light that showed her contact with Roberta was still open. She caressed the blue light as if it were a lock of her daughter's unruly hair and said, with tones of sadness in her voice, "Roberta, please, come home. I'm going to hang up."

"No, mom, wait." Roberta's voice was abrupt. "There is one thing I need to tell you. Dr. Milton says that Waldo Kurtwood died yesterday. He thinks the news might be important for our Panamanian friends ... Mom?"

"Yes, dear, I hear you. Waldo's dead. Another bump in the stream. Come home." Po pressed the button on the steering wheel and the call ended.

Po guided the car into the garage, juggling in her orderly, organizational mind which of her thoughts were the most relevant, and which actions should be addressed first. As she stepped out of the car, she chose to address them in the reverse order her mind ranked them in importance. Groceries came first, greeting her guest was second, Waldo news was third, Roberta's puppy love was fourth, and her quickly coagulating mix of intuition and a premonition of doom would wait.

34

A CALL TO THE BULLPEN

B IG, BLOWOUT GAMES ARE NOTHING NEW in the shrinking world of sandlot. Whichever side of the score you happen to be on, the game breaks down to the individual level. If you're on the winning side, with the outcome no longer in doubt, the team becomes a secondary concern to the goal of personal bests. No worries — just man against himself, trying to satisfy the happy muse that calls you to achieve ever higher levels of performance.

If you're on the losing side, there is no muse, only you and the inner voice that whispers, *You suck.* If you're not in the category of people who throw the towel into the ring, blame your teammates, or believe competition ends with the last hope for victory on the scoreboard, you play on. One play at a time, each victory over your own disappointment, every inning after reality has set in, you hone your grit. You enjoy the opportunity to play. You realize the experience is as close to living the short life as it gets.

On the day after Berti got her mother's signal to steal home, she watched the other kind of game. Since the last days of May, it became a routine event for Freddy to find time to leave the bench and steal moments of chit chat with his favorite fan. After games, they spoke for longer periods.

The usual seven-inning game, on this day, was holding fast to a one-one tie. In the eleventh inning, with two outs, Freddy McPheeters watched the green ball, from the pitcher's hand to the barrel of the bat. He shifted weight to his front hip, followed his hip movement with the forward motion of his elbows, then snapped his wrists, increasing his bat speed at the moment the ball entered his wheelhouse. The synchronized body movements directed their energy perfectly into one location, just in the moment bat met ball. The impact resulted in a loud *whomp* — similar to the sound of an un-aerodynamic Freddy McPheeters dead duck of an exploded tennis ball on a short flight path.

Bob looked up from his position at third base and tried to track where the dead, flopping bird would fall in the infield, but he couldn't spot it. Behind him, in left field, the call was made even before the ball sailed over the fence.

"Mercy," his left fielder exclaimed.

"Holy shit," the center fielder added.

"Save your big swings for when the game is on the line," Freddy crowed to Bob as he rounded third

Slapping hands as he crossed home plate, Freddy kept trotting until he reached the bleachers. "That one was for you," he told Berti as he reached her perch.

"That one was *because* of me," she corrected, slapping his outstretched hand. Dryly, pointedly, she added, "Don't forget to play the bottom half of the inning."

As they traded smug looks, a muffled ping from the diamond announced an infield popup. Freddy told Berti, "I'll see you in three more outs." Then he ran to the bench to retrieve his glove.

As he trotted past Bob, he goaded him again. "If you have a big swing, old man, use it now."

It took but two pitches to record the first two outs of the inning. The next batter, fake lawyer Michael Dixon, sent a double into the gap.

Bob was next up. He was known to be a line drive hitter with little power. Behind him was the girl the gang at the diamond called, Wet Betsy. She was from the alcohol rehab unit, seldom sober, and always ready to swing. From the bleachers, to the benches, and in the field, everyone who knew the players would have to assume Bob needed to smack one of his rare home runs to win the game.

On the way to the box, Bob stopped to whisper to Betsy. "Do what I do."

What Bob did, was watch six pitches hit the catcher's glove. On the sixth pitch, the umpire pointed to first base and hollered, "Ball four."

For two pitches, Betsy kept the bat on her shoulder. On the second pitch, a called strike-one, Dixon stole third and Bob took second on the muffed throw.

"Oh, I got this." Betsy nodded and winked, pointing a finger toward second base. She crouched, bat held high, shooting darts of determination from her eyes. It was apparent she was going to go for the gusto. The groan from the bench could be heard in the bleachers.

"I'll pitch it underhand, if you like," the pitcher shouted to the batter, rubbing a little insult into what looked like an easy win.

Betsy snorted and pawed at the ground with her back foot, then crouched, raising the bat like an executioner's axe. The pitch arced toward the plate, and she whiffed, swinging so early she made contact on the backswing. Incredibly, the ball popped into the air, dropping three feet in front of home plate.

"Infield fly rule," shouted the pitcher as Dixon flew toward home and Bob chugged toward third.

"Infield fly rule," the pitcher repeated, as the english on the tipped ball spun it backwards toward the plate.

The catcher lunged, stopping the ball from going foul, and fell on his face. Dixon bore down and scored ahead of the catcher's effort to spin around and make the tag.

"Infield fly rule. She's out," the pitcher hollered again.

Bob rounded third, slowly, while Betsy jumped up and down on first base, shouting above the call from the pitcher's mound. "Tie game, tie game."

Taking up the pitcher's call, the catcher turned to the ump, "Infield fly rule, batter's out, we win," he pleaded.

The ump put his hands on his hips, just like the real umps do when bracing for a one-sided argument, and stood silent behind the plate. The pitcher ran toward the umpire. The catcher slammed both glove and ball into the dust. Both benches stood and inched forward to hear the upcoming argument.

From the outfield, Freddy tried to alert his team they were about to lose both game and argument. "Dammit, play ball! Time out!" he screamed, while pointing toward Bob.

Bob joined the players at the plate by walking calmly from third base to home and tapping the catcher on the shoulder. asking the catcher to "excuse me."

Finally finding words to more appropriately call the attention of his team to the on-field situation, Freddy shouted, "Tag him, tag him dammit, tag Bob!"

It was too late. Bob grinned at the catcher, both feet on the plate.

"Runner is safe. Game is over. Home team wins." The umpire threw his hands in the air, as if signaling a touchdown, and laughed.

The home team mobbed Bob and whooped in celebration, as Betsy flew into their circle, screaming, "I did it. I did it."

Open-mouthed and confused, the losers trotted in from their positions. It took a while, but they, too, began to grin, and finally, they laughed. One of the finer lessons of sandlot was in play. Today's rivals would be tomorrow's teammates.

Freddy walked over to the bleachers and sat next to Berti, chagrin covering his face.

"What just happened?" Berti asked.

"Sandlot, that's what," Freddy answered. "Lucky old fart is going to give me hell about this one."

"Well, don't let it ruin your day," Berti said while stifling a laugh. "Whatever it was, it was fun to watch."

"Only one thing can ruin my day today. I've worked up the nerve to do something scary." Freddy sucked his lips in and wrinkled his face. "Would you go out with me? I know you like movies. Dinner and a movie? You and me? I really like you … a lot."

Berti mirrored the look on Freddy's face. After a long pause she answered. "I'd like to get permission from my father."

"You … I'm not sure what you're saying. I can wait … how long?" Freddy stumbled over his words, more confused by the archaic answer than the rules to the infield fly rule.

Berti touched his knee and stood. "I'll call him right now."

Heads turned on the bleachers when she made the call. Everyone on the field stopped what they were doing when Berti sucked in a long breath and began singing:

Bake be bout boo ba ball bame.
Bake be bout boo ba browd.
Buy be bum beebuts band bracker back ...

She stopped singing and put one hand over her lips.

Freddy never knew the history of the Killer Bees, but he saw Berti's hands trembling and tears began to well up in her eyes, so he reached for the hand that dangled at her side.

On the field, Bob stepped toward the bleachers. Tears didn't wait to well, they spilled as quickly as he recognized Po in Berti's almond eyes, and understood the call of the song.

"Bi bon't bare bif Bi bebber bum back," he sang. He meant it.

He never came back to Harbinger. He approved Freddy's offer to date his daughter, and, at least for that moment, he let his spirit soar farther than a Freddy McPheeters bomb.

35

HOME SCHOOLING

P O WAS PUTTING AWAY BREAKFAST DISHES when Roberta arrived at the house in late morning. "You should have called," she said in her mother's reproach voice. "Hayak and Velas just left for the post office. Are you hungry? Sit down; I'll make another pot of coffee."

"You drink too much coffee when you're worried, Mom." Roberta broke off the hug and turned toward the drawer with the coffee filters. "So do I."

In the four minutes it took for the coffee to brew, Pɔ peppered her daughter with questions about the man she met in Kansas, finally circling back to her biggest issue. "So, if there is one place worse than a singles bar, for meeting men, would that be a mental institution?"

"What took you so long?" Roberta stirred the cream into her coffee with her finger. "I think it's cute that you worry and Dad trusts me completely. It gives me balance. Freddy is in New York to interview a trainer and sign papers with his agent. He's looking to sign on with the Yankees. You should meet him first, then get all motherish with me."

"Okay, fair enough. What about Bobby? He didn't come to New York with you guys?"

The toaster dinged, and Roberta popped up as fast as the toast. Juggling the hot bread all the way to her plate on the table, she sat down and reached for the butter knife. She was spreading the butter on bread before she answered.

"It's weird. You still call him Bobby."

"I slip sometimes and call him Robert. I can't get used to Bob."

"Are you ever going to call me Berti? Freddy calls me Berti."

"It's not important." Po broke eye contact with her daughter and bowed her head, tapping her coffee cup with her finger.

"What is important, Mom? I took a red-eye get here. What is so wrong?"

"I can't say."

"What do you mean? You didn't tell me to come home to bask in silent worries. What's up?" Roberta pushed herself back into her chair and folded her arms.

Po stood and paced a circle around her chair, fidgeting with her hair, then sat back down again. "I haven't cleared my list of issues. Let's deal with them before I get to the worries." She reached across the table and offered Roberta her hand. "Please?"

"Fine, Mom. Let's see ... Father is flying to Panama to see Otis before he comes here. He knows you think the house is his. He doesn't want it. Freddy is donating a chunk of money to Harbinger with a proviso that gives Jarvis Douglas the recreation director's position. The ball field stays. Jarvis will have Father's room as his office, and he inherits Dr. Milton's secretary. I still plan on going to college. I plan on going to Panama to talk to Huana about her children's relocation project. I'm a happy, busy bee, and my only worry is you. Does that shorten the distance between the issues and the big hairy worry?"

"Dr. Milton is giving up his secretary?"

Roberta stood up and retrieved the coffee pot, bringing it over to the table and topping off both cups. "I know the doctor called you about Father. He didn't tell you he's resigning from Harbinger?"

"No. He said he was going on vacation. He and his wife are going to drive coast to coast with the wind in their hair. He had nice things to say about you."

Roberta didn't respond. She waited, motionless, for Po to continue.

Suddenly, Po burst like a dam, no longer able to hold back a reservoir of muddy water. "We've been lying to you. Otis lost his marble. Velas has everything ready, but there is nothing to do. It's Asitr all over again: Get to the finish line and fall over dead. Heaven has withdrawn protection. The chain is broken, I don't know where. I can't sleep without seeing horrors, I can't pretend anymore. Young men will have visions; old men will have dreams. I'm middle-aged. I get both. The drums of doom are getting louder, and the world is withdrawing from its design to serve us. Someone close is planning to betray us. Everything I believe in is fake. Satan has all the evidence he needs for a successful prosecution. Everyone I love is going to die, and, on the street, everything looks normal. I think, maybe, it's menopause."

Roberta sipped from her cup and sat it down, repeating the act again before opening her mouth. No words came out, and she sipped again. Finally, she said, "Menopause? Is that what I have to look forward to?"

"Maybe not." Po sighed.

"You and Dad lied to me?"

"For your own good. We didn't want to distract you. You were so focused on your father."

"Someone is going to betray us?"

"Yes."

"Is it Velas?"

"Why do you say that name?"

"I have your instincts, Mom. There are so many gifted people in Asitr's chain. He is the odd piece. The X-Club didn't have surveillance tech on the island, but they knew things about Dorothy, Lock, and Willa. He's guided Huana from the start of the awakening. If the X-Club has an insider, he's the most likely suspect."

"I hope you're wrong. No, I hope you're right." Po lifted an empty cup to her lips, then she poured another cup from the pot. "I haven't drank this much coffee since I thought Asitr was the devil."

36

REUNITED

"ADMITTEDLY, FLYING HERE WAS UNCOMFORTABLE," Bob told Otis, after they smiled their way through the reunion on the island and peeled away to be alone together. "It wasn't the claustrophobia of the airplane, it was realizing the loud, clatter-trap nature of a box, made by human hands, wasn't as safe as Kae'Lairy's contraption."

"At least you had a rough estimate for how long the flight would last." Otis grinned and hugged his old box-mate. "We're like two old war veterans, eh? I'm glad the war is over for you."

"Is it?" Bob pulled away from the hug and mingled doubt with surprise into his reply. "Do you feel like it's over for you?"

"No, not for me. I have to finish Dorothy's war. The angels gave me the marble, and, I'm convinced, I'll get it back in time to get the job done." Otis tightened his jaw around the grin on his face and stepped forward, embracing Bob in another hug. "You have your daughter. Enjoy her. She's a real peach. Tell me about her."

"She's nothing like me. She has good instincts. We drove from Lawrence together, on our way to the Kansas City airport. She arranged a little side-trip first. We stopped at a cemetery in Blue Springs. My parents are buried there. I would never think to do that after they betrayed me."

"She didn't warn you ahead of time?" Otis looked shocked at the thought.

Bob put a hand on Otis's shoulder. "I was half-way to forgiving them. At least I opened up about them on Bill's last broadcast. You still won't mention your family. I recommend you sweep out the cobweb in your closet. When I knelt between the graves and felt the grass over them, I realized I forgave them. I wish they could have had time in a box to rethink their path out of the short life. I was lucky."

Otis laughed out loud at the idea. "Lucky? Tell that to little Bobby McKinney, all curled up on the moon, sucking his figurative thumb and holding his spiritual breath until he turned blue. What's happened to that little brat?"

"He's gone. I forgive him, too."

"Otis smiled the warm involuntary smile that makes the eyes sparkle and said, "I'm so happy for you. I'm going to talk to my head spirit in July about my family. I want your peace of mind."

"You have time to rethink that. I'm not sure you can arrange that trip into binary solutions. Nobody can, but ... enough about us. Show me around the island."

"Lunch first?"

"Do they still serve chocolate pudding, black beans and blue liqueurs?"

"Oh," Otis blushed and twisted his lips to avoid the embarrassed grin. "Roberta told you about that?"

37

PRELUDE TO A DANCE

H AYAK AND VELAS RETURNED FROM THE POST OFFICE with a mixed bag of news. Packages were shipped to the wrong locations, but unexpectedly, Guapo Legumbres received two credit card offers.

Hayak set a heavy package on the kitchen table and motioned for Velas to set his package down as well.

"Is funny," Hayak said. "Nine days a temporary worker, and now, Guapo has offers to owe the banks. God bless America. And, there is this." He reached into his shirt pocket and pulled out two orange cards. "UPS leave on gate. They have two packages for Guapo. Both too big for post office. Some equipment is astray, shipped to island, not here."

"What's in the boxes on the table?" Po tested the weight of the larger box by pushing it with her hand. "It's a heavy thing."

"That is an industrial boring engine." Velas answered. "The other is a gas-powered hacksaw. I need them for work on the island."

"What got shipped to the island?" Roberta asked from the doorway, surprising the two men.

"Roberta! You're home." Hayak crossed the kitchen and lifted Roberta's feet off the floor with a hug.

"It's good to see you again." Velas smiled. "How is your father?"

Roberta ignored the question. "What got shipped to Panama?" she repeated.

"A mass spectrometer," Velas answered. "It's for fine-tuning elemental analysis ratios before we analyze crystalline structures near the metal-nonmetal border."

"You have a mass spectrometer already set up in the basement." Roberta was matter-of-fact with her statement. Her face was humorless.

Velas didn't seem to notice the serious look on Roberta's face. He smiled through his explanation. "The one in the basement is an older model. It's trustworthy to within .04% deviation in analysis. I'm not sure that is good enough."

"What's waiting at UPS?" Roberta probed with more questions, like a lawyer poking an off-balance witness.

Velas didn't let the grin slip from his mouth, but his eyes showed he was puzzled. He stared at her, slow to respond.

Hayak jumped in with the answer. "Is one set of titanium hacksaw blades and some drill bits. We find both online. Now, I want know too, how is your father?"

"He's fine. Blades and bits too big for the post office to ship?"

"Too long, sweety," Hayak answered, holding his arms spread in front of him, his hands marking the ends of an invisible tape measure. "No worries, we get all straightened out. Is no more than setting right a messed-up fish order." Hayak turned Roberta toward the door to the garage and announced, "We have pizza in the car. We have two sacks of movies, DVD, VHS, all for movie-night library on island. Come, help bring everything in, then we talk about your father."

"I'll carry the boxes to the basement," Velas called after them.

"I'll start coffee," Po added, winking at Roberta as she exited the kitchen.

"Hayak hooked arms with Roberta as they walked through the entryway between the kitchen and garage. When they stepped into the garage, he asked, "What now is up I am the last to know?"

"Did Velas tell you he spoke to Huana about Wally's death?" Roberta asked.

"Yes, he called that very night."

Roberta stopped walking and shook her head from side to side. "Huana says he didn't mention it. We talked to her just fifteen minutes ago."

Hayak slowed his steps but didn't turn to face Roberta until he reached the car. "What this mean?"

"This means Velas is playing games. How many fish orders have we messed up in all the years we've handled them?"

Hayak opened the car door and the smell of garlic escaped. "What has Velas done? Is need to worry?"

Roberta continued with questions. "How does each separate shipping transaction go to the opposite location?"

"Here, you carry movies, I carry pizzas." Hayak put his weight against the door until it closed. "Is this about losing marble? These pieces not fit into picture of ugly thinking."

"If Velas is going to reship his tools, why is he taking them to the basement? Is the drill bit long enough to penetrate the room in the basement?" Roberta peeked into one of the bags of movies, and her serious expression turned into an amused, sardonic grin. "*Mosquito Coast*? How appropriate. Who chose this movie?"

"I read cover. Is about man who invent a magic ice machine and go to Central America to hide from world. I think, hey, is that funny coincidence. This man go crazy and he die, so no, not funny, but coincidence, yes. I choose movie. Now, maybe you suspect me of some wrong thing?"

"Dad, I'm going to Panama tomorrow. Don't tell Velas. Don't tell him Father is there either. When you get a chance, listen to Mom. You need to listen to Mom. Promise?"

"I think you catch something at that loony bin, but I listen. I lie to good man Velas and listen, but I see no games being played. Velas is big part of chain." Hayak secured the warm pizza boxes and started walking toward the door. "Come, be nice to our guest. All will be fine."

As Roberta reached for the doorknob, Hayak stopped her. "Wait. How you go to Panama?"

"Freddy's chartered a plane. It's our first date."

"Is crazy. You kids today. First date." The expression on Hayak's face was like a man looking for a place to spit.

"What did you and Mom do on your first date?"

"I take her to baby doctor for checking out if you abnormal from tense, supernatural experiences. He say you all right and I kiss her from happiness. I think of it as first date, because she kiss me back."

"Aw. Dad, that's sweet."

"Yes, but maybe tests not so conclusive."

Hayak and Roberta stifled laughs as she opened the door. By the time they walked the distance to the kitchen door, they both settled into their game-faces.

38

LUNCHING, WITH THE LANGUID

THE CAFÉ ON SAM'S ISLAND no longer operated on a schedule for tourists. There were no tourists on the island. Sparse fare was available at the buffet for the two American guests and the workers who were dismantling some of the island's structures.

With the workers busy at the fish processing center on the far end of the island, Bob and Otis were the only diners in the building until Huana came in and sat at their table. Without trading social niceties, she abruptly got to the point.

"Caspi is bringing Velas's wife to eat lunch with you. Stay with her until I return. I might need a half-hour." Huana stood up and leaned in Bob's direction. "Your name is Carlos."

"My name is Carlos?"

"Here they are now. Don't forget: your name is Carlos. That's all she needs to know." Huana passed the two women on her way out the front door and fast-walked across the square.

The two men watched as Caspi filled a plate for the other woman and sat at their table.

Caspi sat stiffly in her chair, no food in front of her. "This is Luap. She's Velas's wife."

Otis smiled. "Yes, we've met. How are you?"

Luap acknowledged the greeting by turning her eyes.

"I'm Carlos," Bob said, and he offered his hand.

Luap raised her arm and barely brushed against Bob's extended hand with her own. She returned immediately to her vacant smile and motionless pose.

"Eat your fish," Caspi said softly.

Luap picked up her fork and looked at her plate. "Okay," she said, and cut off a piece.

"Try the beans," Caspi suggested before Luap could get the fish on her fork.

"Okay." Luap slid her fork from the fish to the beans and lifted them toward her mouth.

"Did you already eat lunch today?" Caspi gave Otis and Bob a worried glance across the table and waited for Luap to return her fork to the plate.

"Yes, at eleven o'clock."

"What time did you have lunch yesterday?" Caspi asked.

"At eleven o'clock."

Caspi folded her hands in her lap and addressed the men across the table. "Is it okay if we sit here until Huana returns? I don't think we'll be joining you in dining."

"If you girls don't mind. The company of two beautiful women doesn't bother me," Bob said. "Is that okay with you, Luap?"

"Yes."

The rest of the lunch consisted of silence, uncomfortable glances between three people, two men pushing food around on their plates with a fork, and one person ignoring the glances and the rearranging of food. Luap sat still at the table, her face placid, steady, vacant.

The uncomfortable arrangement continued until a tight-jawed Huana returned and spoke to Otis. "I'm going to walk Luap back to her house. When I return, I'd like to talk with you."

"I'll wait right here," Otis answered.

When Luap stood and turned her back to the table, Otis tilted his head and spread his hands, palms up in front of him, silently asking, *What's up?*

Huana reached into her sweatpants and displayed a single flash drive, then tapped her pocket, drawing attention to a bulge, suggesting there were more.

"It was nice to have met you Luap," Bob said, with a note of compassion in his voice.

"Yes," she responded.

39

WIND IN THE HAIR

A ILEEN MILTON SUCCUMBED to the vibrations of traveling at steady speeds after escaping the stop and go of the metropolitan spider webs of travel between the Big Apple and the Washington beltway. The sometimes left, sometimes right contours in the sometimes up, sometimes down rolling of the wooded highways relaxed her body, but energized reveries in her mind.

"Where are we headed to tonight?" she asked.

Her husband, transfixed on the road more than the scenery, answered like a man with an organized strategy for not making plans. "I thought Charlottesville, Virginia. Skip the Monticello tour, ask some locals where the good food is, and catch sunset in the mountains."

"Hmm, Monticello." Aileen held her right hand above her head and pointed her fingers into the wind streaming over the car. "It's hard to imagine what it was like, traveling this road back then. Rickety carriages with wooden wheels, bumping and jerking over stone, uneven timbers, mud, and sketchy pioneer-made bridges," she said sleepily. "Those old guys with gout and rheumatism must have been miserable, even in the good weather."

"Which old guys?" Dr. Milton shouted above the radio and wind.

"You know, Madison, Hamilton, the Adams family, all those guys who won a revolution and got together at Monticello to figure out some new ideas for governing the country they won."

"The Adams family traveled to Monticello? Who knew?"

Ignoring her husband's attempt at humor was second nature after fifteen years of marriage. She undid her seat belt, pulled herself up in the seat, and poked her head over the window into the air stream, letting the wind hit her face. "I wish I had floppy dog ears," she shouted over the wind.

With her seat belt unbuckled and her back to the driver, Dr. Milton couldn't resist. He slapped her hard on the backside and ordered, "Sit down and buckle up, young lady. Doctor's orders."

Blushing, but smiling, Aileen buckled her belt and put her hand on her husband's knee. "Don't think that just because we're in vacation mode, a slap on the backside is going to get you some hotel sex tonight."

*   *   *

During dinner at Shadwell's, the vacationing couple watched the sun sink over the mountains to the west of Charlottesville. Afterwards, they sat in the hotel hot tub and pried the cork on a bottle of Monticello wine, silently sipping, and sliding into a peaceful, sleepy, semi-consciousness, both of them stared at a billowing pillar of steam rising to the moon above the mountains.

With the bottle emptied, the Miltons wrapped themselves in towels and headed to their room. On the way, Aileen asked. "Where was that steam coming from?"

"Not sure," the doctor slurred.

"You know what?" Aileen muttered. "I've had too much air, too much food, too much wine, and too much hot tub. I'm not feeling as young as I did this morning."

"There's always tomorrow, babe. We have lots of miles ahead and plenty of time to remember how to do that hotel-sex thing. I'll race you to dreamland."

40

THE MEMORY DANCE

P O BENT OVER HAYAK'S SLEEPING BODY and set her cell phone on top of his chest for illumination. She put one finger to her lips, and woke him by laying her other hand across his mouth and hissing, "Shhh."

In the normal confusion between sleep and not-sleep, Hayak managed to recognize the unnatural lighting on Po's face and mumble-blurted, "Isfoamy?"

Po intercepted the hand that reached for the phone and stood straight, pulling on the captive hand while motioning toward the door with jerks of her head.

Once awake, Hayak let Po lead him in silence down the hallway, past Velas' room, down through the foyer, through the kitchen, through the walkway to the garage, finally stopping at the center of the old carriage house.

Po stepped into Hayak's body and raised her hands, linking fingers behind his neck, swaying back and forth to inaudible music. "Remember the first time we danced?"

"There were blue lights around the dance floor," Hayak whispered. He joined in the sway, pulled his wife closer to him, and set his cheek atop her head. "Over there," he continued, while pointing toward the far corner of the carriage house, "cherry red lights, like fruity embers, they bathe the band in just so a glow for their music."

"God, they were good. Where did you find an acoustic band of Polynesians with a song list of cover tunes done in Reggae?"

"Albania."

"Huh." Po, long accustomed to finding eclectic curiosities in surprising places, huffed her lack of surprise. "Do you remember the song we danced too?"

"It was our wedding night. It was first dance. Your mother say she won't accept me until she see us dance."

"So you don't remember the song?"

"Of course I remember song." Hayak continued to dance, but didn't offer a title until Po poked a finger into his belly. "Okay, okay," he said. "It was … Is test? Song was *Jeremiah he's a Bulldog*."

Po stiffened and stepped back, her face in full pout.

"Come here," Hayak said, and pulled her to him, taking her chin under his palm and tilting her ear toward his lips. "Oh, she may be weary," he crooned into her ear.

"That's it. *Try a Little Tenderness*." Po rejoined Hayak and rested her head on his chest. She added some swing to her hips upon hearing the reggae version in her head. "You could hear the whole band. You could hear the feet scrape sand on the dance floor. I could hear your heartbeat when the dance began. The acoustics were perfect. Sound traveled to every corner of the room."

"I try dance like Fred Astaire, but song it just won't let me." Hayak added a shoulder shimmy to Po's hip swing. "I end up like a wild and crazy Michael Jackson … or Jose Greco." Hayak snapped his fingers and stepped away from Po, striking the matador pose.

"I thought you were more like Elaine, from Seinfeld."

"Your mother like my dancing," Hayak boasted. "She dance jitterbugs with me."

"Mom loved you." Po stopped dancing and reached for Hayak's hands. "I want to talk about the acoustics. Remembering the dance gave me an idea."

"Is a dangerous thing."

"We have cars in the carriage house. You built your big tool closet on the back wall. Do you think the acoustics have changed much?"

"What is, you are up to?" Hayak asked.

"I put a recorder in the room, up high. I brought you out here to do a test."

Po walked to the stairs that climbed over the tool closet and ended at a storage loft. The two of them ascended to the loft and Po pulled her digital recorder out of its hiding place. After donning a set of ear buds, she pressed a button to listen, then stopped the recording.

"Wait, I'll rewind," she said.

Hayak took the ear buds from Po's head and adjusted them to fit into his ears. "Is okay," he said, while lifting one thumb up to emphasize he was ready to listen.

"It's sound-activated," Po told him before pressing the start button.

Hayak didn't listen to the whole recording; he removed the headphones as soon as he recognized the words.

"It works very well, no?" Po erased the conversation while asking.

"I hear you ask me, 'Remember the first time we dance?' Then I whisper, 'There were blue lights around the dance floor.' Why is important?"

"Because, Velas comes to the carriage house when he talks on the phone. I don't think all of his calls go to Panama." Po placed the recorder back into hiding and folded the ear buds, slipping them back into her pants pocket. "We need to know what he's up to."

"If he is up to anything ..." Hayak stopped talking and turned his face in the direction of the door to the kitchen entrance.

Po turned her attention toward the door as well. "What is it? Did you see something?"

"I think I hear a something, but maybe is willies."

Hayak and Po both sucked in a breath at the same moment they saw light suddenly appear under the door to the kitchen walkway.

"Someone just turned on the light in the hall," Po whispered.

"Was on when we walked through," Hayak said. "Who turn off, then turn on light?"

"Bump." Po pressed against Hayak and exhaled into his chest. "I'm glad Roberta got out of here on time."

"What you mean, 'Bump, glad Roberta not here'?"

"Our boat is scraping bottom, dear. Velas knows we suspect him."

"Suspect of what? In four days he go back to Panama. I watch him good."

Po double checked the recorder to make sure it was on and sighed. "You watch. I'll listen."

41

A COLD CAMPFIRE

"I T'S RIGHT TO QUESTION A SPEAKER AT THE CAMPFIRE," Huana began. "It's right to ask why the children could not attend. It's okay to wonder why we are here early, before Velas returns. It's okay to wonder where Luap is. Why have I asked for the fire to remain unlit?"

A murmur rose in the circle around cold wood. Huana didn't circle the pile of cold wood to silence the voices. She spun slowly around, meeting the gaze of all who didn't avert from her famous stare. Like the wave at a ballpark, the effect was dramatic. Murmurs fell silent in each section her eye fell upon.

When all was silent again, she spoke. "The children have finished their relocation project. I was fond of two of the suggestions."

A happy murmur rose, but Huana ended it before it grew to a celebration. "None of their suggestions will be considered," she said loudly and abruptly. "Ears on a familiar face have heard their ideas. Their choices are not secrets. If our new home is not a secret, we accomplish nothing but a different location for where we will perish."

Gasps rose but all went quiet again. Her tribe didn't give in to more murmuring questions. Huana took another spin in place, then shouted a name. "Velas!" The effort seemed to wear her out. She blew breaths between her teeth like she was training to breathe for childbirth. The look in her eye was virulently angry. "Our Velas, who we love ..."

Huana kicked a loose piece of wood with her bare foot and swiped a hand defiantly at a stray tear rolling down her cheek. "Our Velas is not one of us. He is a Mr. Wally, a Sam, a Shori. He is X-Club, and for that, I will take his life."

More gasps rose, but they didn't fall. Murmurs returned. A single voice with the spirit of a Missourian, shouted, "Show me."

Another voice bellowed, "What have you done to Luap?"

Huana walked to where Caspi sat and retrieved a sack and a tube for darts. "Luap is not aware. She sits in my house, in the chair I told her to sit in. She is as dead to her own thoughts, as many of you once were before Dorothy came. Dudes, we have until the second day of July to leave this island."

Huana opened the sack and turned it upside down. Flash drives spilled onto the sand. "This is more than twenty years of X-Club communication with Sam, Mr. Wally, and Velas. We don't have time to debate their meaning."

Huana rolled the tube between her fingers and announced, "It's ready." Next, she took a knee and held the tube in front of her like a Samurai offering his sword to his master. "I claim the power of an emperor," she said solemnly. "Until we leave this island, I recognize no authority but my own. Because this should be unacceptable, I offer a way out. If you agree to follow me to our new home, without question, leave this cold campfire and wait in your houses. If any one of you can't trust me, take the tube. The dart is a kill-dead option. No curare, no second chances. This is how strongly I believe in following my course. If you feel I'm wrong to do this, exhale strongly. Let the dart bite deep, and bury me next to Dorothy in the graveyard of failed heroes."

With head down and eyes closed, Huana listened to the footfalls of her tribe as they left quietly for home. When she heard no more movement, she opened her eyes. In front of her was Caspi. Next to her was the little girl with the Baba Yaga complex.

"Why aren't you home?" Huana asked in surprise.

"Everyone was acting so weird, with changing routines and all. I thought you might need a shaman."

42

THE FUTURE IN THE CLOUDS

SUSPENDED IN THE COMFORT of two fishnet hammocks on the open porch of the tree house, Bob and Otis sipped blue drinks while they watched the night sky. In between long moments of silence, they spoke together like two wounded veterans, removed from the battle but worried about events on the front lines.

Otis's voice garbled while upending his glass to let the last of the liquid drain through the ice and between his teeth. "I don't owe wuttshay doon," After righting the glass, he rolled to his side and set it on the floor before finishing his thought. "But, I'm worried."

"Worried about what?"

"Buncha paranoid kids. Why shut us away and guard us like criminals?"

Attempting to sit, Bob groaned, trying to gain leverage by pushing on the taut outer string of his hammock. After giving up on the idea, he pulled against the string and swung one leg over the edge. "Dang flippin' ding fobs!" he snarled to the spreading wetness on his shirt. "What kind of devilish mind invented the hammock? You get too comfortable to move, then you have to be a contortionist to get out."

"It's easier without a drink in your hand," Otis observed. He snickered and grinned while watching Bob strain to swing his other leg over the side. Slowly, the look of amusement on his face changed.

Once Bob managed to pivot his body into a position to stand, he sat up easily, but he dropped his glass onto the hammock while completing the maneuver, letting its contents spill through the netting. The splash of liquid and clatter of tiny, falling ice cubes sound-tracked what looked like an exaggerated struggle to stand up straight. With his feet on the floor, Bob added a musical run of sound that cut through the rhythm of liquid and ice. It couldn't be called a groan. The tone was wrong. It was a higher octave note, prolonged, wending into a low moan before trailing into silence. When the silence came, Bob was standing, but not upright. He was bent stiffly forward, one hand on his left knee and the other on his hip.

Otis, with weeks of practice in the art of retrieving himself from the comfortable clutches of a hammock, swung his long legs easily over the side and froze. "Are you okay?" he asked. His body leaned forward, ready to rush to his friend's side if he showed signs of toppling.

Bob, frozen into an unnatural, gravity-defying position of a toppled letter L, twisted his face to peer over his shoulder. Light, seemingly a focused beam, fell across his face.

In the white spotlight provided by the bright moon, he smiled, forcibly and eerily, toward Otis. Veins on his forehead popped. His face darkened with the redness of stressful pain. "That was the worst one yet." He pushed his words through clenched teeth.

Otis lunged forward as Bob straightened and suddenly took awkward steps, forward, then backward, forward again and finally to his side, where he steadied himself by grabbing onto the post supporting a clothesline. Once steadied, he held his head between his hands.

"What's wrong, Bobby?" Otis walked briskly to where Bob's transformation from stiffness to limpness hinted he may be sliding toward unconsciousness. "Is it the alcohol?"

Without looking into his friend's face, Bob answered. "Three or four sips into my first taste? I don't think so."

"Something's wrong."

Bob placed a hand on Otis's shoulder. "It's good to see you can still spot a subtle tell." He smiled, but the humor fell flat. Recognizing concern in his friend's face, he sighed. "It's over for now. Let's sit."

After sitting, Otis folded his arms across his chest and leaned back, balancing his chair on its back legs.

Wiping beads of sweat from his eyebrows, Bob attempted to hum a melody, stopping, starting, then finally giving up. "Do you remember the songs you sang with the angels on the moon?"

Otis grinned. "I remember the angel voices. Sing it high; sing it low. It was sweet, like syrup from a French cantaloupe, comforting, like chicken and dumplings, and as strong and thick as Olphrenjii's coffee."

"Cantaloupes, chicken, dumplings, and coffee?" Bob rolled his eyes, grinning like he was trying to hold back a laugh. "Are you hungry?"

Otis shrugged. "What do you remember?"

Bob closed his eyes and folded his hands beneath his chin. After sitting quietly, he raised his head and looked toward the moon. "I remember the journey of the first note. It pried open the shell I built around me and reached in like a trusted hand to a panicked child. I visualized the note's run as an image of a soaring bird, gliding downward to a lake in the mountains. I saw the bird skim the water, rise, brush the water again, then ease onto the surface, gliding across the water, buoyed by a chord from the guitar. If I can quote Asitr, I had my moment. It scared me, because I thought it could be the cruelest trick yet on stupid old Bobby McKinney."

"Wow." Otis lowered his eyes away from the moon and stared across the table until Bob met his gaze. "When did you decide to trust your moment?"

"My first night at Harbinger. I was back in my body and crapped my bed. I realized the universe didn't crap my bed. I decided to take responsibility for what I do, accept the probability that others would do me harm, and not blame God for the hard rules in the short life."

Otis threw his hands in the air and huffed. "How did you do that? You put a lovely image into my mind, then turn it into an image of stinking brain-crap. How does anyone find God in a pile of freshly-thawed twenty-year-old stink?"

"I don't think of it like that. I found God in the first note of a song." Bob tapped the side of his forehead with his finger. "Up here, I think everyone has a pile to clean up."

"Okay, backtrack. You haven't answered my first question. What is wrong with you, other than image-mangling? You know what I mean. What is wrong with you?"

"Can you keep a secret? It's important." Bob leaned in to Otis and repeated himself, a look of desperate pleading on his face. "It's important."

Otis returned his chair to the solid balance of four legs and laid his forearms on the table. "Try me."

"Misfolded prion proteins, originally infected before our time in the box, the growth rate exacerbated and expedited like the bacterial growth in meat that's frozen, thawed, and left out too long before cooking. That's my problem."

Otis stared across the table with an unblinking look of blank helplessness.

Bob attempted a clarification. "Transmissible spongiform encephalopathy." The blank look from across the table continued. Bobby tried to clarify. "*Kuru.*"

"Bobby, stop. I'm not a doctor, I do numbers. What the hell is wrong with you?"

"I've been infected with the human version of mad cow disease."

Otis waited to speak. The tell in the lines around his eyes gave his silence more impact than any words he could choose. After he gathered his thoughts, he had questions. "How …"

Bob cut him off, clearly indicating he was done talking about his condition. "Stop."

"When did …"

"Don't."

"But, why …"

"Otis! Stop."

"What was …"

"Enough!"

The strength of finality in Bob's command landed like a gavel in the tree house. In the silence that followed, the two men stared across the table, faces drawn tight, eyes alive with the fire in the hot coals of their opposing agendas.

In unison with the cooling ashes of Otis's determination to get answers, his posture softened, and the night sounds intruded into the uncomfortable silence.

Finally, he surrendered, but breathed life into the conversation with a detour from the focus on Bob. He gently offered a new question.

"Roberta?"

With a sudden puff of air from his lungs, Bob deflated. "I don't know." As he shrank into his chair, his eyes returned to scanning the night sky. "Our conversation was easy. I don't want to tell her. She's tougher than you."

"She's a determined young woman," Otis said. "And smart. You won't be able to fool her for long."

"Just until September," Bob agreed. "When she starts college, I'm going to explore the world. It's very romantic to disappear in the Alps, don't you think?"

"If she sees what I just saw, exploring the Alps would come across as plain stupid."

"Yeah." Bob folded his arms in front of him like a man with a chill, all the while maintaining his gaze on the night sky. "I can get away with calling it a bad reaction to medicine, maybe." He pointed to the dark horizon over the trees. "See the silver lining of that little cloud on the horizon? No matter what I decide to tell her, that cloud is me."

Otis followed the pointing finger until he spotted Bob's cloud, a small formation, visible only as a silhouette framed in moonlight. "I see it."

"Now look up there." Bob pointed to a white puff, glowing as it approached the face of the moon. "That's you brother, in the wings, waiting to step into the light. I want to watch from the balcony while you take your bows. When the applause ends, my little cloud will have fallen off the stage and be gone."

"If this is a play, I wish somebody would give me my lines." Otis continued to watch his cloud inch its way onto the face of the old man in the moon. After a moment, he stood up, walked to the rail, and looked over the edge. "Have anything special you want me to say at your fake funeral?"

"Yeah. I want you to lie."

"Don't ask too much, Bob."

"Tell everybody I loved to travel."

A laugh burst from Otis's mouth. "Hah! You're secret's safe with me."

"All right, then." Bob held a fist toward Otis. "Kings of cool?"

Otis walked to the table and bumped fists. "That is so 2005" he said. "Kings of cool."

43

CHECKOUT TIME

T HE SOUND OF THE PULLEY on the tree house elevator bled into Bob's final moments of sleep. When he opened his eyes, the gray fog and dim golden light of morning let him know it was earlier than his usual waking hour. He glanced toward Otis's hammock. It was empty. The sound of footsteps made him turn toward the elevator, where Otis peered downward at the device as the pulley continued to squeak.

"Who is it?" he asked.

"I'm not sure." Otis said, after stifling a yawn. "I think it's Caspi."

Bob swung his legs easily over the side of the hammock and threw his weight forward at the zenith of the backswing, landing on his feet. "I think I've got it," he crowed.

Otis didn't comment on the improvement from the night before, he updated information about who was on the elevator. "No. No, it's Huana," he said, glancing at Bob with confusion on his face, while stepping back to allow the bamboo door on the platform to open.

It was Huana. The eye patch gave her away, but her clothing was different. Her usual red sweatpants and yellow T-shirt were gone. In its place, she was clothed in a traditional, pleated pollera skirt, untraditionally simple in the choice of a single shade of green. Her blouse billowed with pleating at the shoulders, but the hand painted design of architectural lines and vibrantly colored, flowering vines made up for the skirt's simplicity. Sitting on top of her head like an oversized place mat, a Willie Nelson-style bandanna clung to her hair and drooped almost down to the eye patch. In the surprise of recognizing the new-look Huana, the little girl behind the billowing skirt almost went unnoticed.

"Good morning, ladies." When Otis spied the face behind the dress, he brightened noticeably and stepped around Huana to extend his hand to the hidden child. "Good morning. What brings you here so bright and early?"

A tiny arm reached out and held onto the hand Otis offered. "Huana brought me. Nobody brought her. She came 'cause she wanted to."

Bob grinned at the sound of the tiny voice. He broke into full smile when she stepped out from behind the dress and looked at him. Her head tilted and bent down as if she was staring at a distant object over the rim of reading glasses.

"I think you are Berti's other daddy," she said. "I already miss talking with her."

Huana abruptly interrupted. She put her hand atop the little girl's head and spoke directly to Otis. "Take a walk with me." She turned to Bob and spoke a question. Her tone gave it the sound of an order. "You will want to babysit until we return?" She didn't wait to get an answer from Bob. She nodded toward the elevator while looking at Otis and said, "Let's go."

The two men traded confused looks, but Otis followed quickly as she stepped back into the elevator and reached for the pulley rope.

When Huana and Otis began to disappear downward, Bob walked to the platform gate and watched them as they descended.

"I've never seen you wear the native dress before," Otis said as they dropped. "What happened to the red and yellow sporty look?"

Huana looked up at Bob and rubbed under her eye patch. "Patience, Dude. You'll see."

A tug on Bob's pant leg brought his attention back to his little charge. "Let me look," she said.

Bob scooped the girl up and held her so she could peek over the gate. When the elevator touched ground, and the two riders stepped off, she hugged his neck, kissed his cheek, and said matter-of-factly, "I hope that helps. You didn't have the chance to be little Berti's daddy, so I wanted to give you one of those lost moments you missed. You can put me down now."

Bob didn't lower the girl to the ground immediately. He searched her eyes, his body frozen, his face wrinkled in surprise. "How old are you?" he asked.

"Older than you think, Mr. Bob. In two more weeks, I'll be eight-and-a-half. I was a preemie baby, so I look like a kid. I'm a shaman … if they let me."

Bob lowered the little shaman to the floor and suddenly laughed. "Oh, I see. You're the Baba Yaga kid."

"No, no, no," the little one said. "Baba Yaga doesn't have her own kids. She's not even real. I'm Baba of Sam's Island."

"Oh, I see." Bob scratched his head. "Where are your parents?"

"My mama died when she brought me into the world. My daddy is a mystery man. Mama liked a lot of men."

"Oh." Bob was, again, at a loss for words.

Baba seemed to know what questions were cycling through Bob's mind. "Huana likes to teach me. Everyone likes to see me come when they make meals. I go where I want to go." Baba motioned around the tree house with outstretched hands. "This is my favorite place to come when I want to think."

Bob's face took on the look of a man with no bridle, riding a runaway horse.

Baba, after an uncomfortable pause, let him off the hook. "I've had breakfast. Why don't you make yourself some coffee? That will give me some thinking time."

She left Bob standing and walked to the rail, sat cross-legged on the floor and pushed her head between two posts.

While coffee brewed, Bob couldn't avert his eyes from the motionless little shaman. When the brew was finished, he hesitated to interrupt her, but finally, he gave in. "What have you been thinking about?"

"Amoebae," Baba answered. She spun in place, still sitting, to face Bob.

"Amoebas?"

"Yes … and Mr. Darwin. But you should know the plural for amoeba is amoebae."

"Okay, I'll bite. What about amoebae and Darwin?" Bob sat down on a porch chair and sipped his drink, waiting for the answer.

"Well, Roberta says the founding fathers of America had to come up with a plan for a good government. She says they didn't compromise, but reached a consensus of principles, then patched together the shape of their creation, like a quilt is made. I think those old amoebae must have had it much harder. They had to figure out how to agree to a sustainable system of ecological cooperation that could support a world where future man could be at the top of the food chain, and everything else would support it."

Baba paused and fidgeted with her fingers before continuing. "Do you know what amoebae do when they're surprised?"

"No, I don't," Bob answered.

"They try to run away, always choosing five different directions to run. They look like five-pointed stars. People who look into microscopes call it their startle response. I was thinking, when those old amoebae called their evolution congress to order, how did they foresee the skazillions of ways to build their governing system? I mean, can you see all those big, YIKES moments when so many of them tried to run in five different directions? What would you do if it was decided you were one of the chosen strains that had to evolve into the organism that eats the waste in a septic tank. Would you cooperate? Why did they need a platypus? I don't think Darwin thought the whole thing through … or maybe he had something else in mind."

Bob's coffee cup balanced on his bottom lip. He stayed frozen in the pose until the balance slipped and coffee ran down his chin. He set the cup on the floor and used his shirt to wipe his chin dry before he spoke, a cautious note in the question.

"What else is on your mind, Shaman?"

Baba looked at her crossed legs. "I'm worried. Velas is coming back tomorrow and something bad is going to happen. That's what Huana thinks. I don't like to see something bad happen."

Bob knew it was time to change the subject. "Can you think of something fun we can do?" he asked.

*   *   *

By the time Huana and Otis returned, he and Baba worked out a routine. They were ready to perform when the elevator reached the top and the two serious-looking adults stepped out.

Side by side, Bob and Baba stood, in half bows, each with one foot forward, toes pointed at their partner, one palm extended as if introducing each other, then they performed.

"*Baba*," Bob began his introduction.

"*Bob*," came the little girl's reply. Then they sang.

Baba

Bob

Bob, Baba ran

Baba

Bob

Bob, Baba ran

While Baba took off and ran circles around Bob, he sang the first verse, then they bowed.

"Most fun I've had since the Killer Bees," he said.

Otis applauded.

Huana shook her head. "She has a way with silly, doesn't she? I'm sorry to ruin the mood, but she and I have an appointment. You and Otis have things to talk about, then you'll have to pack up. You're leaving today."

Bob looked at Otis for a clue and got a *not-now* look in return. To Baba, he said, "Excuse me if I look like a startled amoeba. Will I see you again, before I leave?"

Baba looked up at Huana.

Huana shrugged.

Baba smiled and said, "There's your answer."

<h1 style="text-align:center">44</h1>

<h2 style="text-align:center">THIS OLD HOUSE</h2>

Like any good, carefree road trip, the wandering of the Milton family didn't follow the GPS directions. They didn't chart the straightest line from sea to shining sea. They didn't calculate distance by as the crow flies. They chose roads that weren't congested and, generally, they headed west.

One big dip to the south was purposeful. They set a course for Kelford, North Carolina. Aileen Milton had roots there

Before their arrival, it was apparent the childhood memories that flowered in Aileen's mind had longer life than the roots that grew them. On the way into Kelford, they passed through the neighboring cities of Roxable and Rich Square. Building after building on the main streets of the two towns were shuttered.

A peek into the windows of the old bank in Rich Square brought a gasp from the doctor's wife. The big safe that was the western wall looked to be still intact. The counter, made of polished walnut and oak, was littered with the rubble of the collapsed ceiling. A look upward, past where the second floor used to be, showed an unrepaired hole in the roof. A staircase ascended the northern wall. Its railing, as well as the floor at the top of the staircase, was gone.

"Somebody should have sold the innards," Dr. Milton remarked. "That counter would have brought a pretty penny. Those uptown bars in ..."

"Shut up, dear." Aileen muttered the uncharacteristically harsh words almost apologetically. "Those lawyers don't deserve the spoils. They belong here, in Mayberry, with the dead."

It didn't take years of psychiatric training to recognize Aileen was in an uncomfortable frame of mind. The doctor asked a gentle question. "So, to you, your memories are like the TV show?"

"No, not like the show. This is Opie's world, dear. Andy Griffith was from here. Here or Roxable — I don't remember. The town of Mayberry was patterned after this town ... or Roxable. Our politicians used to argue among themselves about which city was the inspiration. Now, they deny the culture ever existed."

Dr. Milton waved to the curious clerk at the window of the hardware store. "How can we keep the world as we know it?" he asked, rhetorically. "None do," he answered, without waiting for a response.

"Hmm?" Aileen barely acknowledged she'd heard what her husband said.

"Just something from ..." Milton saw his wife's face in the glass of the bank window and ended his attempt to share the undeniable observation of fleeting cultures. "Are you sure you still want to see your grandparents' house?"

"Does a duck have lips?" Aileen marched to the car at the curb and smiled as she slid into the passenger's seat.

Dr. Milton sat in the driver's seat and hesitated before turning the key. "Well-l-l," he drawled. "The truth is, a duck doesn't have lips. He has ..."

"And the Pope doesn't shit in the woods. And the bear isn't Catholic." Aileen blurted the messages, heading off the attempt at mansplaining the obvious. "The next stop sign will be Roxable. After we cross the tracks, we're in Kelford. I'll give you directions to Grandpa's house ... if it's still there."

For the rest of the short ride, Dr. Milton treated his wife like a patient. He listened. He listened as Aileen pointed out decrepit structures along the side of the road and her descriptions of past glories.

"That was the ice house. That foundation was the old sheriff's office — the real Andy Taylor's office. No Barney, just Andy for the entire county. See that antique shop? Aw … It's out of business. It used to be the old general store. I'd walk there with grandpa. He bought his cigars, and I was rewarded with a peach soda. Eight-ounce bottles of ice-cold heaven."

The travelogue ended when they stopped in front of a two-story frame home displaying more exposed wood than peeling paint. The gate at the front walkway to the wide porch was unlocked. Despite the big "No Trespassing" sign, they entered the yard.

The over-sized front porch felt unsafe to walk on. Its foundation of old bricks no longer held it up evenly. The slant was noticeable. The tilt of the house was equally pronounced. None of the safety issues, from foundation to sagging ceilings, kept the couple from breaking in.

Dr. Milton walked the house, relying on his memories of old photos to get the feel of the place.

Aileen went silently from room to room. She didn't speak until she walked into the kitchen. "The old pantry is still here," she said. "Grandpa grew it. Grandma canned it. When I visited, I shucked more corn and shelled more peas than the Jolly Green Giant."

Dr. Milton listened to his wife, but his eye wandered to the window. A plume of steam rose upward, whiter than the weak gray clouds. Three structures, like giant barrels with fluted tops, peeked above the tree line. From the fluted barrels, the steam rose and spread.

"What are you looking at?" Aileen bent sideways and pulled back the dirty, yellowed curtain on the kitchen window. "Oh, my God!" she exclaimed. Aileen jumped in the air and clapped her hands. "They're still here."

She ran to the back door and turned the handle. When the door didn't budge, Aileen reacted without thinking. Her body remembered what to do. One hand pulled against the door handle, the other slid the dead bolt. Her right knee forcefully nudged the door enough to make the sticky bottom corner release its grip.

Dr. Milton followed his wife out the back door. He stepped off the porch just in time to see Aileen disappear under the fruity canopy that covered her grandfather's grape arbor.

"So far, this is the highlight of the trip," Aileen said. The two of them lay under the shade of grape leaves for nearly forty minutes, sucking the sweetness out of ripe, green and bronze scuppernong grapes.

Milton spit out the tough outer skin of a used-up fruit and popped another grape into his mouth. "So, this is where you ate lunch with your dollies?"

Aileen sighed. "Not all the roots are dead here. On our way back, I want to stop again and take some cuttings. We have room in the yard for a few grapes."

"Good idea."

Aileen rolled to her knees and crawled out of the shade, standing when she reached the sunshine.

Doctor Milton followed his wife. When he stood in the sunlight, he saw his wife pointing toward the steam.

"What is that?" she asked.

Without looking to where Aileen pointed, Dr. Milton answered. "Nuclear reactors. New ones. We should leave before Barney Fife comes by."

45

SHELL GAMES, SCARECROWS,
AND WEIRD NEWS FOR THE BLIND

B OB AND OTIS WALKED from the tree house to the guest house and sat on the creaky stairs. Between them, a scarecrow, stuffed with loose mulch and palm branches, rested wooden elbows atop its puffy, misshapen knees. In his red sweatpants and yellow T-shirt, he was unmistakably a caricature recognizable only by its tribal uniform.

"Eerie, isn't it?" Otis lifted the arm of the scarecrow and put it back onto its lap. "Judging from how many of these things are scattered around the island, and all the clothing they distributed to the fisherman from the other islands, Sam stocked the warehouse with a lifetime supply of red and yellow."

"Who buys in that kind of bulk?" Bob asked.

"Huana said she read on one of the flash drives that the X-Club used the uniforms to track the tribe's movements by satellite."

Bob looked around the plaza at the motionless scarecrows. "How many of us living folk are still on the island?"

"By now, Baba should be on the way to the mainland. That leaves me, you, and Huana. By this evening, you'll be gone, too. Roberta and Freddy should be arriving in New York by this evening. Maybe not together. Huana says they've had a falling out."

"Oh, yeah? What about?"

"Freddy started worrying about being played for a sucker. Roberta was coordinating a business deal with fishermen from the neighboring islands. It was Huana's idea. The fishermen met at the processing area and donned the red and yellow. Huana's people dressed in more standard clothing, groups of them mingled with the fishing crews and shuttled around the area until they embarked to the mainland. Each boatload had a single group leader who guided them to a rendezvous point."

Bob scratched at his ear, confusion on his face. "So, it's a shell game?"

"Yes."

"But, why did Freddy get upset?"

Otis shrugged. "He got suspicious about money offers. He told Berti he wasn't going to stand by while she and Huana made nation-building plans on his dime."

Bob leaned forward to look across the scarecrow at Otis's face. "Is that what they were doing?"

"No, but they couldn't tell him where the money was coming from. Roberta didn't know, and Huana wasn't free to say. I insisted it be a secret." Otis tapped his knees with the palm of his hands. "They'll get past it ... or not. They're young."

Bob echoed Otis's knee tap by repeating the motion. "And, where is the money coming from?"

"I'm the only one who knows where Lockjaw stored the rest of the gold from the Arizona cave. There's plenty. I told Huana she had a blank check, as long as she didn't reveal the source."

"That much gold is a powerful lot of temptation." Bob shook his head and snorted like a dog getting rid of a bad odor. "Is the stash richer than the golden room?"

"For sure." Otis stood up and hopped off the stairs. "I hope Berti doesn't think she can shave enough off the walls to fund the moving project. When you see her tomorrow, let her know she doesn't need to find funding. Just don't tell her ... you know."

"I wouldn't worry about her." Bob stood and braced against a stab of joint pain, followed by a flash of headache. "Let's take a walk through the scarecrows and see that petrified *shem* of yours."

"First." Otis reached in his pocket and pulled out a flash drive. "Huana wants us to see this. She cut and pasted some things from Velas' drives. There's a computer on the kitchen table."

Bob smirked. "A little light for the blind?"

"Or, as Huana put it, when she gave me the drive, 'Here's some weird news for weird dudes.' You should learn to speak Huanaese. She grows on you."

Otis laughed, but it was a short chortle that choked in his throat. He crept up the stairs, choosing his steps deliberately, avoiding the creaker boards. When he reached the doorway, he stopped and spoke so quietly Bob asked him to repeat it.

"I said, she's too tough to let Velas live, and she's too soft to kill him." He faced Bob and added, "Tomorrow, I might have to do it myself. You know, to save her the guilt."

"I should stay." Bob said it as if it were both proposal and final decision. "Huana ain't the boss of me." He folded his arms across his chest. "Roberta can do without me for one more day."

"Sure." Otis said. "The three of us will kill him. You go home and soak up your time with Berti. I dissipated an angel. Velas won't be a problem."

Bob walked through the doorway and spotted the computer on the kitchen table. "Okay. Before we decide anything, let's pop in some weird news for the blind."

46

THE SLIPPERY SHAMAN

B ABA NEVER TOLD ANYONE she liked to go into the jungle alone at night. Her night vision was remarkable. She pretended to be a jaguar and never felt fear. Never ... until the night of her second escape.

When she walked up the gangplank to the last fishing boat to leave the island, she didn't give it a second thought. She waved to Huana, walked to the prow, slipped overboard, and swam to shore, unnoticed, just as she'd done the day before.

The second time was different. The night was different. Scarecrows in shadow morphed into sinister lurkers. The empty houses felt unwelcoming. The whole buzz in the air was different. The stars felt smaller to her eyes, more distant. There was no home to drop in for dinner. No comfortable, familiar place to hide.

While waiting for night to deepen, she retreated from a stare-down with rats in the empty warehouse by climbing onto the stubby wing of the *shem*.

Tired from being a bad girl for two days straight, she fell asleep while saying her prayers.

"I try to be clear, Lord. Tomorrow, somebody's going to need a Shaman. Amen ... and set all this stuff straight, please? I don't like to see bad things ... And don't let Huana die ... or grow mean ... and one more thing ..."

She dozed just half an hour before Bob and Otis, fresh from trying to make sense of weird news, woke her up two hours before midnight.

47

THE SECRET VELAS

SOME OF WHAT HUANA DECIDED the two men should see was a smash of obvious facts. Some of it, mysterious teases — like the bits of communication between Velas and his pen pal in Laurel Canyon. Why did he continually mix references to Bob and Otis as a single John Doe? Why did he exclude mention of the *shem*? Why did he paint the marble project as a search for meaning in the *quipus*? What game was he playing with his long-time sponsors?

One item in particular, not shared with Laurel Canyon, was a bolt from the blue. Otis literally slapped a hand across his forehead when he read it.

Bob exclaimed, "Of course! He was here when they put her body on ice.",

"I should have caught that," Otis said, while he paced. He rushed back to the screen and read the information again before saying it out loud. "Baba is a Dorothy-clone."

"No, Bob corrected. She's an in-vitro baby from Dorothy's cloned egg, inseminated by Velas, and planted in an unfortunate, sacrificial surrogate."

All of the news items and revelations on the drive needed to be discussed. Otis needed to sort it all into binary stacks of information. Bob needed to sort through the reference points until he visualized a three-dimensional sense of place on the event map.

Bob brewed coffee. Otis brewed a pot of *yerba mate*. Everything was over-discussed until, after hours of jabber, Bob suggested they take a break and hike to the *shem*.

48

MOVIE NIGHT IN NEW YORK

THE CREDITS FOR THE MOVIE *12 Monkeys* began to scroll on the TV in the Asmudi living room. Hayak offered his review.

"I don't understand. Why could that lady not come before Brad Pitt had to die in front of himself? Why she wait too late on plane?"

Velas offered an opinion. "I think you have it wrong. I think she was there to ensure the past didn't change. The plague was the event that brought her circle of maniacs into power, after all."

Po stood from the couch and pressed the eject button, addressing Velas as she removed the DVD. "Tomorrow, you leave for home. When are you going to reship those tools in the basement?"

Velas put his palms together, and tapped his fingertips against each other in a rapid rhythm. A half-smile raised a dimple on his right cheek.

Hayak stood up abruptly. "Hey, I make popcorn. What we want, cheesy or butter powders?"

"You decide, dear." Po answered while placing the DVD into its holder, watching Velas in the shadows of the blackened TV screen. "I'll pick another movie. We haven't watched *Mosquito Coast*."

Velas twisted his neck, looking over his shoulder toward the door, and waited for Hayak to leave the room. "Let's skip that fiction," he said, after watching him leave. He pulled his hands apart and rested his elbows on the soft arms of his cushy chair, crossing his legs as he sat back. "Yes, I appreciate the irony of a story about a man trying to build a better civilization with nothing more than a miraculous invention and an isolated land to hide in. The truth is, *12 Monkeys* is closer to reality in our predicament."

On the black screen, Po watched Velas tilt his head and scratch the side of his neck. "What is our predicament?"

Velas, once again, put his fingertips together and drummed. "The best thing for everybody, to avoid the bump, bump, bump of your boat of doom, is to cooperate with my plan."

Po sat on the couch and leaned into the corner between the wide arm and high back, showing no outward signs of her pounding heart and racing pulse.

Velas swiveled in his chair to more directly face Po. "The real story of the Moskito tribe is interesting and relevant. If you like to walk the tangents toward understanding what's going on, it's as good a place as any to begin."

"I want to know what's going on, no matter ..." A tremor in her voice betrayed Po's anxiety, and she paused to inhale. "No matter what path we take."

"You're doing fine, Po. When Hayak comes back, try to avoid saying anything that raises the hackles of his protective instincts. Instincts can kill."

*   *   *

In the kitchen, Hayak tore open the packages of flavored powders and set out two large bowls and three small bowls. He set a roll of paper towels next to them and pulled a chair over to the cups and glasses cabinet. After stepping onto the chair, he reached to the top and found his revolver.

With pistol in hand, he walked through the carriage house, over the river-stone path, and to the front door.

"Van," he whispered in a sharp tone.

The reply came from within the dark cover of shade engulfing the bench by the gate. "I got you, bro."

Back in the kitchen, Hayak placed his revolver into one of the large bowls and waited for the timer. Ding. The hum of the microwave ended. Hayak pushed the button again and waited, ignoring the smell of burnt popcorn.

Ding. He pulled overdone popcorn from the microwave and placed a second bag inside. The contents of the burnt bag, he emptied on top of his revolver, then poured the cheesy powders atop the contents and stirred the yellow color into the pile of smoky-colored puffs.

Ding. He removed the second batch of corn and poured the contents into the second large bowl, stirring in the butter-flavored dye. When he finished, he placed the three individual bowls on the spoiled heap and tucked the paper towels under one arm.

"Done," he said out loud and picked up the two bowls, closed the microwave door with his elbow, and walked to the living room.

49

TWO CALLS IN A CAB

BEFORE BERTI'S CAB EXITED THE AIRPORT GROUNDS, her phone rang. She was politely cold in the conversation, listening, but contributing only three words. Her questions were nil; her hang-up, "So, goodbye, then," was abrupt.

"Fight with new boyfriend, young miss?" The cab driver adjusted his mirror and adjusted his turban, eyes darting back and forth between merging traffic and his fare in the back seat. "Is he your future?"

Berti sat back violently and snarled a frustrated, "*huuunh!*"

"Trust me, young miss, Sandeep, know these things."

"Do you? What do they call you, Sandeep, the Sikh Psychic?"

"Oh! Thank you for knowing my culture. I get weary of fraidy-faces."

"How did you know he was a new boyfriend?"

"I'm Sandeep, I know these things."

Berti leaned closer to the partition between front and back seats. "So maybe you could tell me ..."

The ring of the phone surprised her. "Oh, show a little backbone, mister," she said, while lifting it to her ear.

Sandeep put his foot to the floor, found the traffic flow, and inserted himself into the lane going north. "Give the boy a bone to ..." He stopped without delivering his advice.

In the mirror, he saw Berti, with her head tilted toward her phone, as if pressing into the device would shut out the interference from the driver in the front seat. She thrust her free hand toward him, palm forward, in the butt-out signal.

Sandeep knew about these things, so he shut up and listened to Berti's side of an increasingly tense phone conversation.

"Huana, yes, hi.

"Who?

"Why Dr. Abrams? He wasn't ...

"Knight? From the X-Club?

"Alvin Chomuk? They have it wrong.

"John Doe, in return for what?"

A pause, long and deep, pulled the cab driver closer to his mirror and frustrated his ears. He strained to hear the voice on the other end of the phone. In the distracting immersion into his rider's business, he missed the turnoff on the highway. While adjusting lanes to take an alternate route, Berti came back into the conversation.

"Those warrants, those records, they aren't him.

"No! Tell them he can't read *quipus*.

"In the guest house? Right now? Go tell them.

"Yes. Whatever Velas is doing, it's going to see him dead. Everybody's on to him about something. He's the only one who doesn't know it.

"Oh, yeah. I won't let on. Sure. Dead dude walking. He's your kill.

"Those eugenic schmucks won't believe he can't interpret. He's been through too much to go out like that.

"Like dyin' under torture because the monsters won't admit they screwed up.

"Okay, Huana, keep your darts drippin' with the kill-dead stuff. I'm heading home right now."

Berti let her head flop backward and fall limply on the headrest. She closed her eyes, opening them again when she heard the partition slide shut.

Muffled by the closure of the divider, Sandeep's voice sounded hollow, but the words were legible. "Sandeep knows nothing about these things."

50

FWEEP

HUANA LAY HER PHONE DOWN ON THE TABLE, next to an unattached cylinder of a .22 caliber target pistol. She looked for the ash tray among the gun parts, spotting it under a package of swab cloths. With a flick of her pinkie, she ejected the package and ground her cigarette into a one-day accumulation of cold butts.

"Damn foreigners," she moaned, while she reached to grab a corner of the red and white cloth covering the uncluttered table closest to her chair.

When she jerked on the tablecloth, a clean ash tray rattled across the floor and settled against her foot. She kicked it away and pushed her chair back, standing to drape the cloth over the contents on her table.

Before the air fully billowed out from under the descending linen, Huana was taking her first steps toward the front entrance of Rick's Café.

As soon as she stepped onto the narrow porch, she saw the lights were on in the guest house, but two flashlight beams caught her attention, making her realize the guesthouse was empty. The twin beams played up and down against the trees on the path to the warehouse, fading as they moved around the turn on the trail.

"Hey!" Huana yelled toward the path, but the flashlights maintained course and their beams disappeared.

Huana walked briskly back to the bar and retrieved a flashlight. After a glance around the café, she hustled to the porch, descended the stairs, and speed-walked across the plaza and up the stairs to the guest house.

The computer was still on. Secrets, newly learned, were displayed on the screen.

Huana began to pace, but froze when she began a conversation with herself. "I'll wait 'til they get back. No, they may have gone to the tree house for the night. Think. Was that Knight dude gaming me? Did I slip up? Intelligence is hard."

Huana began walking again, slowly. She stopped once more to ask herself a question. "What would Dorothy do?" Immediately, she stiffened, then took off, walking with energy around the table. Before quickening her pace into a trot, she hiked up the hem of her long dress and launched herself through the doorway.

When she caught up with the boys at the warehouse, Huana's good news-bad news mission took a backseat to the sight of Baba, standing on the metallic wing of an un-petrified *shem*. Both machine and girl looked ethereal, outlined in the cold white illumination of three LED flashlight beams.

Behind Baba, inside the cockpit, a small blue puff of light shimmered, then was gone. The color of night snapped from cold to warm, as the headlights of the *shem* glowed. Their warm yellow beams overpowered the white LEDs. In the silence of the surprises, a clear, but gentle *fweep*, announced the opening of the cockpit.

Standing in the center of the warm halo of light, Baba giggled at the sound.

"Now, that was an acoustic reality," she said, pointing toward the cockpit with an over-the-shoulder jerk of her thumb. "It said *fweep*. For a second, I thought I was still dreaming."

51

THE HOME VERSION OF *JEOPARDY*

"SO, WHAT IS MOVIE?" Hayak stepped into the living room and leaned toward Po. "Take little bowls off top. Ignore bad smell. Cheesy no good."

When Po removed the three bowls, Hayak leaned closer, to set the buttered batch next to her on the couch. He slowed his motion, noticeably, at the sound of metal scraping against ceramic. Involuntarily, he darted his eyes left, toward Po, then right, toward Velas. Neither of them reacted to the sound.

After regaining control of the lop-sided weight shift inside the cheesy bowl, he slowly stood straight. "*Mosquito Coast*?" he asked.

Po robotically transferred butterish popcorn from the large bowl to the small ones. Her eyes darted from the popcorn, to the end table next to Velas, and back to the popcorn.

Hayak dropped into Po's old rocking chair and set his bowl of spoiled popcorn on his lap.

From his days of escorting artifacts through airport security, he knew nervous chatter was a bad idea, but he didn't seem able to help himself. "I eat cheesy. Burnt popcorn is like roasted termite of Sudan. Cheesy powder is luxury. I like. No, can't say like. I enjoy, for memories of good times in bad places."

Hayak's screen of babble ran into a hiccup when he reached into the big bowl of burnt popcorn and followed Po's eyes to the end table by Velas.

At his end of the couch, Velas dropped his air of indifference. "Relax," he said. "I'll give you the program."

He shifted his eyes from the ceiling to the spot on the end table, where his hand pressed flat against a line of five tubes, each slightly wider than a cigarette and as long as a dollar bill. The slow motion of rolling the tubes back and forth was like a caress. His smile, as he turned his gaze toward Hayak, was confident, like a bully's threat.

"So, no *Mosquito Coast*?" Hayak pulled his fist from the bowl. He opened his palm and shook off excess kernels before popping the crunchy burnt yuck into his mouth. "Or, maybe play a game. Is your last night, Velas. Choose."

52

LOSING THE DIMPLE

O N A WHIM, HENRY AND AILEEN MILTON jagged back to the north, their top up, due to a line of rain clouds ahead of them.

For Aileen, a day intended for planting her feet on familiar, solid ground turned melancholy. She told Henry, "The memory phantoms were fun, but I'd like to end the day heading toward somewhere we've never been. Maybe somewhere wildernessy? Or, somewhere that doesn't show scars from living past its shelf life."

"You can't fight change."

Aileen huffed. "I don't want to fight it. I want to understand it."

Doctor Milton studied the green road sign ahead and made a snap decision. "Okay. West Virginia, here we ..."

The radio chimed, and Henry stopped, mid-sentence, waiting for his Bluetooth to announce who was making the in-coming call. Through the radio, they heard: *Call from ... Jarvis.*

Aileen leaned into the radio speaker and greeted their friend. "Hey, Jarvis, what's new?"

Jarvis was abrupt, interjecting himself at the tail end of her greeting, leaving no room for pleasantries, ticking off the things he wanted to say one-by-one.

"Doc, those people who brought Waldo Kurtwood here have a new project goin' with Dr. Abram. They gatherin' up all the records they can find on a patient: John Doe. Abram wants you to send everything you have to him today. He say to send it to Rishard.

"And, one more thing, Doc. Hugh want I should wish you a worry-free vacation."

"Message received, Jarvis. Refer those curious gentlemen back to Dr. Abram, thank Hugh for me, and pass this message to our esteemed master of elegant linquisticity." Dr. Milton cleared his throat. "'Forcefully exhale it out your dorsal sphincter muscle.' Is the message clear?"

"Yes, sir. I'll have maintenance on stand-by."

"You're a funny man, Jarvis."

"Have a good vacation, guys. Bye."

Dr. Milton pressed the button on his Phablet device, and music returned to the radio.

Aileen turned the volume down and asked, "What's going on with Jarvis? He sounded different."

"I think he was in a hurry."

"Who is Hugh?"

"He's a guy who ran some tests for me a while back."

"Are those the records they're looking for?"

"They're just fishing."

"What kinds of tests?"

Milton shifted in his seat. "This is why I don't tell you about the weird stuff."

"I know. Medical tests?"

"Hugh tested a patient for *Kuru*."

"Oh, ugh. Thanks for protecting me from that. Don't you have a filter?"

"Yes."

"You have a brain-eating patient?"

"He didn't do it."

"Can you get *Kuru* from a toilet seat?"

"I'm using my filter."

"Okay, fair enough." It was Aileen's turn to shift in her seat. "Who is Waldo Kurtwood?"

"Filter."

"Oh?" A raindrop hit the dusty window. Aileen waited for the second drop. "John Doe ..."

"I'm using my safeword, doctor-patient-confidentiality."

"Ooh, wipers. It's coming down hard now. Jarvis isn't a patient. Why is he ..."

"Would you find an oldies station? And, turn it up."

"So, it's like that?"

"Yes."

"I liked how you gave it to Dr. Abram. What's that rift all about?"

Henry Milton pulled the car to the shoulder and closed his eyes, listening to the rain beat down on the canvas above him.

Aileen put her hands between her knees and stiffened. She faced straight forward with her eyes shut tight, like a person waiting for a pie in the face. "Ready," she said, a playful dimple from a suppressed grin appearing in her cheek. "Let me have it."

Henry blew out a puff of air and sagged, waiting more than a couple beats to answer. "I have good news."

"I like good news," she said. "Is it good, good news, or is it silver-lining-in-a-cloud-of-crap good news?"

Henry held his fingers out straight, put his palm down, and waggled his hand. "Meh. Boring news from my old life. I think Nurse Rishard made a filing error, but Jarvis was letting me know it's all worked out." Henry turned sideways in his seat and smiled. "I don't have any paperwork on a patient, John Doe. I don't work for that pompous ass anymore, and I'm on vacation. All good news."

Aileen returned the smile. "And, the bad news?"

"To make room for a deluded club of humans with power, money, and superior intellect, the world, as we know it, is going to suffer in ways my most insane patients haven't dreamed up. That is, unless John Doe does something about it."

Aileen lost her dimple.

53

PIN THE TAIL ON THE DON QUIXOTE

VELAS LIFTED HIS HAND and studied the tubes on the end table, tilting his head and squinting while he surveyed them. "I don't want to get these mixed up. If I make one mistake," he said, while rubbing his chin in a ponderous pose, "the opportunity for a mutually happy outcome is lost. Ah, here it is."

Po leaned over her knees and paused, appearing to be unable to decide whether to stand or sit back.

Hayak reached into the popcorn bowl. He held his breath, locked his eyes on Velas, and explored the gun at the bottom of the bowl with his fingers, finding the barrel first, the chamber, and finally, the hand grip.

Velas picked up a tube and held it to the light from the lamp on the end table. "This is it," he said. "Damn dots. Light-blue and gray look alike with indoor lighting."

In one fluid motion, he pulled the tube out from under the shade, and put it in his mouth, letting it dangle like a cigarette. The movement was so quickly made, it looked like a magic trick or a filmed sequence, with several frames missing. "Demonstration dart, don't be alarmed," He said, while shifting the tube to the right side of his mouth.

Po slid back into her corner and raised her hands to her breasts. Her voice squeaked. "We're not alarmed, are we, Hon?"

Hayak found the trigger and turned the pistol to get his thumb and trigger finger into position to fire on reveal.

"*Fwit!*" From the six-inch tube, to the puff of popcorn lying on the rug was a distance of more than nine feet. Velas pinned the kernel to the carpet with his dart, demonstrating his ability to cover a medium-size room with dart power from a six-inch tube.

Po and Hayak moved their eyes from popcorn, to each other, then to Velas. Already, he had a fresh tube between his lips before the spent tube bounced on the floor.

Velas sat back and crossed his legs. In the same series of movements, he waved his hand across his face in a motion that ended with his elbow resting on the arm of the chair. Plucked from his lips, again as if by magic, the tube now rested between two fingers. "It's game time," he said, wiggling the tube between his fingers. "Are you smart enough to win?"

Hayak finalized his grip on the pistol and slowly raised it out of the bowl.

Po pounded a fist into the couch cushion. "What do you want?" she screamed.

Velas swiveled toward Po, his lips on the tube before Hayak could point his barrel in Velas's direction. Thus, it was the popcorn bowl that was first to fly across the room with bad intent.

Hayak pushed the bowl toward Velas and pointed his pistol into the curtain of falling popcorn. He zoned in on the mass of his target and squeezed. An impotent *click*, lost in the clatter of a ceramic bowl colliding with a heavy table lamp, was all there was to indicate Hayak pulled the trigger.

A hush lingered while Velas and Hayak traded long looks.

Click. The silence was broken.

Fwit! Hayak slapped at the sting he felt under his ear, just below the jaw line.

Click. The sound of hammer on empty barrel was the result of Hayak's last voluntary response, before pitching forward from the rocker.

Po reacted to the final *click* like a sprinter, jumping at the sound of a starter pistol. Kneeling at his side, she rolled Hayak's limp body onto his back.

Velas flicked the light-blue tube onto the floor and chose another. "Red dot," he announced, as if Po would know the color code.

Velas reached under his pillow as he stood and pulled out a device of clear plastic, attached to a small pump and a tangle of straps. He tossed it onto Hayak's chest and paced while Po scramble to untangle the straps.

With the tangle cleared, he began to give instructions. "Fit it tight to his face. Make sure you get that shoehorn over his tongue. That's good. Shove it in all the way down his throat. You have it."

With the mask in place, Velas clapped his hands "The rest is self-explanatory. The heart will beat as long as you can keep pumping oxygen into his lungs."

When Po began to work the pump, he leaned over and smiled into the wet eyes of the paralyzed man. "Never bring an unloaded gun to a dart fight," he said. "I took the bullets out this morning."

Po set the pump on the floor and pressed on Hayak's chest, reverting to her CPR training.

"You're not listening, girl." Velas slapped Po on the back of her head. "The heart will beat as long as the lungs have air ... That's it ... Slower. In and out. I gave him a half-hour dose, give or take a few minutes. It's all the time I need to explain what's going to happen. Just so you know, we're going to beat the X-Club, with almost no sacrifice."

Po pushed and pulled the plunger. The squeak of plastic on plastic, the gentle click of the in-out valve, and the back and forth movement of air was quiet enough to allow the sound of her growl to elicit a backward, defensive step away from Hayak's body.

Velas returned to his chair and sat. "Okay, class. If you're done tilting at windmills, let's start with who we should all be afraid of and end with why we shouldn't be afraid. Are you listening, Po? I know Hayak must be on pins and needles to hear the good news."

54

SEARCHLIGHTS ON A MERRY-GO-ROUND

BEFORE HUANA COULD DELIVER HER NEWS, Baba leaped from the wing of the *shem* and onto the tower. Even with the yellow backlighting from the *shem* and the white beams of three searching flashlights, only hints of movement in the vines and leaves of the hanging branches behind the warehouse could be detected. Sounds from rustling vegetation suddenly ended.

Like searchlights in an air raid, the flashlights criss-crossed the rooftop, but there was no sign of Baba.

"Baba?" Huana's voice, directed toward the roof, called out.

Bob cupped his free hand to his mouth and raised his voice. "Are you okay?"

"Do you have my marble?" Otis hollered louder than the other two adults waiting for a response.

Bob whistled a puff of air and marveled at the speed in which she moved. "She's like a monkey."

"Muscles like a howler monkey." Huana whispered. "Eyes like a jaguar. She's Dorothy."

"She's also Velas," Otis added with serious intonation. "She has my marble."

Behind them, Baba spoke up. "No, sillies, it's me, Baba."

The three adults swiveled and guided their beams onto Baba's face. She raised both hands to cover her eyes.

In the glare, she opened and closed slits between her fingers to peer back at the surprised trio. Beneath her hands a big smile, with a full array of white teeth, slowly shrank when Huana asked sternly, "Why are you here?"

"Where should I be? You might need a shaman." She looked at her feet and dragged a toe across the sand.

"How did you get down from the roof?" Bob turned his light behind him and scanned for a clue.

Baba's smile disappeared. "I broke the window to climb onto the funny sculpture. I went back through the window, into the warehouse, out the door, and ..."

"Did you see my marble?" Otis interrupted, while sweeping his light toward the *shem*.

"I didn't see a marble, but I smell smoke. It's not a campfire." She licked a finger and held it in the air, and then pointed. "It's coming from over there. I have a nose like a mouse."

"Is the ladder in the warehouse?" Otis started down the path, to the turn by the door but stopped. "Can I get through the window?"

"Screw your marble, dude." Huana kneeled in front of Baba. "Are you sure there's a fire?"

"No, but I'm sure there's smoke."

The four of them walked briskly around the corner, past the door to the warehouse and around the next bend before they saw the hazy light in the distance.

Huana broke into a run. "It's the guest house," she shouted.

The speedy Huana pulled away, followed closely by the long-legged Otis and the leg-churning Baba. Nobody noticed that Bob had fallen to the ground, seized in pain from his joints and an electric jab of pain in his head.

Too dizzy to stand immediately, Bob forced himself to one knee and took a breath. He poised himself to get back on his feet, but stopped upon hearing an oddly familiar high-pitched hum. As he turned his body awkwardly from his kneeling position, something tapped against his foot and the hum ceased.

"Peace," a voice called to him from the shadows. "It knows where to go."

Bob strained to stand. His progress ended altogether when a crackle of small explosions from the direction of the village green made him flinch.

A figure stepped out of the dark, toward Bob, and offered a hand. "What you hear is the sound of exploding bullets. No one will be harmed. Huana has set the café ablaze with an ash tray, a table cloth, and cleaning fluid."

"Kae'Lairy?" Bob asked the question in spite of recognizing his face. "What is going on?"

"I'm a messenger, not a teacher."

Bob waved-off Kae'Lairy's extended hand. "I want to speak to Olphrenjii."

"The mighty Olphrenjii has entrusted me to speak to you. Be at peace with that."

Still refusing to take the hand of his former tormentor, Bob asked, "What's the message?"

"You need to take that big swing you've been saving. The game is on the line."

In a blink of blue light, Kae'Lairy was gone, leaving Bob with a marble, a *shem*, a sense of urgency, and no game plan.

55

REALITY IN SMALL DOSES

"**Y**OU'RE DOING WELL, PO." Velas relaxed into his chair and crossed his legs. "I was hoping you could adjust. I'll stop hovering."

Po continued the rhythm of the in-out pumping of air without responding.

"I'm an engineer by skill set, a romantic dreamer by nature, and most of all a survivor. What's a man like me supposed to do with the reality I've been fed in small doses?" Velas reached out his arm and began rolling the remaining line of tubes back and forth on the end table. "Black," he said, and picked up the chosen tube. "If I have to use this dart, you won't need the mask. You'll just have to lie there — or is it lay? It's the little things that can trip you up. Lay, lie, lie, lay: what's the difference? The important thing is for you to learn your role, trust the structure, and embrace the rewards of cooperation. Clear? Good. That's enough about you. Let's hear more about me. You'll be more comfortable after you find out what a swell guy I am."

Po looked up briefly to steal a glance toward Velas when he paused. She shivered upon recognizing how comfortable he appeared, legs crossed, head back, eyes on the ceiling, a tube between his fingers, lips pursed as if he about to whistle and one foot swinging like a metronome at the end of his leg. In this setting, the sappy, self-contented posture screamed insanity.

"It's lie," she said, and turned her eyes back to the pump.

"Now, you're talking. This is progressing well, but don't use up any more time. I want to tell you about me."

Velas unfolded his legs and leaned toward Po. "I think you might be familiar with my father." A long drawn out chuckle ended with a clarification. "His photo, I mean. You may have seen his photos in the 1980s. He was the grinning man with a shovel." Another chuckle escaped from Velas, and he returned to his staring-at-ceiling position. "Every photo, in the company of armed men, but always with the shovel. You might say he was a poster boy for Reagan's Contras. Maybe the photographer liked him because he was always smiling. Maybe he appeared in so many news photos because he was a message for villagers who might vote again for the Sandinistas. Was my dad the happy latrine digger? No. My dad was the executioner. When the Contras visited a village with Sandinista voters, they had a protocol. Influential voices for the government were forced to borrow my father's shovel for digging their own grave. When finished, they were forced to lie ... I forget, again, is it lie or lay?"

Po caught herself pumping faster and forced herself to slow down. She bit her lip and didn't respond to the question.

Hayak's eyes took on a discernible look of life-on-fire, a shining burn of urgency. The intensity added pressure to Po's determination to stay calm. She smiled at him and winked to give him some comfort in knowing she was staying steady.

"I will say lie ... lie down in the holes they made. My father would put his shovel to their throats, all the while his friends and family wailed for forgiveness of their choices, then he stomped down hard, over and over, until, ugh ... separation. It was very effective. Very few villages participated in the next election."

Velas lowered his gaze from the ceiling and twiddled his tube between his fingers. Before he spoke again, he flicked a popcorn kernel off the end table. "That was my dad, the shovel man. He was a patriot of the modern Moskito tribe, fighting to earn the reward promised by the Americans. We were told we would receive our own land, part of Nicaragua, but independent of their government.

Velas pointed to the DVDs on the entertainment center. "He was not one of those Moskitos. Not the back-country traditionalists of the *Mosquito Coast* movie, and not the black Moskito, descendants of Africans, shipwrecked on their way to be sold in New Orleans. Their history is one of men, escaping slavery by the whim of nature, then becoming slavers and slave hunters themselves. What a fine kettle of flesh that is, huh?"

Velas flicked another kernel onto the floor and sighed. "Father. He was a ... How did your Henry Kissinger put it? 'Dumb, stupid animal to be used as cannon fodder for Realpolitik.' Old Henry had a way with expressing his void of emotions, didn't he?

"The lesson learned? Don't bring a tribe to a war of nations. Win or lose, nobody respects you in the morning, especially yourself. Dad killed himself after the war.

"It was my second father who crystallized early lessons in my mind. He was a helicopter pilot for Air America. He saw something in me and began my education into the bigger, wider world of small dripping doses of reality. You know him as 'Pineapple Sam'."

Po couldn't ignore Velas any longer. "Can you stop this crazy game and get to how this turns out well?"

Velas reached for the TV remote and turned it on, making a comment before shutting it back off. "Clock says we have twenty-three minutes before Hayak can move again. Shut the hell up and let me go on. I have more small doses of reality for you before you have to make a decision. We have to go through a dozen betrayals, state-sponsored terrorism, gifts of weaponized anthrax to a madman, the running of a world-wide drugs cartel, mind control experiments on the innocent, assassinations both foreign and domestic, the war on belief in God, the institutions of education, the institutions of the American constitution, and to seal the deal, construction of walls to babbleize human communication. Did you think these were all disconnected? These things aren't rogue coincidences."

Velas let his ugly stew of modern American shames simmer in silence, then he laughed. "Did I mention what's next on the menu? The upcoming solution to overpopulation? Pandemics are sloppy and not easily focused on the right people. Already constructed is an easy-button, in plain sight, lurking in The Cloud. The safekeeping, entrusted to the masters of logical horror. The keepers of the paradigm of Realpolitik. Keep pumping, Po. I'm going to connect the dots for you. I can show you the spider behind the web. It's the X-Club. This is who you should be afraid of. I am the man who can save you. Maybe your spunky little girl, as well."

56

I KNOW THAT HAT FROM SOMEWHERE

WHEN ROBERTA'S CAB PULLED UP TO THE GATE, Sandeep pointed to a man looking in the window of the pizza joint. "I am happy for you to have a policeman in the dark street. You'll be safe."

Roberta looked up from her purse and smiled. "Comforting," she said. "You don't see beat cops anymore."

"No," Sandeep said without humor. "You see video of cops beating."

"Skewed sample size," Roberta mumbled after finding her ETM card. "Add twenty percent. Thank you for the ride."

Sandeep returned the card and smiled. "You get that boyfriend to respect you, young miss, and good luck with your monsters."

Roberta watched the cab drive off and stepped through the gate, noticing the light was on in the living room. On the way to the front door, she fumbled again with her purse until she found her entry key. The distraction took her eyes from the low-lit path and she jumped when she kicked an obstacle on the paving stones.

"God," she said when realizing it was a hat. "Who the hell ..." She bent down when she recognized the overly long peculiar feather in the band of the fedora. "Uncle Van? I haven't seen you in years."

When she picked up the hat, she was surprised by its sticky feel. Goose bumps erupted when she realized the stickiness came from areas of dark liquid, spotting the gray material. She put a hand over her mouth to staunch a rising scream when she noticed the pool of liquid at her feet. Swiveling toward the street, Roberta searched for the policeman, but decided it would be better first to see what was happening inside her home. Things were complicated.

With pepper spray in hand, she took the river stone path to the garage and entered, picking up an autographed Freddy McPheeters' bat on her way to the kitchen entryway.

57

ANOTHER ALL-NIGHTER

MRS. KNIGHT WAS ALMOST FINISHED combing out her long, platinum blonde hair. On the sink in front of her, the day's choice of jewelry lay atop a washcloth. She turned slowly in a circle to admire her new kimono in the bathroom mirror. The young woman was ready for the usual Wednesday bedtime. It was hump-day. The scheduled time she'd agreed would be set aside for the uber-organized Mr. Knight to engage in what he liked to call intimacies.

On the other side of the master bathroom door, a chime intoned. The lady of the house put her ear to the door. It was the sound of an incoming call on Mr. Knight's important phone.

"A fire?" Her husband delivered the question in his usual monotone.

Lengthy pauses ensued, each pause punctuated by Mr. Knight issuing a series of instructions.

"That won't be necessary. Wind the satellite images back to an hour before the blaze.

"Not yet. Call New York. Confirm the surveillance on the fish business partners.

"No, Dobbins is good. Send him photos of the family. Send a good picture of Velas as well.

"What do you mean?" Mr. Knight's voice changed from slow monotone to a rapid clip of questions. "How do you accidentally kill someone under surveillance? Is there an incident to control?"

After listening, his voice returned to its normal drone. "Call Dobbins. Tell him to contain it. Notify the cleaners. I'm going to the office."

Mrs. Knight stifled a giggle and silently fake-clapped her hands before opening the door.

"Another all-nighter, dear?"

"Yes."

"You work so hard to keep the country safe."

Her husband slipped into his shoes and headed toward the door. "I like that robe, wear it next Wednesday."

58

THE GREAT MANDALA

CONSIDERING THE SIZE OF THE FIRE, the smell of smoke was surprisingly faint, a savory note in the sweet smell of light, tropical rain. On the porch of the guest house, Huana and Otis sat silent in the steady drizzle. Their moods mingled like cough syrup over rotten potatoes.

Huana leaned forward, resting her elbows atop her knees. She looked fierce. If not for the forlorn appearance of her soaking-wet pollera skirt, clinging to the shape of the stairs, she would have looked like a pirate, scowling to intimidate the crew of a defenseless ship.

On the opposite end of the stairs, head tilted upward, elbows resting on the top step, Otis nodded in rhythm with his tapping foot, rain drops splashing on his face while he scanned the sky from horizon to horizon, his facial affect stuck in the vicinity between bland and forlorn.

Baba sat between them, looking pensive. She was buoyant after returning from the warehouse to check on the missing Bob. "He's okay," she told them. "He told me we shouldn't worry, because he was ready to take a ride on the great mandala. I helped him with the ladder, then, *whoosh*, he was gone."

Any almost eight-and-a-half-year-old child would recognize her message wasn't well received. As she sat between the two down-in-the-dumps adults, she twirled a lock of hair around a finger. "When you're ready to talk," she said, "you can explain to me, what's the deal. And maybe why we care about a building we'll never see again. Maybe you can tell me what a great mandala is ... or something. I sorry."

Huana stiffened at hearing the phrase from Baba. Then she hugged her. It was as if a spell of gloom was broken. Two words, so common in Dorothy's vocabulary, never before heard from the mouth of Baba, snapped Huana out of her funk. "No, Baba, I sorry. Would you go into the guesthouse and stay until Otis and I have a talk? It's adult stuff."

"Then you will feel better?" Baba returned the hug and sprang to her feet, patting Otis on the head as she bounded toward the door. "If you need me, let me know."

Huana watched her skip toward the kitchen, then she slapped her hand against Otis's shoulder. "Dude, we have to talk."

"I need to get some sleep, Huana. You stay here with Baba. I'm heading for the tree house. I want to be fresh when Velas arrives tomorrow."

"That's the reason we have to talk. Everything's changed." Huana stood up, gathered a handful of her muddy pleats together, and squeezed water from the soaked cotton. "I chased after you, all the way to the warehouse, to give you some news. I don't know what to make of it."

Otis stood up and shook his legs, splashing Huana in the process. "It can wait? I want to get out of the rain."

"I got a phone call tonight. It was a man who called himself Mr. Knight. He says his organization will guarantee my people can live here without worry, if we tell him where Velas and John Doe can be found."

Otis sat back down on one of the creaky boards and wiped water from his face. "He what? What did ..."

"Hold on, dude." Huana looked through the doorway to check on Baba, then put a finger to her lips. "Keep it down. Let me finish."

In hushed tones, Huana went through the highlights of the call. "I've already told Roberta. She'll be seeing Velas tonight when she gets home. She'll keep it a secret, but something weird is going on. Mr. Knight said he's run down Mr. Doe's history, and he won't contact the police if I turn the two of them over to his team. He mentioned Alvin Chomuk and serious crimes. He's looking for Bob, not you."

"That can't be right. Velas knows the truth."

Otis blurted the words too loudly for Huana. She reached across the stairs and pinched his nose between two fingers. "Dude, do I have to beat you with a stick? Keep it down." She let go of his nose and continued. "Velas is playing everybody. That Indian is jumping more than one reservation. I thought if I showed you the rest of his flash drives, you could figure some things out. I don't know what he's doing ... or why."

Otis wiggled his nose between two hands and whispered. "Show me what you have."

"I'd like to." Huana put her head down and pointed to the steaming remains of the café "I left them under the bar, along with the cell phone with Knight's number. I was supposed to call him in the morning ... or else."

"Or else what?"

"I don't know, the dude was giving conditions, not negotiating. He has a scary voice, like a Golem or something."

"That's okay. It doesn't sound like he's on top of things. He doesn't know the tribe is gone, apparently. He doesn t know ..." Otis jumped to his feet, leaned into Huana's ear, and whispered. "He must know that Velas needs John Doe for the *Silver Book* project. Does he know about the marble? He thinks John Doe is Bob. Bob's in trouble."

"Okay, Sherlock, what can we do about it?"

Otis offered an observation. "You don't need a box to be boxed in."

Huana added, "Or be boxed out."

The two of them returned to their original sitting positions on the steps. Neither of them offered a suggestion. They sat that way until Baba called from the doorway.

"I've been snooping on the computer. What's a cloned egg, and how did Velas fertilize me?"

With one less reason to stay on the porch, whispering in the rain, Huana suggested they all go inside.

"We should go to the tree house," Baba said. "That's the best place to think."

59

A BREAKDOWN IN BACKUP

ROBERTA TAPPED THE HEAVY WOODEN BAT with her knuckle. It was heavier than the aluminum bats from her days in the softball league. Adjusting to the weight, she gripped it around the handle, raised it over her shoulder, and took a slow-motion swing, the arc ending head high.

After three practice swings, she put her ear to the door. Hearing nothing, she eased the knob a quarter turn. Behind her, the sound of footsteps on concrete caused her to stop.

The policeman she saw on the street stood behind her, beneath the light above the garage doors, scowling, his hands on his hips. "Do you have business here, young lady? It looks to me like you're sneaking around in the dark."

From a holster on the back of his belt, the officer removed a flashlight and lit the dark corners of the garage. "Is anyone with you?" He turned and illuminated the bushes in the yard.

"No, nobody, officer. I mean nobody but my family. We live here." Roberta leaned the bat against the door and reached for the purse at her feet. "I have ID." Her voice trembled and her face flushed.

"So why are you sneaking around?" The officer stepped toward her, placing the flashlight back into the holster. "You seem nervous."

Roberta stumbled over her words. "I don't think anything is ... No, something is wrong, but ..." She snatched the bat again and placed it on her shoulder.

The officer placed his hand over the handle of his sidearm the moment Roberta reached for the bat.

"We have a house guest. There's blood by the front gate. I'm going in."

The officer drew his weapon. "Okay, listen ..."

"I have to check on my parents."

"What you have to do is listen. Put the bat down. I'm calling for backup. Miss? Put the bat down."

Roberta reached for the doorknob, the bat still in her hand. "I can't wait, officer. Would you go out to the street to make your call? If there's trouble inside, I don't want to announce us."

The officer lowered his weapon and pulled his body-mic to his mouth, speaking to Roberta as he did. "Wait. I'm coming in with you."

"I can't wait."

"Seven-eighty. Immediate entry. Need backup. No sirens. Going silent."

The officer pressed a button on his radio and pointed to the dark space where a red light had been. "It's off. Stay behind me. Just show me where to go." He pointed his weapon toward the ceiling and stood next to the entry door, nodding when he was ready for Roberta to turn the doorknob.

Once again, Roberta grasped the knob and began to turn. Then she stopped. "You didn't give an address," she said in a whisper.

The officer tapped a pouch on the side of his belt. "GPS," he said, and nodded again toward the doorknob. "

As quietly as she could manage with nervous hands, Roberta opened the door and pointed down the small hallway. "This is the entryway to the kitchen," she whispered. "Down the hall and through the kitchen door on the left, is another hallway. The living room is the first door on the right. I should hear a TV from there. I don't."

As the policeman slid past her, into the hallway, Roberta touched his arm. When he turned toward her, she whispered, "Thank you." She read the name on the officer's nameplate. "Thank you, Officer Dobbins."

*   *   *

In the kitchen, Dobbins threw his hand up in the universally recognized halt signal. The sound of a single voice filtered down the hall. Dobbins turned and whispered, "Is that the TV? Do you recognize the voice?"

Roberta answered immediately. "That's our house guest. His name is Velas."

"Velas? Is that a first or last name?"

"Both. He's from Panama."

"How do you know him?" Dobbins took a Phablet from his belt, and they both cringed at the loudness of the Velcro as the device was removed.

"He's a business associate." Roberta leaned around the officer to see the hallway. "Fish. He's a fisherman."

"Spell that, please." Dobbins held his thumbs over the Phablet keyboard.

"F-I-S ... Oh, God, I'm nervous. You meant ... V-E-L-A-S. Right?"

Dobbins tapped on the keyboard, his attention glued to the screen.

Roberta cupped her hands to her ears and inched closer to the door. The more she heard, the bigger the wrinkles on her forehead grew.

"What's he saying?" Dobbins whispered the question while still watching his screen.

"He's talking about Aliens and their books in the Vatican library. He's crazy."

"Roger that, Miss."

Officer Dobbins reached to his belt with his free hand and peeled off what looked like a miniature, old-fashioned nightstick. With a snap of his wrist, a four-foot appendage, as thin as a fishing rod, extended from the handle. He set the Phablet on the kitchen table, and, going once more to the belt, reached into a pouch and removed a device the size of a small grape. He attached it to the far end of his four-foot rod, reached again into the pouch and uncoiled a cord, attached one end to his Phablet, and the other end, he plugged into the base of his nightstick.

"Ready," he said, and grasped Roberta's arm, guiding her to the sink.

Roberta didn't argue. "I had no idea you guys were so prepared," she whispered, "so well-equipped.

"Protect and serve, Miss. Say 'cheese'." He held the extended end of his rod to Roberta's face while he watched the Phablet screen on the table. "It's a go. You stay here while I get eyes in the room."

Dobbins crept into the hallway and disappeared around the corner.

Roberta watched the wallpaper pattern of the hallway go by on the Phablet screen as Officer Dobbins made his way toward the living room. When the image settled into a still shot, she could see a view from the hallway floor. Only a hint of movement at the top of the screen evidenced there was more than a back side of a couch in the room.

Unsatisfied with the view on the screen, she once more went to the door and cupped her ears. Velas was talking about the alien technology of a blue orb.

"Dream catcher," he called it. A device to hold the entire content of the human brain for "safekeeping, until another brain could be drained and refilled. "Immortality," he said. "We have enough yellow pigment to make twenty or more."

Once again, Officer Dobbins moved her to the sink. "Stay,' he ordered and returned his attention to the Phablet.

With the tip of his finger on the screen, he raised the angle of the camera until Velas came into view. He was partially blocked by the couch, but he could be seen clearly gesturing with his hand, talking, and staring downward at the top of Po's head.

On the screen, Po was rocking rhythmically back and forth, her image blocked from the shoulders down by the couch. Roberta stepped to the table to get a closer look.

Dobbins slid his thumb across the screen and a text page appeared. "Stand back, Miss," he said and put his hand over one breast, squeezed, and pushed her back to the sink. "You don't want to see this, Miss. Parents are entitled to their secret lives."

Roberta had to put her hand to her mouth before she spoke. She stepped backward until her back pressed against the kitchen counter. An involuntary expression of sudden rethinking marked her face.

From the moment she accepted the leadership of Officer Dobbins, she clung to the bat like a security blanket Now, she slowly adjusted the bat's position and wrapped both hands around the handle. "Are you NYPD?"

Dobbins turned to her with an inappropriate smile, "I don't want to mess with the image you have of your folks," he whispered through his slanted grin. "But it's clear to me they like gettin' it on while some immigrant preaches voodoo at them. Don't judge."

"You're making such a stupid mistake, mister." Roberta transferred the bat to her shoulder while moving away from the sink to find room for a backswing.

"I was just funnin' around, Miss." Dobbins reached to his belt once again, and, with practiced speed, retrieved a canister similar to a purse-sized breath freshener spray, and puffed vapors toward Roberta's face. While Roberta melted downward and slid unconscious to the floor, Dobbins secured the bat before it could rattle noisily to the ground.

Walking back to the table, he slid his thumb again and tapped on the keyboard. After a short series of texts, he zip-tied Roberta's hands and feet, removed his gun from his holster, and proceeded to the living room. On his way by the Phablet on the table, he saluted.

"Yes, sir, Mister Knight. Velas is yours."

60

COOKING, FROM THE INSIDE-OUT

O N THE WAY TO THE TREE HOUSE, Huana warded off Otis's questions about flash drives and phone conversations with Knight.

"Zip it until Baba goes to sleep, Dude."

To Baba's persistent questions about cloning and fertilizing, she said, "When we get to our new home, ask me again. I can't sit down with you for the birds-and-Petri-dishes talk until I know we're safe."

After reaching the tree house, Otis made hot chocolate. Huana wrapped Baba in a dry blanket and placed her in a hammock.

The mixed sounds of a wooden spoon, stirring and bumping against the deadened walls of a pan filled with milk, the light patter of rain on the palm leaves below them, and the rhythmic squeak of the hammock's toggle-hook against the eyebolt blended into a soothing lullaby. Huana's gentle nudging of the hammock added movement. Resistance to sleep seemed futile. Baba's eyes flickered and closed before Otis had the hot chocolate poured into cups.

With a toss of his head, Otis motioned for Huana to join him at the kitchen table.

She turned her chair to keep Baba in view, then sat.

Otis flipped open his laptop and tapped on the keyboard. "She looks so small, bundled like that," he whispered.

"She looks like a cocoon trapped in a spider web," Huana said darkly.

Otis closed his eyes and shook his head. "Yeah, bright shiny wings, glued down before they can fly." Otis tapped again on the keyboard. "Let's see if we can cut some of those sticky strings. I want to word-search your memories. Any word, any phrase, anything you can remember from the flash drives. Anything Knight said in his phone call. Give me everything."

Huana didn't respond.

"Anything," he pressed. "Any little scrap. I'll see what we can bundle. Start with the call. He was threatening. Did he make a specific threat?"

"She's not sleeping." Huana turned her head to Otis and put her finger to her lips. "She's snooping with her ears. That's what Dorothy called it when she gave me hiding lessons."

"Baba is just a little girl. A very clever, headstrong, little girl. She's not Dorothy." Otis turned the computer around and pushed it toward Huana. "Type what you remember. I'll bundle the words."

Huana stared at the keyboard, plucking at her bottom lip before letting out a sigh and squaring up to the machine. "Spider webs," she groused, before typing.

When finished with the keyboard, she spun the machine around again, pushed it back toward Otis, and turned in her chair, focusing again on Baba. Over her shoulder, she said, "That's what I remember from the phone call."

Otis read what Huana typed and stiffened. He didn't formulate a word bundle for searching. He read the list out loud. "Neutron Drone ... Six-thousand focused rads ... tomorrow morning ... ionize your worthless asses."

Huana twisted quickly in her chair. "Dude, I'm going to sew your mouth shut."

"Dude," Otis said mockingly, "We are getting off this island tonight. Right now, tonight." He took steps toward the hammock. "I'm taking Baba to the boat. If you want to stay and kill Velas before Knight kills all life on the island, I won't stop you, but Baba and I are leaving now.

Huana leaped from her chair and put herself between Otis and Baba.

Before she could speak, Baba interrupted. She sat up and whistled between her fingers while kicking at the blanket around her. "Sure as we breathe," she said, "we're leaving now. I don't want to cook from the inside out."

"Baba, what do you know about this?" Huana walked to her side and helped unravel the rest of the blanket.

"I know what happens to tissue when neutrons impale their atoms. I'm a shaman." She squeezed Huana's neck. "I read the medical journals. They outlawed neutrons for healing and put it in a drone. I won't let you stay, Huana. I love you too much to let you stay. If you want to live for thirty not-real-happy hours while you cook, cell by cell, from the inside out, you won't do it today. Shaman's orders."

"Okay," Huana said while putting Baba on her feet. "Grab the flashlights and follow me to the boat." She kissed the little shaman's head and let her go.

Otis waited by the elevator. "She reads medical journals?" he whispered.

"I do," Baba answered from the other room. "And I wasn't snooping with my ears. You whisper too loud."

61

SO, YOU LISTEN WHEN I SHUT UP?

T HE FIRST THING BOB DID, after the *shem* reached the clouds, was pick up the marble. He held the orb in front of his face, searching past the blue surface, squinting into its center, and scanning for any sign of the workings inside. Like staring into Vladmir Putin's eyes to see his soul, the exercise was a folly.

Bob lowered the marble and cupped it in one hand. He rolled it over, again and again, poking it with his finger and asking questions.

"Can you hear me? Where are we going? What's the game? Am I poking you too hard? Is it a touch thing?" Before the shem broke through the rain clouds descending on the island, Bob was working the surface of the marble in a grid pattern. He poked and touched the entire circumference, asking one question after each contact, "Can you hear me, now?"

Bob let his hand drop to his lap and he closed his eyes. When he opened them again, he saw the heavens. Above the clouds at the tail end of the Caribbean storm front, the sky sparkled with stars. The moon showed off its powers of reflection, full and silver, smiling back at Bob with a face sculpted from eons of impactful history. Bob pulled his shoulders and limbs tight into his body, reflexively shrinking in size at the sight.

"How could I forget so soon?" he asked, but he wasn't asking the marble. With both hands pressed against the cockpit window, he began to cut himself down to size. "Here I sit, looking at a tiny moon, revolving around a tiny planet, warmed by one tiny sun that rules a single, tiny solar system in an ocean of solar systems."

Bob looked into the marble again. "I don't have to tell you. You get around. In the cosmology of the galaxies we've seen, this Milky Way isn't all that big. Do you know what I'm saying? I'm sayin' …"

Bob closed his eyes and entered into a state of formal prayer.

"God, our father and creator, to whom no evil can be attributed. Thank you for this world of chaos, which we can never tame.

"Thank you for my sliver of time between the always-was and the ever-shall-be.

"I thank you. I recognize you. I surrender.

"I am so small. You are immeasurable.

"Amen."

Bob ended his prayer with head down and eyes closed. He lingered in his meditative state long enough to add a personal plea. "And if it's in your will, Lord, could this cup of mad-cow disease be removed from me?"

When he opened his eyes, the *shem* was motionless, hovering over a familiar spot on earth. Beneath him, one city block in the metropolis of New York, defined by a rectangle of weak city lights around a compound of buildings, beckoned him to come play the game without rules. "So I get home field advantage," he said to the marble. "Nobody knows this field of play like I do."

A glance at the rooftop gave him a thought. Before he could express it to the marble, the *shem* moved and settled onto the roof, next to a hatch that made entry into the main house undetectable.

Bob raised the blue orb to his face and chuckled. "So, you listen when I shut up? What am I thinking now?"

The answer came with a *fweep*. The cockpit opened. Bob was ready to stroll from the on-deck circle to the batter's box. He took the route down the ladder beneath the rooftop hatch to get there.

62

IT'S ALMOST MIDNIGHT

"A ILEEN, WOULD YOU TURN THE TV DOWN? If we leave early, we'll have the sun at our backs when we drive through the mountains."

"Sure."

"And maybe change the channel? That's three times through the news cycle."

"You scared me today, Henry."

"Sorry, I should have gone with the meteor-hits-the-earth story."

"Oh. Your Dr. Strangelove meets Pinkie and the Brain scenario was a ploy to scare me into your arms? Was that the game?"

"You see right through me, dear."

"Will you check under the bed for monsters?"

"No. They'll eat my face off if I look. Maybe they'll stay put if we ignore them. Maybe they'll kill us in the night. *Que sera*."

"*Que sera*?"

"Yes. *Que sera, c'est la vie*, and *viva la viva pequeno*."

"Oh, look at Captain Fatalist, There's no monsters under the bed, are there?"

"That's Dr. Fatalist, please, and no."

"No asteroid screaming toward earth?"

"Not that I'm aware of."

"Dark plans by deluded fiends are real though?"

"Yes."

"Then there's only one thing to do."

"Sell our stock portfolio?"

"No, Henry. It's almost midnight. If we might not live to see tomorrow, we better not waste a moment. This could be our last chance for hotel sex."

"Aileen, I like the way you think."

63

THE WALLS HAVE EARS

THANKS TO THEIR KILLING in the tulip-futures scheme, the Vanschnabely family had a gargantuan pool of funds to draw from when they set foot in the New World metropolis of New Amsterdam. They had big dreams and solid plans.

They understood that people who dream big dreams often find the infrastructure of the dream is more costly than a gargantuan pool of funds can buy. From observations during their time in France and Switzerland, they were aware nothing kills a big dream, or shrinks a pool of funds, as quickly as dealing with governments.

Among big dreamers, the family was second to none. They were also Dutch masters at the game of gathering wealth ahead of need. To that end, they designed the big house, in what would later become the Bill Elliott compound, as a functional work of art.

As the city grew into what would be called New York, the elegance of the home, the large area for the safe sheltering of visitors' carriages, and the quality of the expected spread of gourmet fare made an invitation to a Vanschnabely *soirée* a status symbol among the privileged elite.

Bob learned the history of the house from Bill. "The walkways behind the walls mined more resources from the swamp of movers and shakers in the political and socially elite class than all the bulbs in Versailles," he said. "You can reach into your pocket and pay bribes for as long as there's money in your pocket. If you have knowledge of one indiscretion, you hold a lifetime of, 'I knew you'd see it my way.'"

Bill led Bob on his first exploration of the passageways, but Bob returned often to explore. He knew every inch in the dark. With no light to guide him, he descended the ladder from the roof to the second floor and found his way to the back wall of a guest bedroom closet. After sliding open a panel, he crept through the exit, into the room, and out into the hallway.

His eyes focused in the direction of the stairs that led to the first-floor foyer. Voices filtered from that direction. Maybe people talking, maybe the TV in the living room; he couldn't tell.

Holding the marble tight against him with both hands, like a running back determined not to fumble, Bob slow-walked to the head of the stairs and stopped to listen. When he couldn't make out the words, or identify the voice of the speaker, he dropped to a knee and stretched his neck to glance down, around the corner, in the direction of the living room.

In the hallway, with one foot inside the living room, a man in a policeman's uniform pulled his body mic toward his face with one hand. His other arm was outstretched, as if pointing his weapon into the room.

Low to the floor, Bob could hear the words spoken. He watched the officer swivel his head, continuously, back and forth, glancing down both ends of the hallway as he spoke.

"Tell them to knock on the front door when they get here. I'm not sure how much wet work they'll have. There's a wet under the tree by the gate. How many more? It's not reasonable to juggle this many marks. Velas's curare drop is close to coming around. The girlfriend will be out another hour, but she's bundled. In total, that's two marks on the floor, the girlfriend, and Velas. I would feel safer if we reduced the number."

The tone of Dobbins's voice gave Bob a chill. It didn't carry any more emotion than you would expect from a forklift driver discussing the movement of boxes in a warehouse.

Velas's voice boomed up the stairs. "No, wait. We need one of them to get Chomuk here. We should keep the girlfriend alive. Trust me. Let me talk to Knight."

"Sir? Did you hear?" Dobbins asked into his mic. Silence followed the question.

In those few seconds of silence, Bob waited, with a list of mysteries to ponder. *Wets and drys? Chomuk? Girlfriend? Reducing the number?*

"Velas," Dobbins barked. "Sell it in one sentence."

"Thank you, sir," Velas began. "It's like this: Chomuk *aka* John Doe, possesses the very same orb mentioned in the Vatican books. He possesses the language skills to read the usage manual in the *Silver Book*, and enough raw material to make twenty more just like it. There's no reason on earth to come to this address if we wet his girlfriend, who won't cooperate if we wet her parents."

A bead of sweat dripped from Bob's brow and splashed onto the marble. He wiped it dry on his pant leg and waited, listening for more clues as to why Velas was playing his elaborate game of lies that seemed to argue for keeping the three Asmudis alive. He didn't wait long.

"Velas," Dobbins barked again, "Mr. Knight says he wants a 'holistic' answer to this question. Where have you invested your loyalties?"

Velas didn't hesitate. "Myself, sir, but I'm mindful of your reach. I planned to give you one marble and keep the rest for myself. If you knew everything this marble can do ... Excuse my presumptions. Even without being briefed fully, you understand the temptation."

After another interlude, Dobbins relayed a query. "Which of the temptations has you flirting with assured destruction?"

"If I had to choose one, it would be from a list that hasn't changed since childhood. Immortality, invisibility, or the ability to travel in time. Each of those magic wishes require the attention of a single marble. On the other hand, if I were motivated to further the aims of the organization, I would consider using it to supply self-renewable energy for powering a fully functioning Skinner Box of continental size."

A long silence followed.

Finally, Dobbins spoke. "Do you follow Kurtwood's color code for identifying your tube content?"

"Yes, sir." Velas answered. "I have a red and two blacks remaining."

"Use the two blacks."

Po's voice followed. "No," she said, loud and sharp, like the bark of an excited seal.

Bob froze in position, waiting, waiting, waiting for Po to speak again, but Velas ended the wait. "No need to worry about those two anymore."

Dobbins gave instructions. "You take the woman, I'll take the guy," he said. "We'll drag them outside and dump them next to the old man by the bench. The cleaners will take care of them."

"What are we going to do with the girl?

Dobbins sounded annoyed by the question. "You and I are going to get my equipment from the kitchen and set up the TV for a face-to-face with Mr. Knight. The girl can wait. She has an hour of sleep time left."

Bob dropped caution from his list of concerns and moved quickly, barely attempting to hide his footfall volume. From bedroom to bedroom, he criss-crossed the second-floor hallways, flipping on the lights in each room he visited, looking into closets, under beds and pulling the curtains back in the shower. He tried the door to the old radio station. It was locked.

"Don't worry," he told the marble. "I know another way in."

Without finding Roberta on the second floor, he dashed back into the walkway and climbed to the attic. There were three rooms in the large attic, and, as he quickly discovered, only the first room had a working light.

Standing in the dark of the second room, Bob addressed the marble. "Do you do illumination? Of course not. Wait ... I'm not asking, I'm requesting."

Bob held the ball above his head and gasped when the room lit up. He took a step toward stacks of boxes on the other side of the room and stopped after noticing the only disturbance of the dust in the room was his own footprints. He bound to the third room and held the marble into the gloom. When the light revealed undisturbed dust on the floor, he walked back to the rabbit hole, held the marble tight against him and descended again to the second floor.

After emerging into the hallway, he paused to listen. What he heard was the mumbling of men trying to direct each other to the completion of a project. Bob smiled and loped into the master bedroom, headed straight for the closet, and ducked into a different, shorter walkway to the area young Bobby McKinney once called Baal Alayat's man cave.

"Two doors and a getaway exit," Bob said when the marble lit the short walkway. "First, we go to the radio room."

He'd learned his round blue partner didn't respond to chatter, but nonetheless, the chatter continued.

"Follow me," he said, when he stood in front of the entrance to the studio.

"Damn," he swore in disappointment after sliding the door and stepping into the room. Dangling from the ceiling, a burnt, distraught Icarus still dangled between a fiery, unforgiving sun and a hard, unforgiving earth.

On the desk beneath the mortal Icarus, kneeling in prayer, eyes looking upward, arms spread wide, a glass angel appeared to be, by will and prayer alone, holding the hapless human aloft.

As if he recognized the kneeling angel as the instrument that split his head open during Po's attempt to protect the unborn Roberta, Bob rubbed the scar tissue on his forehead while he sorted his thoughts.

"Damn," he swore again. "She must be in the kitchen."

He placed the marble on the desk and backed toward the exit. After glancing again at the frozen Icarus, he addressed the marble. "If I don't return ... Never mind, you know what to do."

With all the speed he could muster, Bob scurried down the escape hatch to the walkway that exited into the carriage house. He felt his way to the door and slid the panel. No light shown through. He felt in the darkness and discovered the reason. Thick plywood, the new back wall for Hayak's tool closet, sealed him in. Slamming his shoulder into the wall caused the tools to rattle on the other side, so he stopped.

With no marble to confer with, Bob spoke to himself.

"There's nothing left to do. If I want to get to the kitchen, I'll have to walk past the living room. What could go ..."

He stopped before finishing the jinx of a sentence and turned toward the ladder to the second floor. As he spun, jolts of pain struck his joints, sweat poured from his body, and he lost his balance.

While he gathered himself, on the floor, waiting for his strength and balance to return, he laughed aloud and made an attempt to speak.

"R-R-R...R-right ..."

The next symptom in the steady decline that is mad cow disease made its first appearance. He waited for the stutter to subside and finished the sentence he started.

"Right on schedule," he said defiantly, while struggling to his feet.

64

MIDNIGHT

CONTRACTUALLY, TWO MINUTES REMAINED before Sandeep had to abandon his airport station at midnight. With only two minutes, a little luck and hustle would be needed if he was to snag one more fare.

Pushing through the doors of the terminal, a large man with an armload of flowers turned toward the cabbie stand, providing the luck. Sandeep provided the hustle.

"I have room for you and your messengers of love," he said, after opening his rear door and sweeping an arm toward the back seat. "Relax, you have found the cab of Sandeep."

With his fare settled in, Sandeep slid the partition between seats and asked, "Where did you fly in from, sir?"

"I didn't fly in," his fare answered with an edge of grump in his voice. "I rode here in an auto-Uber. I didn't know they weren't allowed past long-term parking."

"Oh, I see." Sandeep pressed the gas, and the taxi swerved, tires squealing, into the moving traffic. "You can trust Sandeep, sir. Give me the address and I will get you to the girl you have angered."

His fare did a double-take. "How do you know I pissed off a girl?"

"Sandeep know these things. You did not fly in. You hike in corduroy slippers. Did you purchase a ticket?"

"Well, no. I ..."

"Don't tell me, sir. Sandeep know these things. You come here and fly nowhere. Is too late to shop for apology gift, so you buy big bouquet of expensive stink-pretty's from airport vendor. You leave without the girl. Maybe you missed her flight? Maybe she don't like your slippers more than she do like your flowers? Either way, dot Is, cross Ts, add two and two ... you get angry girl. See? For me, this is easy. Sandeep does not know where you want to go. This you must tell me."

Sandeep locked eyes in the rear-view mirror with the man in the back seat, waiting for an address. After hearing the destination, he held his stare, distracted from the road, until his passenger lurched forward, eyes wide, and yelled, "Hey! Hey!"

Sandeep recovered in time to avoid a collision, but he lost his turban in the process and took his eyes off the road again to fish it from the floor.

"For the love of God, man, will you watch the road?" His passenger reached past the partition and tapped him on the back.

Sandeep sat back up and turned on the dome light. "I don't like to be a confrontation man, sir, but I'm a Yankee fan. For the love of God, will you keep your eye on the ball this year? Sandeep is not happy my team will sign the Bum of Mexico. I see who you are, Mr. Freddy McFeebles."

"McPheeters. The name is ... aw hell. Now you know, and now you can turn your eyes around and drive."

"Oh, sir, I am not staring at you because you are historical disgrace of a man with ugly reputation. You have much bigger problems. Sandeep know."

Freddy continued to lean forward, watching over the driver's shoulder. "I see your point. Getting to my girl's house alive is my biggest problem."

"God willing you don't go." Sandeep watched himself in the mirror while he attempted to reshape the loose turban on his head. "I will not take you there. I fear for you. I fear for me to go there again."

"What are you talking about?" Freddy leaned back into his seat and waited for an answer.

"Don't fall in love with pretty almond eyes that know murders, monsters, death dripping darts, John Does, dead men walking, and likely has tall-tale-telling tendencies. Sandeep know these things are not good for relationships. Back in Kashmir ..."

"Wait. What?"

"I was saying, in Kashmir ..."

"Kae'Lairy?"

"No, Kashmir."

"Olphrenjii? Is that you?"

"Where are you lost in this conversation, sir? I was in Kashmir when ..."

Freddy poked his head into the front seat. "Forget Kashmir. Almond eyes, dripping darts, John Does, that's what I want to hear about. What does Sandeep know about these things?"

"Sir, Sandeep know to tell you he won't go to that address."

"If you can make it there in a half-hour, I'll set you up with season tickets."

"For two season tickets, maybe I can get there in twenty minutes."

Sandeep bent forward again, fishing for something under the seat. When he popped up, he held a revolver in front of Freddy's face, barrel pointed at the roof of his cab.

"But you should know what Sandeep know, and Sandeep know he is captain of his cab."

65

WADE UNDERWATER

B OB'S CLIMB UP THE LADDER to the studio was painful. His joints ached and his fingers tremored when he extended his arms above his head. Emerging in the walkway, he stumbled through the studio door and lunged forward to the chair behind the desk.

In the last two steps to the chair, the prickly-numb combination of sensations that precedes loss of consciousness teetered toward immersion in the abyss. Sitting ebbed the flow toward unawareness, but it was understood, like a retreating wave at the shoreline, it would return.

Bob reached across the desk and rolled the marble close to him. "Any last thoughts?" he asked. "No? Okay, thanks for the ride. I've gotta roll."

After several deep breaths, Bob placed the marble inside the vaporizer bin and stood. He put a foot on the chair, and stepped onto the desktop, reached above his head, and latched onto Icarus, freeing him from his string with a jerk. "You've hung around long enough," he said, as he lowered himself to the floor and laid Icarus next to the glass angel.

Bob walked from the studio, into the walkway, and opened the second door in the section he called the man-cave. A flip of the wall switch illuminated Bill's secret library. He didn't reminisce old storytelling days. He walked directly to a tall, wall-mounted bookshelf and selected an ancient text with stories of a long-dead culture, written in a long-dead language. Two things recommended the book. There was nobody alive who could read the long-dead language, and the sheaf was enclosed in a goatskin binder with bold silver lettering.

After tucking the book under his arm, he pressed a wooden block beneath the shelf, and the bookcase swung into the room like a door. "The trophy room," Bob whispered as he flicked the light switch and entered. "Every sumpin' has a story, don't it."

Because Alayat never tired of revisiting better days with his audience of one, Bob knew the story behind every trophy in the room. Everywhere he looked, his eyes were tempted to linger as the memories of their story kept popping up, but he forced himself to search for one item in particular. He scanned the shelves and looked over the items sitting atop the packing crates on the floor. No luck. No round profile among the other shapes. He was searching for a six-inch orb of occlusion-free beryl, once used as Lucretia Borgia's scrying ball. To speed his search, he lifted the wooden lids from the packing crates and tilted them on their sides. On his third crate, Lucretia's marble rolled across the floor.

"Mushka," he said, as he shuffled through the mess of priceless artifacts at his feet and picked up his book with silver lettering. With fake book and fake orb in hand, Bob walked back to the studio, unlocked the door to the hallway, and stepped out.

The next door down, on the way to the foyer stairway, was a guest bedroom. Bob entered and placed the book with silver lettering under the mattress, straightened the bed linens, and hustled to the window. The street below was illuminated by the blue flashing light of the pizza joint, and the headlights of a vehicle parked near the gate, on the near side of the street, and invisible behind the high wall.

"Oh, no," Bob spoke like a man who realized his parachute failed to open. "The cleaners." In his rush to reach the kitchen before the cleaners rang the doorbell, he placed the scrying marble in the center of a dried flower arrangement and entered the hallway.

Never had Bob walked with a stride as long-stepped as he did at that moment. He reached the stairs and slowed from stride to glide while descending to the first floor. From the bottom step, he could hear Velas and Dobbins in the living room. His ears caught comforting words from Dobbins. "Idiot, I don't give a shit what you know about AV communications. You don't know my system. Just plug the damn male into the female. It's not sprocket science." They apparently had no idea he was there.

Rounding the turn through the foyer, his eyes darted back and forth between the front door and the hallway. Sliding across the doorway to the living room, his eyes focused full-left.

As he passed the doorway, Bob must have felt relief. Velas had his head buried behind the big TV screen, and Dobbins had his back to the door. It was clear sailing to the kitchen.

When he arrived, he found a bound and unconscious Roberta on the floor. In the corner, by the sink, he spotted Freddy's bat. After some quick decision-making, he tucked the bat under his arm, and dragged Roberta by the armpits all the way to the carriage house.

At the bottom of the stairs to the kitchen hallway, he stopped. A car door slammed. Bob put the bat on his shoulder and peeked through the garage door window.

On the street, at the edge of the sidewalk, a man with an armload of flowers stood with one hand cupped over his eyes, surveying the house beyond the gate.

"Why the flowers?" Bob muttered. In the moment the question escaped his mouth, the man on the street lowered his hand. and the headlights of the parked vehicle bathed his face.

The instant recognition brought on by the sudden illumination caused Bob to two-step, involuntarily. He took one step toward the doorway to the courtyard with his right foot, and stumbled when his left foot tried to carry him in the direction of the bundled Roberta. Another peek through the window settled the question over which direction to move his feet. He saw Freddy step onto the sidewalk and move toward the house.

Bob burst through the door and broke into a dead run toward the darkness of the courtyard. "Don't press the button, don't press the button," he pleaded in whispers, while he steamed forward.

Freddy bent toward the modern electronic gate lock and lifted his hand. It hovered over the keypad until he spotted the call button. His forefinger pointed, ready to push, but the intrusion of his name, hissed from somewhere in the darkness of the courtyard, caused him to step away.

"Freddy, Freddy," he heard, then, startled by a pounce out of the dark, he recoiled before recognizing his friend.

"Don't press the button," Bob said breathlessly as he slowed his charge. "I don't want them to know we're here."

Like a harsh rebuke to a prayerful wish, a horn honked. Sandeep's voice bellowed. "Is okay?"

Freddy turned toward the cab, his thumb-up message giving an ill-informed diagnosis.

Bob let out a frustrated breath and slumped. "Is not okay," he said. "I don't have a plan for this."

Filtering through the bushes of the courtyard, light from the foyer escaped through an opened door, and sprinkled through the leaves around the bench. Behind the lightly illuminated foreground, movement in the form of black shadow passed from the doorway, heading in the direction of the gate.

"Damn," Bob gripped the bat with both hands. "No matter what you see, no matter what I do, this is justified. Roberta's in the carriage house. Get her out of here."

At the edge of shadows, a human form took shape. "Bobby?" it whispered. "It's me, Velas. I need you to listen, and fast."

"Tell it to the Asmudis."

Bob rushed at Velas, the bat arcing from down low, and pausing at its zenith to gather power with a double pump and a skip in the step for timing. A whoosh of air sound-tracked the big whiff.

Velas dove under the swing, falling face down onto the sidewalk. He didn't try to get up. He covered his head with his hands and pleaded. "Don't. They're not dead. They're not dead."

Bob lowered the bat.

Freddy rattled the iron gate. "Who's not dead?"

"Po and Hayak. I used a black dart." Velas raised himself to his knees. "It's a Wally mix. Mostly puffer fish zombie juice. There's an antidote." He stood up and brushed himself off while walking toward Freddy. "No time to explain."

"Explain something," Freddy said.

Velas walked to the gate and tapped on the keyboard. After six taps, the gate unlocked.

Freddy stepped forward and shoved Velas to the ground again with a push to the chest.

"Listen to me. This is what we have to do." Velas sat up and covered his head again while he talked. "Freddy, give Bobby the flowers and stay out of sight until we go into the house."

"Why?" Freddy asked.

"Bobby." Velas spoke rapidly, like a man in need of slipping the information contained in a book into the time needed to speak a single sentence. "Trust me. You are Alvin Chomuk. Your girlfriend is Roberta. The flowers are for her. Follow my lead. We have all the power if you let me do the talking. You won't believe how close we are to getting everything we want. The X- ..."

"Where's Roberta?" Freddy interrupted.

"She's in the kitchen, unconscious. Listen to me. There's ..."

"Velas?" A voice boomed from the front door. "Is everything okay?"

"Yes, sir," Velas answered. "Mr. Chomuk has arrived early. I'll show him in."

Velas turned and whispered. "That's Dobbins. Be very afraid of him, but follow my lead. This is it."

An excited look slid across his face. He put a hand out, palm up, and splayed his fingers. Staring into his palm as if it held a magic visible only to him, Velas slowly curled his fingers, like squeezing a shrinking ball, until his hand was a fist.

"Come," he blurted suddenly and walked toward the house without looking back.

After an exchange of glances, Bob held the bat out to Freddy. "Roberta's not in the kitchen. Go to the carriage house," he whispered. "Get her out of here."

Freddy traded flowers for the bat and nodded agreement. "Get hold of that antidote. I'll be back when she's safe."

Bob turned on his heels and followed Velas into the dark, catching him before he reached the door. At the moment he caught him, he grabbed a shoulder and spun him around. When they were face to face, he gripped Velas's shirt at the neckline and pulled him close.

"The antidote," he said.

Velas didn't struggle. "We have three hours from the time of penetration. Wally was very precise in his concoctions. Play along and you'll have it in time."

"Antidote first, or I don't play." Bob turned his hand to twist the collar tighter, but Velas held a steady-eyed, defiant sneer, until Bob let go his grip.

Velas straightened his shirt and put his finger in Bob's face. "Keep this in mind. Dobbins is dangerous, Knight will need to be humored, but eventually ... putty. Within an hour, this meeting of the board will conclude by naming me the chairman. After that, I'll give you the antidote."

He held his pose long enough to be satisfied Bob understood the rules, then the two of them walked to the door. When they stepped into the foyer, they saw Dobbins leaning against the rail at the bottom of the stairs, his arms crossed, eyeing Bob like a street thug sizing up defenseless prey.

"This way, Mr. Chomuk, Mr. Knight is anxious to see you." Dobbins waved his hand toward the hallway and followed behind as they stepped into the living room.

Freddy watched the shadows move in the patches of light behind the leaves until the door closed and the images disappeared. He propped the bat against the gate to keep it from closing shut, shot another thumbs-up to Sandeep, then ran to the carriage house.

66

A SHOUT-OUT ACROSS THE BOW

HUANA WATCHED THE SKY as she steered the fishing boat through the water.

Baba, on tiptoes, stood at the stern, watching the island shrink in the distance.

Otis leaned against the rail, ignoring both destination and backward looks. His eyes were on the list of recent contacts in his cell phone directory. Among his options, he ruled out Bob, who left the island without his phone. He was afraid to call the Asmudi household, for fear of stirring curiosity in Velas about a late-night call. One number was left, so he pressed the button and waited for Freddy to pick up.

The phone rang four times before the call was answered. The voice on the other end left Otis with little to say. After a pause to gather himself he asked, "Is Freddy there?

"Will you inform him that Otis McKinney needs to speak with him?"

And finally, "Good skies to you as well."

Baba noticed the concern on Otis's face after he hung up. "Is something else wrong?"

"I don't know. I think someone has Freddy's phone and he's impersonating Hayak."

67

CAPTAIN OF HIS CAB

AFTER SANDEEP WATCHED FREDDY RIG THE GATE and dash into the compound, he called his wife.

"Hello, my spicy curry pot. I will be late, but with big surprise."

"No. I want to be surprising when I get home.

"I would rather you steep in wonderment like a tea bag.

"Have you no shame? Grrr. You have me growling like tiger. I tell. I have tickets for baseball match. Not one tickets, but all-season-long tickets.

"Yes, I would not lie. The Yankees.

"No, my Punjabi sunshine, Yankees are all I can get.

"Oh, dear. I hear the disappointment. Wait, I have to go. A phone is ringing in backseat.

"You should know I am clueless until I answer. Yes. Goodbye my little jasmine pollen. Home soon, God willing."

Like a choreographed dance, Sandeep swung open his door and spun his legs around. He slipped onto the pavement and rotated, all the while depressing the down button for the driver's-side rear window.

After completing his turn, he reached through the window, into the back seat, and gathered up the ringing phone.

"Happy thoughts. I am answering service for Mr. Freddy McFeebles. How can we help you?"

Silence from the caller lasted longer than was comfortable, so Sandeep chided. "I see. What more have you phoned to not speak of?

"I would not tell you. Mr. McFeebles enjoys with me a curtain of confidential expectations.

"Yes, Mr. Otis Beckley, He will know you have called as soon as I tell him.

"Yes, of course. I await with meter running. Good skies where you are."

Sandeep shut the phone off as he slid back into the front seat. "Bothers," he said. "Best to call again when Sandeep is not here." He picked up his revolver and laid it on his lap, took the turban off his head, and turned the mirror toward him. "Hat hair. Should Sandeep die tonight, he will not be looking like his head was poured from a frozen soft-serve appliance."

Sandeep rewrapped and tightened his turban until he was satisfied with the fit. When he turned the rearview mirror back into place, bright headlights reflected into his eyes and he squinted through the glare until the vehicle passed him. "Police. Where will you be when I needed you?"

He watched the disappearing taillights until a movement by the gate caught his attention.

Freddy trotted up the sidewalk, a bundle draped over his shoulder.

After recognizing Freddy's over-the-shoulder burden, Sandeep slapped at his lock-doors button.

Freddy, hauling the bound and unconscious Roberta over his shoulder, pulled at the door handle in the back of the cab. When it wouldn't open, he slid to the front window and looked in. Inches from his face, a revolver touched the glass in the window.

Sandeep hollered, "I do not kidnap!" To add emphasis, he swatted the flag on his meter and huffed, "You no longer enjoy the safety of Sandeep's attention."

68

MUSICAL CHAIRMEN

THE FACE ON THE GIANT TV SCREEN spoke in monotone. "Greetings. I've been looking very hard for you, Mr. Chomuk. Please, take a seat. You, too, Mr. Velas. Sit."

"No, thank you. I'll stand." Bob held the flowers toward the TV. "I'm here to visit Berti."

"Alvin Chomuk." Knight spread papers across the top of his desk and leaned close to read them. "I see you burned down your own house at the age of eight." Knight chuckled. "With your father inside, no less. You're what I call an early bloomer." He lifted a sheet of paper, with a photo of young Alvin Chomuk in hospital whites, and held it up to the camera. "You certainly know how to be institutionalized. Countless violent events. Forcible rape. Two times, the prime suspect in suffocation deaths?"

Bob sat down on the couch and laid his flowers on the end table. This was the first he'd heard of the incidents during his youthful incarceration in the mental ward.

"Go on," he said, trying to appear unfazed.

"I can forgive childhood transgressions, Mr. Chomuk." Knight pushed the fan of papers off to the side and pulled his lips into an expression of disgust. "Ugh," he said emotionlessly, but with a quick shiver. "Your adult record ..." Knight shook his head without finishing the sentence. "Well, I can't say I'm not impressed with your ability to disappear."

Bob looked over his shoulder at Dobbins, then stared at Velas in the easy chair. When no one spoke, he turned toward the TV. "Okay, how did you find me?"

"Are you serious?" Knight narrowed his eyes and tilted his head. "You found us. We couldn't help but notice. Why were you after Wally's flash drives in Panama? How did you know Waldo Kurtwood? How did you pull off communicating with him at Harbinger?"

"I meant," Bob sat forward on the cushion. "How did you find my past?"

"John Doe's fingerprints, but that's enough about your memoirs. Let's get to business and settle our futures. Velas says we need you. Is that true?"

"It depends on what you need." Bob turned to Velas and gave him his best attempt at a where's-your-follow-my-lead look.

Velas responded, "Mr. Knight wants Wally Kurtwood's flash drives, the blue marble, and the *Silver Book*. I've informed him the flash drives are my insurance policy against betrayal. He knows I have access to the marble and the material to manufacture more. You have the book, as well as the ability to read it. He understands we all need each other."

"That's interesting." Bob raised himself off the couch and gave Velas a hard stare before turning back to the TV monitor. "I'm not clear about the path to needing you, Mr. Knight."

Knight grinned. "Mr. Dobbins?"

The instant Knight called his name, Dobbins reacted, "Chomuk!" he said in a tone of impatient authority. "Sit down." He unsnapped his holster and placed a hand on his firearm.

Velas pivoted in his chair to get a look at Dobbins. "Slow down. Slow down. Everybody, breathe. We're too close to mess this up now." He put his hands atop his head and appealed to Bob. "We need Mr. Knight so we can continue to live. Everything will be fine once we let him know what we're offering."

Knight spoke the name again, "Dobbins, stand down."

He leaned back into his chair and opened a drawer on his desk, removed a cigar, snipped it, sniffed it, and leaned to reach off-screen. When he centered himself on the screen again, he held a golden figurine.

"Look familiar?" he asked. He held it toward the camera, briefly. It looked like the bull in front of the stock exchange on Wall Street. "I have the original in my antiquities collection. It's nice, but it doesn't do this." Knight flipped the head of the bull backwards and flame erupted. "Butane," he said. "A gift from Roy Cohn, in appreciation, as they say. He held the flame to the end of his cigar and puffed until his face was shrouded in smoke. After a long exhale, the screen cleared and Knight was once again in focus.

"The Bull of Heaven," he said, as he leaned off-screen again to return the lighter to its place. "Myth tells us he was the creature who delivered Hammurabi his code of laws. I like myths, Mr. Chomuk, but I like functional tools better than stories. What do you think? I've read books in the Vatican library that tell tales about a blue orb and what it can do. I've read ancient rumors of a *Silver Book*. I would characterize the descriptions as a user's manual for alien technology. What am I chasing? A myth? Or do we have functional tools?"

Bob turned toward Velas but answered Knight. "What do you mean by we?" He looked at Dobbins, pointed at him and turned his face back to the TV. "Is he a we? He has nothing to add and I don't like him in my business. Me and Velas, are we the final we? I know, between the two of us, we have one functional tool and the ability to make more. What can you offer me to make us the we? Lay it on the table. I don't do threesomes."

Velas spoke to the image on the screen. "Isn't this what I've been telling you, sir? Chomuk doesn't understand the value you bring. He's a loner without vision, but he can read the instruction manual."

"How is it that you have this ability, Mr. Chomuk?" Knight placed his cigar into an ash tray and began rubbing the back of his hands, moving them over each other like he was washing them in slow motion. "Are you an alien?" The motion of his hands ceased and his eyes narrowed as he awaited the answer.

Bob didn't leave him waiting long. "I'm an inmate, born to this asylum we call earth, just like you." Bob grinned, paused for effect, then added, "But I've spoken with angels."

Velas rolled his eyes, Dobbins stifled a chuckle, Knight clapped his hands together and laughed, gleefully. "Relax, gentlemen, our Mr. Chomuk has a sense of humor. One man's little green creature from Mars is another man's messenger of a bearded old goat in a cloud. They're all alien to earth. You should know what I know, Mr. Chomuk, and I should know what you know. Show me yours and I'll share mine."

Bob walked toward the door, keeping his eye on Dobbins. "Easily done," he said, as he walked past Velas. "I'm going upstairs, I'll be right back."

Velas stood, stammering, "N-no. Wait. You're not going to let him leave the room without an escort. He'll disappear again."

"Dobbins? Let's trust our prospective new partner. If Velas speaks again, strangle the obnoxious worm."

At the moment of the threat, a shrill, electronic facsimile of bells rang through the house. Movement ended until the sound stopped. "It's the doorbell sir," Dobbins announced. "The cleaners are here."

Again the shrill ringing began. This time it lasted longer, stopped briefly, and began again. The insistence of the call to come to the door didn't feel like an announcement of arrival by a team of stealthful enablers of murder.

Knight glanced at his watch and looked up. "The cleaners are twenty minutes away."

Bob prompted Knight to make a decision. "Do you want to answer the door with a uniform?" He waved his hand at Dobbins. "An obnoxious worm?"

The doorbell rang again, longer, more insistent, annoying to the nerves. "Or should I get it?"

69

YARD WORK

NEGOTIATIONS BETWEEN FREDDY AND SANDEEP went smoothly. The cabbie demanded what Freddy most wanted. "Unbind the young Miss and buckle her into the back seat. Sandeep will take her to the hospital."

Freddy's request for Sandeep was also agreed to. "Her parents are in the courtyard, unconscious. All three need to go with you."

"They go. You stay." Negotiations concluded.

Freddy found Hayak first. As strong as he was, it took an act of adrenalin to get Hayak lifted off the ground, over his shoulder, and to the cab. Once Hayak and Roberta were strapped in, he returned for Po.

Po was lighter, but messier. She'd vomited. Freddy recoiled, but recovered, lifted her, and jogged to the cab.

After the women were belted into the back seat, Roberta began to groan, and the fingers on one hand twitched intermittently. Next to her, Po was motionless. Her head leaned backwards, her mouth hung open, her eyes were half-closed.

Freddy touched the side of her neck. "She feels warm," he said. "Hayak felt cool. Can you feel his pulse?"

Sandeep turned on the dome light and looked into Hayak's eyes. He put his hand to his neck, trying several spots to find a pulse. Finally he groaned a sentence without looking at Freddy. "Is all different, now," he said. "There will be questions I cannot answer. Very hard questions."

"Questions? At the hospital? Tell them it's puffer fish poisoning."

Sandeep opened the glove box and tossed the phone out the window to Freddy. "Is yours. Now, for sake of ladies I must go. But ..." He turned his head to face the road and put his hands on the steering wheel, without finishing.

"But? What?" Freddy turned his phone on, noticed he had a new text, found the button to access his messages, and then looked up at Sandeep. "What?"

"A passenger has gone on ahead."

"What do you mean?"

Sandeep sounded somber. "The gentleman has left his temple." He put Hayak's head upright against the headrest and pressed the gas, slowly pulling away, moving slower than a Yugo driving uphill, the dome light still on.

Freddy watched the cab travel to the next block and make a slow left turn. Even with all the caution, he watched the three heads loll to the left then plop downward, disappearing, as if they'd been decapitated in the same moment. The image made him grimace. "Bad omen," he whispered, while he raised the phone and began to read the text message.

Headlights on his left distracted him again. Recognizing the silhouette of a police car, he put the phone to his ear and walked casually toward the gate. He glanced at the officers when they passed by, then he read the message on the screen. It was advice from Otis McKinney.

> Bob, you don't need to know how.
> You need to visualize what.
> Don't forget the trinary data.
> Ya know what I mean?

Freddy loped to the front door and rang the bell. He rang it some more. He laid on it stubbornly, like donkey on break. Finally, Bob answered.

Freddy turned the phone toward him, pointing at the message. "Oh, Sahib," he said in a terrible attempt at an Indian accent," So sorry to have driven off with your phone. Please forgive." In a whisper, he added, "All are on their way to the hospital."

"Put your hand down. There will be no further tip for you," Bob said. He typed a message for Freddy as he talked.

Cleaners coming. GET OUT! NOW!!!

He turned the phone around to allow Freddy to read his warning. "Good deeds are free. Be off." He huffed the scold, then slammed the door.

Freddy retrieved his bat from the gate and walked to the parking garage. He paused, startled by a sound from three, maybe four, blocks away. The quick, piercing screech of a blast from a police car cut through the air. Scant blocks from where he stood, coming from the direction the cab had turned, someone was being pulled over.

70

HOUSE WORK

A S SOON AS THE DOOR SLAMMED, Bob began deleting his messages. "I'll take that," Dobbins said, as he entered the foyer from the hallway.

From inside the living room, Knight's voice asked, "Who was it?"

Velas answered, "The cab driver, Chomuk left his phone in the cab."

Bob finished deleting the messages, ignoring the approaching Dobbins. On the fifth step up the stairs, he lurched to a stop. Dobbins pushed his arm between posts on the stairway and wrapped his hand around Bob's ankle like a constrictor. Each attempt to shake himself free brought a tighter grip.

"Give it to me," Dobbins repeated. The grin on his face was an insult, threatening to escalate into injury.

Bob quit struggling, but he placed the phone in his pocket and answered smirk with smirk. "Come and get it, Dipnot."

Dobbins looked confused, then laughed. "Dipnot? Is that the best you can do, tough-guy?"

Bob shouted toward the living room. "Your trained monkey doesn't speak alien languages, does he?"

"Mr. Knight, sir, he's trying to hide something." Velas was half in the hallway, half in the living room, shifting weight from foot to foot. "I'll get the phone. Tell Dobbins not to let him go."

"Dobbins!" Knight shouted. "Is this how we're going to trust our new partner? Come here. I have something I want you to do."

The grip was removed immediately. Bob watched Dobbins walk back to the hallway, then jogged up the steps, and headed for the guest bedroom.

Behind him, Velas called his names over and over. Each time, the tone was more desperate, the volume higher. "Chomuk, wait. Chomuk. Bob! Tell them you need me. Bob! Damn you, Bob! BOB!"

Bob sighed. "May the lens of death … Aw, screw it. Go to hell."

On the way to the bed, he plucked Lucretia's scrying ball from the flower arrangement. He turned it over in his hand, spreading his fingers to evaluate different grips. When he was satisfied, he removed the book and held its weight atop his left hand. He placed his right hand, firmly gripping the ball, underneath the book to hide the marble and provide balance. He carried it like a serving tray, back to the living room.

Dobbins came out of the living room to greet him in the hallway. His eyes focused, unfriendly, on Bob's face, but his hands were working to reattach a buckle to his belt. Noticing Bob's interest, he held the device up, twisted it, and with a zinging sound, he pulled two halves of the buckle apart, exposing a wire connected to both sides. As he brought his hands back together, the wire retracted into the buckle. "Two-finger garotte, "he said. "One more for the cleaners."

Bob stopped at the doorway. Velas was on the floor, eyes popped in a wide stare at the ceiling. Across his neck, a thin, dark dent in the flesh circled below his face, bloodless, but deep.

"Take him out to the pile." Dobbins stood away from the doorway to allow exit.

Bob walked to Velas's feet and glanced back at Dobbins. He stared into the unflinching poker face of Knight on the TV screen. "It's like that?"

"It's like that," Dobbins answered. He leaned back into the door jamb and hooked his thumbs on his belt.

Bob sighed, kicked Velas's foot, and turned to Dobbins. "Take this," he said, holding the manuscript out to him.

Dobbins accepted the large book in the manner it was presented. He turned his palms up and slid his arms underneath. As soon as Dobbins took possession, Bob pulled his right arm away, then whipped it back around to deliver Lucretia's marble, to Dobbins's left temple.

Dobbins dropped the book and stepped back to the door jamb. Surprise was in his eyes, but his grin stayed eerily arrogant.

Bob swung again, down and hard with solid contact. They both crashed to the ground. Only Bob sprung up. He hovered above Dobbins, ready with marble in hand. A twitch, a death rattle, the last hurrah of a dying nerve, a something, caused a bit of movement on Dobbins's face, and the third blow left no doubt. One more for the cleaners.

"The book," Knight called from the TV, "it's being destroyed."

Bob pulled the manuscript away from pooling blood and carried it to the couch. "It's fine. It's dry," he said after examining the script. "Now, a question."

"Yesss." Knight let the word slither from his mouth. "What else can that marble do?"

"That's not the question."

"No?"

"My question is: Now that you've killed my engineer, how are we going to make more?"

71

PEACE OFFICERS

"OH, GOODNESS," SANDEEP MUTTERED after seeing lights approaching in his rearview mirror. "Everyone act normal. The police, they have returned."

He put his pistol under the seat, turned off the dome light, and checked his turban in the mirror.

Before traveling another block, the police car pulled up behind the cab so closely, the headlights appeared to dim.

Sandeep rolled his window down and motioned for the car to pass. One block later, blue strobes blasted his eyes and a quick shriek from the siren pierced his ears.

"Bothers," he said, addressing the girls in the back seat. "Is best to say nothing. What can Sandeep tell his wife? No, I did not murder the gentleman and date-rape drug the ladies? She will be in Punjab before Sandeep know what he has not done."

He pulled his cab over to the curb and continued his litany of worries. "I should have continued, like O.J. all the way to hospital, but no. Where can I get an all-Sikh jury? Night sticks will rain down on me until they bloody my face. My turban will unravel. I will be taken to the morgue in disarray. Look, they'll say, this *hashishan* has wetted his pants from fearing repercussions. Oh, and Quantanamo. Sandeep cannot go to Quantanamo. The authorities will pour water up my nose until I say I am Osama Bin Laden, then the death-cult Muslims will remove my head for my choice of religion. The headlines will say ..."

Light swept through the taxi and Sandeep smiled at the policeman at his window. "Yes officer? Was I speeding?"

"Please step out of the car."

As Sandeep opened the door, a second officer appeared at the passenger side and tapped at the front widow, motioning for him to roll it down. With the window lowered, he shined his light in Hayak's face and addressed his partner. "Cyanotic."

"Roll down the rear windows," the officer at Sandeep's door ordered. To his partner he barked. "Clary, vitals check."

"He was not blue when he entered the cab," Sandeep said. "At least, Sandeep did not know he was blue."

"In good time," the officer responded. "Please step out of the car."

"When the back windows lowered, Officer Clary lifted Po's head and rested it upright against the back seat. He looked closely at her half-open eyes and announced to his partner, "Nothing but whites." He placed the palm of his hand on her head. "Atropine." He stepped back to the front window and placed his hand on Hayak's head. "Induce regurgitation, atropine, and necstigmine."

After Sandeep stepped from the cab, the officer on his side of the taxi reached through the back window and laid his hand atop Roberta's head. Immediately, she lifted an arm, chest high, ground her teeth, whistled through her nose, belched, and let loose a long, loud, musical fart, followed by a deep moan. "Body functions normal, she's waking up."

Sandeep couldn't help himself. "Oh, for goodness. If young miss wake like this, she must consider full disclosure before marriage."

"Sir." The officer removed Sandeep's turban and lifted his hand, palm down, toward his bare head.

Sandeep backed away, jabbering as he went. "There is a legal revolver under the seat. It is mentioned in spirit of cooperation. These people were placed into my cab by a Yankee man. They cannot walk to hospital. What can Sandeep say? Sandeep know nothing about zombie families and Yankee men, plagued by monsters of a stripe Sandeep cannot illuminate upon."

As if the officer had Inspector Gadget abilities, he caught up to the retreating cab driver without moving his feet. His arm appeared to stretch and he palmed Sandeep's skull. "Be at peace," he said soothingly.

Sandeep opened and closed his mouth like a fish, but no words came out. He relaxed and watched with a smile as the two officers went to work.

Officer Clary stabbed Hayak and Po in the leg with injectors. He pulled Hayak from the car and held him with one arm around his midsection, horizontally aloft. The other arm extended to his face, his hand holding open his mouth, while his finger probed, pulling his tongue from his airway and inducing a liquid-spewing gag response with his finger.

As Clary finished, his partner had already transferred the two women to the back seat of the cruiser. He fit Hayak in next to them. "Officer Chee? We're ready," he said, as he stepped into the front seat and closed his door.

Chee placed his palm on Sandeep's head again and said, "Well done, cowboy. We can take it from here. All they need now is a little coffee and fresh air in their faces while we drive them around. You're free to go." He put Sandeep's turban back on his head and tapped it in place. "What you've seen here tonight? Keep it under your hat."

Sandeep clasped officer Chee's hand and shook it vigorously. "No need to tell Sandeep. Already I can't wait to get home and not tell the wife what I have seen, but ..."

Chee waited for Sandeep to finish his thought, then let go the vigorous handshake.

"But," Sandeep continued. "Maybe there is more for you to do tonight?"

Chee wagged his head. "It's certain; we are building a rage to stomp through the wicked, lay low the high tyrants, and write the parasites from this life. The Lord will remove them from the next life. Not on this night, but on-time."

"Goodness. Sandeep will write a letter to the police commissioner and wax bountifully in praise of your fervor."

"Better to put it in prayer." Chee sat in the driver's seat and turned off the strobe. "Happy trails, Pardner," he said as he drove off. "I release you to your own authority."

Back in his taxi, Sandeep looked into the mirror, speaking to his image in the glass. "How would you look in a cowboy hat?" He retrieved his revolver from under the seat and posed. "What would Hopabout Cassidy do with his own authority? Perhaps Sandeep should go back to the corral and lay himself down some lawfulness."

72

IT IS WHAT IT IS

"**R**EALLY?" KNIGHT RESPONDED to Bob's concern over Velas being killed. "Did you have a personal, call it a special, attachment to your engineer? I may have misread your relationship. If all you want is an engineer, I can offer them in droves. I'm usually better skilled at picking up on aberrant motivations."

Bob mocked Knight's attempt at casual puffery. "I too, misread your depth of affection for Dobbins. You must feel naked and impotent without your ape."

Knight shook his head in mock concern. "Oh, no. Here we are. Two birds of a feather, alone in the world, naked and impotent. That's a bad combination."

"I need one talented and disposable engineer to regain my potency," Bob said in a serious tone. "What's your Viagra?"

Knight put his elbows on his desk and, at sloth-like speed, leaned toward the camera. His face grew larger on the screen, as if the camera was panning in. While the image grew, the fine lines morphed. From tells displaying mockery, to amused curiosity, and finally, settling into a mask-like image of bland indifference, he cycled through the features that telegraph a serious and confident disrespect. Only the Nixon-emulation of sweat beads on his upper lip involuntarily betrayed his real feelings. Knight was nervous.

"Let's forego pushing each other's buttons," he said, after leaning back into his chair. "I have buttons neither of us wants pushed."

Knight swiveled in his seat and pulled an extension from his desktop over his lap. He pointed his finger straight down over the panel to indicate a spot Bob couldn't see on his monitor. "This little button here, will cause a horrific accident in a nuclear facility near you. You might not care what happens to the population of New York, Mr. Chomuk, but you can't outrun it. There's no reason to fry when you are inches away from godhood, and have a partner who will negotiate. I won't let you walk away with what I want. Let's define what success will look like. Visualize what you want."

Bob wiped blood from Lucretia's ball on his shirt sleeve and set it down next to him on the pillow. He set the book across his lap, opened it, and turned pages. Without looking at the TV, he cleared his throat and said, "Okay, one marble for my life. What's your flavor, big guy? Time travel?"

"I'd like a menu." Knight pushed his tray of buttons back into the desk and rubbed his hands together. "Tell me what you're offering. Velas said immortality was available? He said a power source for a community of the future was possible. Did he lie?"

"Often, but not about those options. You can have alien weaponry if you'd like, or water purifying applications. Would you like to control an untraceable broadcast frequency that will override and hide inside other frequencies? There's more, but choose one. One marble per application. I'm offering only one."

Knight ran his tongue across his teeth and swayed back and forth, like a cobra, before answering. "How many marbles are there?"

"There's this one." Bob lifted Lucretia's ball. "You'll notice it's not blue. Velas was going to make the chamber it needs for activation. I possess one active marble. If Velas's calculations were correct, we can manufacture up to twenty more."

"Why is the supply limited?"

"An element, not found on earth, is in my possession. Choose to fly around the galaxy and search for more, if you'd like. There are instructions for manufacturing the craft in the book." Bob patted the manuscript in his lap. "You arrange the manufacture of twenty marbles, deliver nineteen to me, and I'll send you the transcription for making your spaceship. Of course, future conditions may apply."

Knight scowled, wrinkling his nose, and retracted his bottom lip. His jaw protruded, showing a row of white, uneven teeth. He snarled a warning. "You don't get it. I'm the man behind the curtain. I'm King Arthur, offering you the opportunity to be my Merlin. I'm offering you life in Camelot, not a voice at the round table. Camelot is coming, with you or without you."

"I see. You have options." Bob laid the book on the floor and stood up. "How far out are the cleaners?"

Knight let the angry badger look fade and replaced it with a puzzled expression. "Why do you ask?"

Bob walked over to Velas and picked up his feet. "I want to remove one of your options." He pulled Velas toward the door and kicked Dobbins's leg from the entrance.

"What are you doing, Mr. Chomuk?" Knight placed his elbows on the desk and rested his chin on his hands. "Where are you going?"

Bob stopped in the doorway. "Cleaners come, enter the house, put me to sleep, and I wind up telling you everything I know after getting a little gabby juice. Merlin is not stupid. Merlin can find a shotgun in the master bedroom, there's a pistol on the floor, under the end table, and Dobbins has a sidearm. All of those things will be useful. If I'm going down, it will be nuclear. I'll settle for a gun battle, or a house afire, but not in a melted heap of talking goo."

"Mr. Chomuk, barricade yourself if you wish. I'm ready to make you two offers. Think clearly about what you can call a win. Visualize the unthought of options. I'll be here when you're done with moving the furniture."

"You know what? I'll take that advice. Visualize and explore the maybes sounds like the right path."

"Good man. A decision worthy of Merlin."

"Just one thing. Inform the cleaners who will be in charge when they arrive. Do they know Dobbins?"

"They do not. We keep the ugly fringes compartmentalized."

"Good. The name, Chomuk, should never be spoken. I'm Dobbins, until they leave. Merlin will appear after negotiations are finished." Bob reached to the floor, removed the name tag from Dobbins's uniform, and pinned it to his shirt.

"Agreed." Knight reached for his Phablet and sat back in his chair. "Go about your business. You might want to look under those flowers and find a white tube with a red dot on one end. Roberta is in the kitchen about to revive from an unscheduled nap. Place the tube in your mouth, red dot between your lips, point at your former girlfriend, and exhale with power. You'll have three loads to drag outside."

Bob lifted the flowers and placed the tube in his shirt pocket.

"Oh, and another thing." Knight grinned while tapping on his Phablet. "Don't inhale. The cleaners will arrive in forty-five minutes."

73

I DON'T LIKE MESSY

"I DON'T LIKE IT."
The oldest of the three men sitting in a booth at Waffle Den put his phone in his pocket and showed the waitress three fingers.

"Refills, and more cream."

"Don't like what?" The fortyish man sitting across from him adjusted himself on the bench and leaned forward to hear the answer.

"Was that Grandma?" The almost-adult asked. "What'd she want?"

"Aw Jeez," the middle man moaned. "What did I tell you? No names."

"Grandma is not a name," the young one said, rolling his eyes.

"I just don't like it," the eldest man repeated. "Any of it" He turned to the teenager at his side and pressed a table knife in the gap separating his patella and tibia, applying enough pressure to make the boy flinch with discomfort. "Listen to your father. He learned from the best."

The boy's eyes darted around the restaurant while he massaged his knee cap. "Sorry, sir, I'll learn."

"You don't like what?" The father asked again.

"I don't like changing the schedule. I don't like rising laundry counts. I don't like field training a rookie."

"How long's the delay?" asked the father.

"We arrive in forty-four minutes," the elder said while checking his watch.

"More laundry?" asked the boy.

"We started with one bag. Now, the count is at six. I don't like making live adjustments. That's the bad news."

"There's good news?" the father asked.

"It's an outdoor cleanup. One spot removal. The new laundry only needs bagging and processing." Grandpa tousled the hair of the kid and smiled. "This is the best part. The additional cleaning fees will cover a semester at your fancy college. How you like that?"

"More laundry, less student loans. What's not to like?"

"Fluidity. It makes for messy. I don't like messy."

74

FAITH IN MAYBE

BOB PULLED VELAS INTO THE COURTYARD and lined him up next to the body of the old man by the bench. "Who are you, and what's your story?" he asked, before rushing back to get Dobbins.

After struggling with the heavier Dobbins, Bob's breathing was labored, so he sat in the dark to catch his breath. While waiting, he patted the old man's clothing, searching for an ID. Realizing there wasn't enough light to read the documents in the man's wallet, he slipped it into his pants pocket and regained his calm. In less than a minute, he stood up and hustled back to the house.

On his way to the kitchen, Bob stopped at the doorway to the living room and looked in to check the image on the TV.

Knight was at his desk, puffing a cigar and flipping his golden lighter on and off. He looked like a man who just signed the business deal of his career. When he saw Bob in the doorway, he smiled. "All done, Mr. Chomuk?"

"Be patient," Bob said. "I have to say goodbye to someone special."

"Having second thoughts?"

Bob grinned. "Come on now. Wally wouldn't respect me if I just let her go without indulging in a little fun. Don't worry; I'm not a marathon man."

Knight looked at his watch. Wally was a ..." When he glanced up, Bob was already out of the picture and on his way to the kitchen. Knight's lip curled and he returned to flicking his butane bull. After a few clicks, he spoke into an exhale of Cuban smoke. "Take your time, Mr. Chomuk. I'll just wait here."

Bob hustled to the entryway between the carriage house and kitchen, stopping just long enough to pluck Po's car keys from its customary hook by the kitchen door. Even after Freddy approached with questions, Bob barely broke stride on his way to the tool shed, flipping Freddy the car keys and silencing him with an uncustomary abruptness.

"Don't talk. I know what I'm doing. I need you to help me take down the plywood on the back wall."

Freddy stared as Bob started removing tools from their hangers and setting them on the floor. "Tell me what you're doing," he implored.

Bob stopped momentarily and faced his friend. "I'm stepping up to the plate," he said. "Don't try to understand. Help me pull this panel down, then take Po's car to the hospital. Ask Berti to explain. Get ahold of Otis. He knows more than ... Damn. How many screws does it take to hang a sheet of plywood?"

Freddy stepped forward and picked a claw hammer off the ground. "Stand back," he said. "Do you want fast or pretty?"

"Fast."

Freddy swung the hammer, punching a round hole in the top left corner. After inserting the claw into the hole, he jerked. The corner separated itself from the binds of a half-dozen screws. He jerked again and the wood fractured, leaving a triangular hole in the corner, big enough for Freddy to grab onto the panel with both hands. On the first mighty pull, the plywood ripped through the screws at the top and left side. On the second pull, it hung like a broken door, exposing the original wall behind it. "Okay. Now what?"

Bob nudged Freddy out of the way and felt for a gap between the old panels. When he found it, he smiled and turned his head toward Freddy. "Now, this. That's what," he said, as he slid the panel open, exposing the walkway.

Freddy peered into the dark opening. "What the ..." He reached for a shop light hanging on an adjacent panel but stopped when Bob jogged out of the shed. "Where are you going?"

He watched Bob speed his way to the garage door opener by the kitchen entry. His long stride made the distance there and back seem insignificant. He was back in the shed and speaking in riddles before the door finished its glide up the track into the open position.

'Trust me now. Figure it out later," Bob began. "Things are beginning to gel. Asitr's stories. Things I've seen. It's gelling. He paused, looking into Freddy's eyes. A blank expression answered his gaze. "Sorry, just listen."

He gave Freddy a quick hug and continued his rambling attempt to communicate in shorthand images. "Special people, with unique talents and skills, are not an accident. Like you. Learning from you the role of an individual on a team. Roberta. Wasn't Berti a surprise? Traveling outside our little planet. How do I ignore that? Baal Zebub is dead. Satan is ... How did Asitr put it? He's ruling us by letting us rule ourselves. Malign neglect, that's how he put it. It's not a question of how I fit in or where I fit in. It was always a question of when. When is now. Where is right here, in this house. There's a secret in the basement, a room that can't be duplicated and shouldn't be allowed to fall into the wrong hands. I don't know how I'll do it, but I know it will all happen tonight. I'm the right guy to step into the batter's box. My shelf life dictates my pinch-hitting job is right freakin' now. I need to go upstairs and visualize how. You know, the Otis advice. Visualize and don't forget the maybes in the database. I'm going to visualize what I want to do and ask the marble to supply the know-how."

The two men stared at each other until Freddy grasped Bob in a bear hug. "You'll tell me later?"

Bob pulled away. "Listen to me. I want you to give Berti a message. Have Otis explain it to her. I don't have time left to explain myself. Every day that goes by, I'll become less and less. I'm hoping I don't survive the night."

Freddy took a step back. "What? You can't tell me something like that and ..."

"Hey!" Bob interrupted. "I have to go upstairs and visualize. I don't have more time. Tell Berti to let Chomuk die tonight so her father can be her secret hero. That's all I have. Go."

Bob didn't wait for his friend to shake loose from his stunned silence. He pulled back the plywood and dashed into the dark, leaving Freddy jingling car keys, void of facts but with foreboding enough to let loose a tear for his friend.

Into the blackness behind the opening, Freddy spoke his encouragement somberly. "I'll tell her, buddy. Go win the game."

75

SOMETIMES FAITH NEEDS A MUSE

WHEN BOB SAT IN THE CHAIR behind Bill Elliott's desk in the old radio studio, he lifted the red-dot tube from his shirt pocket and examined the design. The tube itself was nothing like the long, hollow bamboo and reed instruments he saw in jungle documentaries. Visually, it looked like a tiny PVC pipe. Both the mouth end and the business end were plugged with a clear, thin substance that glistened like spun sugar.

On the end with no dot, in the center of the plug, a tiny bump, no bigger than the tip of a fine needle, interrupted the flat surface. The smooth surface on the other end reflected light evenly, without a hint of unevenness. Holding the tube to his eye, Bob looked toward the ceiling light and found no stray beams penetrated the tube. It was tightly packed.

Experimentation continued. Bob shook the tube, tapped it against the desk, and pinched it gently at the center. Nothing in its construction seemed to change. He rolled it gently between two fingers and checked again. Nothing. He applied pressure and rolled it against the desk. The hard surface seemed to soften. A fine dust, like powdered sugar with the gritty feel of fiberglass spilled from both ends. Bob looked again. The film was gone.

He cautiously put the tube to his mouth and placed his free hand inches away from the business end of the tube. "I can't miss from here," he said aloud. "A walk-off sacrifice-bunt. For you fans scoring at home, that's an RBI, an out, and a plate appearance without an AB. Blue Marbles win! Blue Marbles win! Go crazy, folks! Yeah, go crazy. Call it a win without playing the bottom half."

Bob opened the top drawer of the desk and found everything just as it was on the day he was boxed by Kae'Lairy. He removed a pencil and pried the eraser loose. The fit wasn't perfect, but it was good enough. With a little pushing and twisting, he managed to cork the eraser into the end opposite where the dot warned of danger.

"Now what?" he asked. He looked at the clock. "Cleaners come in thirty-eight minutes."

He removed the marble from the vaporizer bin and set it next to the tube on the desk. "I've won a game. What about the tournament? Help me visualize what to do about the tournament. The chain. Is my link finished? Is my big swing a sacrifice bunt, or am I the weak link? The missing link?"

Bob lifted the marble over his head and made two false starts at smashing it onto the desktop. "Talk to me!" he shouted.

The sudden eruption of anger slowly dissipated from his face, and he lowered the orb to the desk.

"Are you recording me? Of course you are. How did Ctis realize he could use you to drive a golf cart? How did you fly the *shem* to the places he wanted to go? Why did you land next to the hatch on the roof at the moment I visualized the best spot to enter the house? I'm thinking of something I said. I want you to play it back."

Bob stared as the marble traded gaze for silence. "Tricky little thing, aren't you?" He pointed his finger at the marble and slowly inched his fingertip closer and closer, stopping before touching it, as if afraid to learn his experiment would fail. His eyes moved toward the clock and he exhaled a frustrated breath, then poked the ball.

In the room, he heard his own voice. "Blue marble wins! Blue marble wins! Go crazy folks!" Startled, Bob jabbed the ball so hard it rolled off the table, but it was silent. He jumped from the chair and chased after it, knocking Icarus and the glass angel sideways as he careened around the corner. When he picked it up, he asked, "What's your range? I can't take you downstairs. I'm thinking ..."

Bob sucked in his lips and once again poked the marble with his finger. Freddy's voice answered his silent command. "I'll tell her, buddy. Go win the game."

Bob put the marble back into the vaporizer door and looked again at the clock. "I'll try," he said. "I can swing the blue bat. I need a muse. Someone to whisper in my ear and tell me how to visualize the swing."

76

BENEVOLENT HYPNOTHERAPY

S IX BLOCKS FROM THE HOUSE, under the dirty-yellow light of a street lamp, Freddy and Sandeep crossed paths again.

Seeing a taxi approaching, Freddy slowed to get a look at the driver.

Sandeep almost passed by, but braked when he recognized Freddy behind the wheel.

Both men put their vehicles in reverse and stopped when they were window to window in the middle of the street.

"What has happened?" Sandeep asked. "Have you left your friend alone with Dobbins and his monsters?"

Freddy got out of the car and approached the cab. "It's complicated," he said. After putting his face to the taxi window, he asked, "Where are the Asmudis?"

"Also, is complicated," Sandeep twisted his face through configurations of thoughtful confusion, then settled on an affect of sudden consternation. "Sandeep has entrusted them to peace officers."

"Peace officers?" Freddy raised his voice, "The police?"

"Is good." Sandeep raised two thumbs up. "The Mrs. has beneficially been stabbed in the leg. The Mr., likewise. Additionally, he has been forcefully regurgitated. The young miss has been relieved of her gaseous contents. All are now having wind blown into their faces. Is good."

Approaching headlights interrupted whatever God-knows-what reply Freddy might have had. He and Sandeep turned their attention to the vehicle. The blinding blue flashers stunned them both.

Blurred by the back-lighting, two officers approached. Each of their shadows fell across Freddy and Sandeep, softening the assault of the police lights. Both men appeared to relax in the officers' shadows. Their postures of relief escalated to grins of obvious comfort upon hearing the phrase, "Be at peace."

In the throes of a peaceful, compliant mind, Freddy watched the slow-moving, silly-grinning Asmudis exit the police cruiser and walk to Po's vehicle. Wordlessly, he opened the doors and ushered them in.

"There's a Waffle Den just up the street," the officer with the name tag, Clary, informed them. "These folks could use a cup of coffee before you take them home. You have a little time to think. Take it."

"Yes, of course," Freddy answered, displaying the same happily vacant expression as his passengers. "We need coffee."

"And you, sir. Deputy Sandeep. You're free to go."

So, with hypnotic suggestions in full effect, off they went.

77

STROLLING UP TO THE PLATE

A S BOB SET FOOT ON CONCRETE, after descending the ladder in the walkway, pain swelled suddenly in his joints. The tremor returned to his hands. He braced himself for the blitzing headache, but it didn't come.

The sweat flowed while he waited for his hands to steady. "Oh, no," he said aloud. It was only two words, but he didn't stutter.

From the ladder to the tool shed, he walked with an unsteady gait, not fluid, but still in control of his balance. He tested his speech as he went.

"*Beauti-ba-boo ... B-b-boolaroo ... Bluba.*" He slapped his hands against his head and braced himself against the bench before trying again, this time slowly, without the impetus of the three-times-fast requirements of the twister.

"*Beautiful blue broadloom rugs.*

"*Beautiful blue broadloom rugs.*

"*Beautiful Blue Broadloom rugs.*"

He looked at the ceiling, toward the studio on the second floor and announced, "Think ahead. Talk slow. I'm ready to play."

78

DOOR NUMBER ONE

N O MATTER HOW COMPOSED a man is mentally, some tells are impossible to miss. Bob's entry into the living room was too forced. He walked a straight line, but his gait was stiff. His facial projection of calm was belied by a white pallor of the skin. Knight picked up on the signals easily, but he misread their meaning.

"Welcome back. You look a bit pale, Mr. Chomuk. Getting too old to handle a wild young thing?"

Bob eased onto the couch and smiled at the TV. "She didn't exactly congratulate me for being a credit to my gender, if that's what you mean."

Knight pursued the question. "You didn't notice any … let's say, an unexpectedly exuberant response?"

Bob paused before answering. "Are you testing me?"

Knight snuffed his cigar in the ashtray. "Whatever do you mean?"

"The dart. Is that what Wally called his 'chicken-dance potion'? I'm a sadist, not a lover of manic thrashing. Her writhing about with a demented grin left me disappointed."

"A shame. You missed Wally's genius. That happy face was nothing more than involuntary twitching. You can be sure you caused her a great deal of fear."

Bob frowned and waved his hand at the image on the screen. "Get to it. We have thirty minutes. What's your offer?"

Knight grimaced and looked at his watch. "I have two offers, Mr. Chomuk. First, you should know something about the club." He removed his watch from his wrist and put the band around his fingers, positioning it so the face would be visible each time he opened his hand and looked at his palm. "Hmm. The fact is: We have thirty-three minutes. The cleaners arrive on my time."

Bob groaned. "Get to it, and skip the list of renowned names. Wally's already given me the pitch."

"Ah, history as a list of names. That's Wally. He never cared about the big picture." Knight pulled the ashtray close to him and picked up his cigar. "You'd be surprised by who we are and what we do."

"CIA, Masons, Bilgeburgers, I don't care. Illuminati? Sam's Club?" Bob threw his hands in the air. "Make an offer."

Knight put his cigar in front of his lips and blew. One corner of the tip survived the snuffing and began to glow under the long, soft exhale of air. With an exaggerated sweep of his arm, he brought the cigar to his mouth and puffed the ember hotter, redder, larger. He lifted a hand to his face and opened his palm to check his watch, wallowing in a display of indifferent confidence. "It's important you know, Mr. Chomuk. I'm going to tell you. Focus. You're behaving like a teenager.

"You don't get to stall me until your boys get here. Make an offer."

"Ten minutes to enlighten you." Knight checked his watch again. "Give me nine minutes. You'll have your offer in ten."

Bob checked his own watch then lay prone on the couch, put a pillow under his head, and laced his fingers over his stomach. "Ten minutes," he said. "Ten minutes by my watch."

"Excellent," Knight began. "Here's a fact. We are not the CIA. We aren't any of the world's intelligence agencies. We are not one of the well-known secret societies, but we do lead them all by the nose into situations advantageous to our agenda. We're just beneath the surface — stealthy, dark, and immune. If you have the proper blood plasm, our agenda is beautiful, even holy. If you're in the mass of unacceptables, we offer images of danger to the warm and fuzzy places you hold in your heart and use the fear of their loss to grow targeted hate. Think of it as brain science turned into art form. Think of us as the man in your head who is Photoshopping your word images. If you don't think it through, our agenda is unstoppable."

Knight took a long draw on his cigar. "Are you following along, Mr. Chomuk?"

"Sure, you're muckety-mucks with an agenda."

"Yes."

Knight flicked ashes into the ash tray and laughed. "So we are, and, thank the holy trinity, we will always muck the mucky bloods." As quickly as he said the words, the upturned grin disappeared and his face returned to his previous display of bored and sour. "Forgive me, Chomuk, I was being obtuse. It's an inside joke."

Bob sighed and twiddled his thumbs. "I got the inference. Darwin, Huxley, and Teilhard being your holy trinity, and mucky bloods being the unworthy. Wally laid out the vision for your brave new world inside a bubble."

"Back to business, then. Let me tell you what makes our founding fathers so revered. It's not their recognition of superstition as the anchor on intellect. Egad. Who can't reason that the biggest existential threat to the human race is the human race? 'Go forth and multiply?' What a holy heap of guano. Our founders recognized a flaw in logic when they saw it."

Knight paused and tilted his head, the lines of a grin hinting at pleasure in his observation. "They saw the future and laid the groundwork to change it," he continued. "How you ask? The churches opened the door when they pressed charges of heresy on scientists, doing what scientists do. Darwin and Huxley bestowed on each other awards and praise from inside the newly prestigious Royal Academy. They utilized the new phenomena of radio and the recently organized guilds for distributing photos and news stories for a world-wide press. They made sure everyone knew they were men of renown.

"Teilhard de Chardin clothed himself in the robes of a man of God and went on world tour. Posing in his robes with photos of faked fossils and bones, he gave interviews touting a phony alternative reality. Ears hear and eyes see. Science and church appear to be in agreement. Is intelligent design disproven? Is there even a God? Divine right is resurrected out of the ashes and rekindled with a scientific name. Eugenics is born and swaddled in the image that any man is free to do as they whilt to do. How else to show you are the fittest? Try to appreciate the impact. Do you see how brilliant are the moving parts?"

Bob checked his watch and sighed loudly.

"Am I boring you?" Knight set his cigar in the ashtray and leaned forward.

"No, I wasn't listening. I was trying to visualize wrapping this up."

Knight glanced into his palm. "I still have seven minutes and thirteen seconds. There is the passing of batons to recognize. Marshall McLuhan vows to take up the mantle of Teilhard. I don't mean he fakes bones and dons robes. He continues the research in how minds are manipulated through mass media. New pipers and sirens, like ..."

Bob checked his watch and sighed loudly.

Knight snorted and turned sideways in his chair. "I don't want to stretch the limits of your attention span. Do you feel like I've left you in the dark?"

"I like the dark." Bob sat back up, closed his eyes, and let his head fall back on the couch. "The monsters I avoid hide in the light. I see what you do, your club that is. Tell me how you fit in. Sales presentation isn't your strength. What's your function, and why should I trust you to offer me a deal?"

"My function? I'm the switchboard operator. I'm the editor of the cloud. I'm the finger on the button." Knight held one forefinger in front of his face and narrowed his eyes. "There is one agenda and one knight to guard the gate. I am that knight. I built the gate. It would be fatal to wait for a second opinion."

Bob raised his head and leaned forward. "You built the gate?"

Knight huffed. "It might help if you understood how we are organized. Each franchise is a finger on the hand. Dobbins's unit is the opposable thumb that holds the franchises to the agenda. The club, the inner circle if you will, is the palm." Knight lifted one palm toward the camera, then turned it. "When necessary, we are the proverbial back-of-the-hand. In the extreme," he formed a fist, "we'll put your lights out. Normally, those decisions are made in council."

"And you?"

"I control the nerve center of the hand. Franchises make proposals, I filter them for council consideration. Problems pop up? People like Dobbins are on standby. Donors need to be handled? It all requires specialized communications. The system that handles the communication between parts runs through me. I decide what the council sees and hears. My system can't be hacked. Communications can't be recorded."

Bob groaned. "I'll take your word for it."

"It's wireless, carried on a miniscule frequency pattern, and emits EMPs enough to scramble even the old-school recorders." Knight reached for the cigar again and smiled, as if to celebrate the good fortune of having such toys to play with. "And, I built it. It's my design."

Bob sat still, open-mouthed, like a man who obviously didn't know what to say.

Knight blew on the cigar again, but it was dead. He put it, unlit, between his lips and rolled it around between his teeth. After a long wait, he spoke. "No comment?"

"No, I was trying to visualize the idea. Kudos, guy. And you put it all together?"

"Yes, thank you." Knight took the cigar stub from his mouth and cleared his throat. "I'm ready with my offer, Chomuk. We finished early."

Bob put his hands up and shrugged. "So go ahead, offer."

"You'll be happy to know you can keep your blue marble. What we get is the material to make more. We house you in a lab where you'll teach our team to read the *Silver Book*. After you've assisted in producing the maximum of new marbles, you're free to go."

Bob threw himself backward against the couch and laughed. "I can't take that."

"I wouldn't either, unless I couldn't escape the penalty. With that in mind, an offer of life is generous."

"The penalty?"

"If we don't deal tonight ..." Knight pulled an instrument across his desk and lifted its top, uncovering a keyboard with a square configuration of button displays. He let a finger hover and circle above one of the buttons and asked, "Don't you remember? There will be a nuclear accident near you. We retrieve everything in that house, and our linguists' crack that *Silver Book* of yours."

Bob lifted the book with silver lettering and stood. "Fine, I have just enough time to burn the pages."

He stepped toward the door, but stopped when Knight called him back.

"You haven't heard what's behind Door Number Two."

79

PARKING THE POSSE

S ANDEEP MADE TWO PASSES AROUND THE BLOCK. On the third pass by the open gate to the carriage house, he stopped. His headlights revealed the garage doors were open.

"I reckon we should giddy up to the ol' corral," he said in an awkward attempt at a western drawl. "It's high noon … somewhere."

On the rooftop, Kae'lairy appealed to Olphrenjii. "Recalculate. You can't manipulate free will like this. The margin of error …"

Olphrenjii cut him off. "I don't recalculate what is certain. This would be his free will if he was allowed to know the facts. He is necessary. We owe it to Bobby."

80

THREE DEGREES OF DISGUSTING

FREDDY AND THE THREE ASMUDIS walked into Waffle Den and took a booth next to three men in blue overalls. When the waitress arrived at their table, she fanned herself with a menu, attempting to chase away the odor of stale vomitus from the customers' clothing.

"Four coffees and cream," Freddy said. "Nothing else."

As the odor wafted to the adjacent booth, Grandpa pulled bills from his pocket and gave them to Junior. "Pay the tab," he said, adding quietly, "We'll go over the job in the van. We arrive in twenty minutes."

At the cash register, Junior complained to the waitress, "Can't you do anything about the derelicts in here?" He hiked his thumb over his shoulder in the direction of the four new arrivals. "Some people are just disgusting."

The waitress shrugged, took the money, and closed the register.

"You forgot the change," Junior said.

"Oh, I thought I was getting a twenty-three cent tip."

She waited for the three men to leave before she sneered at their backs.

"Ass holes. Next time you're in, I'm spittin' in your coffee."

81

THE HOLE IN THE WALL GANGPLANK

OTIS ENTERED THE BRIDGE OF THE FISHING VESSEL and studied the displays on the dash. "So she was right?"

At the wheel, Huana continued to scan the horizon with night-vision glasses. "Baba? I assume you're talking about Baba. The only thing bigger than her eyes and ears is her mouth. She told you where we're going?"

"She said you were trading this boat for a river vessel in New Orleans."

"Three vessels."

"Then you're going upriver. To stay?"

Huana put her binoculars down. "The papers for the transaction are in order. Did you get American papers before you took off in the *shem*?"

"My papers? I'm an American. Why ..." Otis stopped for thought and sat in the swivel chair next to the captain's perch. "What about your papers? You can't stay in the country with papers for a business transaction."

"We're indigenous. We don't need no stinking papers." Huana picked up the night-vision binoculars and handed them to Otis. "Business deal or work agreement, all we need is time to get to our destination. Most of us are using the Velas plan. Dude, if we were illegal and pretty, we could go to parties with the elite and marry a future president."

Huana pointed toward the bow. "Over there. Look over there. That's the US Coast Guard, sitting in the dark. Those eerie green lights on deck are the snared paperless. Once plucked, they stay shackled to the deck until the rounds are complete. I hope that doesn't happen to you. It might be two weeks before they finish their rounds and return to port. Can you take the elements that long?"

Otis scanned the horizon without comment.

Huana put her hand atop the binoculars and pushed them down. She stood in front of Otis, locking eyes. "If they decide to board us, I suggest you think of something to tell them. I'm telling them we rescued you from an overturned cigar boat. The rest is up to you. Your fingerprints will be on file. Maybe amnesia will be good."

"What?"

"Dude." Huana squinted her one good eye at Otis and drew a finger across her throat. "It makes sense to weigh you down and dump you off the gangplank. Betray us and you'll wish I had. You don't get special treatment just because Caspi's sweet on you."

Otis raised the binoculars again and studied the formidable-looking vessel off the bow. "I had more questions about what you would do in the country, but it's best I don't know."

"That's smart. You look good in your thinking cap.'

Otis huffed and smiled. "You don't scare me, Huana."

He returned the binoculars and closed his eyes.

After a few moments of listening to the boat's motor hum and waves slap the bow, he asked, "Caspi's sweet on me?"

82

DOOR NUMBER TWO

B^{OB PAUSED WHEN KNIGHT OFFERED} to give him a second proposal. He didn't look at the face on the TV. He didn't commit to returning to the couch or walking through the door. He stood still, his eyes closed, and his feet stuck in place. He stayed like that until Knight spoke again.

"I'm done with selling. I want to talk to you as a buyer."

Bob opened his eyes and closed them again after raising a finger toward the TV screen as a signal to wait. A faint smile rose on his face, then grew until he nodded his head one time, as if putting his stamp of approval on a decision. He returned to the couch asking a question. "Are you making an offer for yourself, or your club?"

"I'll need to use club resources," he responded. "A single engineer, for production. I can pry him away from his current project and avoid red flags. Only the three of us need to know. After production, it will just be the two of us."

"You would go rogue on your organization, just like that?" Bob snapped his fingers. "You'd give up your seat in the center of the web for …?"

"Immortality. I would give it up, if I had to, but I don't have to. The only thing better than sitting in my seat is staying in my seat. Forever. To do that, I'll need six marbles and the instructions for five applications."

"Name them, and tell me why you need them." Bob opened the book and leafed through the pages.

"Immortality is number one. Water purification. A power source for my bubble inside the bubble. I'd like to overhear the organic communications between members of the club, their private conversations. The fifth application is something we need to discuss. I'd like to replace the thumb. Dobbins's group is a sloppy, risky tool. I want to explore the alien weaponry with you. Perhaps, and I'm just thinking theoretically here, perhaps there is something I could use to target individuals inside the inner circle? I'd like it to be a matter of just pushing a button. Buttons are clean and easily organized. The sixth marble would be a backup storage vault for my brainwave bank. That is how it works, am I correct Mr. Chomuk?"

Bob closed the book on his lap. "You turn very quickly. How long have you waited for this chance?"

Knight's eyes softened from the focused, new-car-shopper stare to the distant gaze of a man reminiscing. "I was a schoolboy, reading bad science fiction books by L. Ron Hubbard and learning the real lessons of the Scopes monkey trial." He unwrapped the watch from around his fingers and laid it on the desk as he continued. "Epiphanies come in the strangest of places."

Bob checked his watch. "I don't need to hear the story."

"A man is criminalized for exploring a theory. If his persecutors were so sure of their truth, what were they afraid of? I was young, but I saw it. If you can learn what men fear, you can control their rage. Most men fear the truth if they have a weak faith in their beliefs. It's an easy game if played with twenty-first-century schizoid men."

Knight threw his hands up, waved them in mock fervor, and exclaimed, "Huhaw!" He sat back after his outburst and continued, in a somber voice, "As our dear departed friend, Mr. Wally would say."

"L. Ron Hubbard?"

"He turned bad science fiction into a religion. It's the flip side of the coin. For those not devout enough to hate for their god, there is an empty spot to fill. Knight put his hands in the prayer position. "I'm ready to use my club's resources to ascend, Mr. Chomuk."

Bob juggled Lucretia's orb from hand to hand, not looking at the screen. "It looks like you have a plan for making the pieces fit."

"You have my final piece." Knight tapped his knuckles on the desk. "Now, let's get to it. What pieces are you missing? Do you need money? You may need to consider where you hide. I could share with you the parts of the world safe from our winnowing events. Wally told you about that?"

"He mentioned it."

"Did he tell you why the American nuclear plants are located in such odd clusters? I have a button for each one. I have a button for all at once. I have buttons for every country in every continent. If it's in the Cloud, it connects to me, right here." Knight pointed to his desk.

"I'm giving this to you free. Avoid the east coast of the United States. Google the locations of nuclear plants in the U.S., and you'll see why. Pay attention to the doughnut hole we call West Virginia. That's where the Pentagon is storing the equipment for colonizing Mars. Between you and me and a handful of those who need to know, it won't leave the state. It's all for the first city of the brave new world.

Bob sucked in his lips and scowled. You're so far ahead of everybody."

"So what will it be, Chomuk? Want to hide in the bubble? Prefer the wild lands? I can tell you where you'll be safe from the winnowing. Guaranteed safety, currency in the tens of billions, and what else will six marbles cost me? Name your price, name your conditions, fix a schedule for delivery. The resources of the X-Club are at our disposal."

Bob stopped juggling the sea-green marble and held it to his eyes. "Your image appears to be upside down," he said, as if the observation would mean something to Knight.

"As it should be," Knight answered after a pause. "Are you trying to make a point?"

"Just an observation. A trick of perspective." Bob shrugged and paused, as if waiting for an explanation for the illusion. He was answered by an empty stare, so he continued, "Sometimes you see the vision and ignore the perspective. One person can claim, 'You're upside down.' The next guy can respond, 'I am not.' They're both right. They're both wrong. The truth is: you need the right perspective."

"Mr. Chomuk, may I be blunt? I believe you have issues with focus. Why did an alien race, superior to our own, choose a sadistic scatterbrain to share their language and magic? No offense intended. I think we can be honest with each other."

"Okay." Bob set the marble on the couch. "Let's be honest. My angels aren't some united empire of little green men, or gray, pencil-necked, bulbous-headed, bug-eyed butt probers. I ..." Bob ran his hand across his mouth like he was trying to erase a sentence on a blackboard. "Skip it. You've been helpful. To put it in fictional alien speech, 'Goodbye and thanks for the fish.'" Bob crossed his arms and stared into the TV.

On the screen, Knight tilted his head and sat up stiffly. He reached toward the camera and jiggled it, causing the image on Bob's screen to quake.

"A minute," Knight said in a hurried tone. "I have an issue."

Bob watched as Knight pulled a control board across his desk and examined his buttons. He pushed the board away and opened a drawer, retrieving a second wireless camera. "Can you hear me?" he asked while switching the first camera off and replacing it with the backup. "I've lost visual. Can you hear me? Did you unplug something?"

"I see you. I hear you," Bob answered. "Check your comm board. You'll see red lights. Your franchises have questions. Your inner circle is concerned. For the last four minutes ..." Bob checked his watch. "No, for the last three minutes and twenty-seven seconds, your former colleagues have seen and heard you as well."

Knight moved rapidly, jerking open another drawer and slamming it shut. "How?" he asked in a suddenly thin voice.

"Your 'unhackable' frequency isn't something you invented. You discovered it. Did you think it was unknown to the angels? You chose the mirage, Mr. Knight. A little rethinking your perspective on the facts would have done you some good."

Knight pulled one board after another from his drawer and desk spaces. He pressed one button at a time, then slapped at entire arrays, finally banging them against the desk. When a thumping sound, an insistent knocking noise, came through Bob's speakers, Knight slumped, then raised his head toward the ceiling, his eyes shut tight. Slowly, with exaggerated purposefulness, he removed his dead cigar from the ashtray and reached for his golden bull. He lit the cigar, holding his inhale for a long moment, as the pounding on the door ended. When he exhaled, he reached into a lower drawer of his desk and removed a gold-plated, .50 caliber Golden Eagle pistol. He hesitated momentarily. "They're going to blow the door," he said calmly.

Bob reached to turn off the TV screen, averting his eyes as he reached. An instant before he pressed the off button, a loud *crack!* resounded from the speakers in the living room.

Bob began to sweat before his finger reached the TV. He jerked forward awkwardly, as if it was he who suffered the gunshot. Tremors ran through his fingers and involuntary ticks in his legs caused him to spill onto the floor. He screamed and clutched his skull. Lying on the rug, his eyes rolled upward into his head. He passed out.

When he woke, he had space-time issues to sort through. Once again, a door was being insistently pounded on. A glance at the TV screen showed it was dark. "Sh- uh-uh ... sh-shot," he stammered, while feeling the side of his aching head. "H-howl on ... huh-how long?" He struggled to talk and think.

The pieces came together when a voice called from outside, insistent. "Dobbins! Open the door."

Now Bob was sure of where he was and aware of the time. He crawled to Hayak's revolver on the floor and struggled to his feet.

The cleaners had arrived.

83

FOURTEEN HOURS LATER

IT'S BEEN SAID, AND OFTEN REPEATED, initial news reports immediately following an event, are seventy-percent inaccurate. The phenomenon of honest eyewitness confusion has to do with the mind's need to fill in blanks, the bias of perspective, or the perspective of bias.

Some statements are simply lies. Pity the policeman who begins the process from eyewitness accounts to jury testimony. Pity the prosecutor, judge, and defense attorney who must play their roles in dissecting the information into usable portions. Pray for the jury who must identify the truth from the deconstructed parts.

In recording the events that followed after Bob opened the door for the cleaners, the first-on-scene officer struggled with his notes. He wrote in his conclusions:

> *The testimonies of four witnesses at the Asmudi crime scene were suspiciously consistent. The fifth witness, the shooter, was consistently incoherent.*

So, on the day after the shooting, New York Assistant Attorney General Mike Donahue interviewed responding officer Jack Wilde in his office, going over the officer's notes in preparation for follow-up meetings with New York Yankee lawyers, ATF agents, and an interrogation of a cab driver named Sandeep.

Donahue swung his legs up to the desk and crossed them at the ankles. "Officer Wilde, from the beginning, what happened here? Don't regurgitate. I want facts." He pointed a pen at the officer. "Go. What happened?"

"You mean at the fire or the shooting?" Wilde answered, while taking a notebook from his pocket. "I've got separate notes. I got the call for the shooting, but I was redirected to the fire while *en route*."

"Go with the fire, no notes. Did you arrive in time to see what was burning?"

"I saw nothing but white light and the occasional fiery orange bucket flying through the air." Wilde shrugged. "Like phosphorus. It was like a phosphorus fire without all the popping."

Donahue tapped the pen against his lips. "Nothing but light?"

"Yeah. Light, heat, and flaming buckets. The streetlight melted. The wires burned through. The concrete pole crumbled."

"You saw that?"

Wilde shifted on his feet. "Well, no. White light and buckets, yeah. But I left for the shooting scene before the fire trucks arrived. I left as soon as I could drive. I went snow blind from looking into the light."

"But you couldn't see what burned?"

"No, sir."

Donahue swung his legs off the desk and leaned forward. "Very good. You saw nothing at the fire. If your notes include anything you haven't seen, correct them. ATF is taking over the fire investigation. They don't want speculation. Understood?"

"Yes, sir."

"On to the shooting, then. You believe the three Asmudis and the ballplayer organized their stories before you arrived?"

"They had enough time to confer."

Donahue bounced his pen on the desktop and stared through narrowed eye slits at Wilde "So, what your notes should say is … what?"

"Uhh …" Wilde shook his head in confusion. "The witness statements were consistent?"

The bouncing pen stopped its *ratatat*ing on the desktop and Donahue grinned. "Excellent. Now, about the cab driver. What can you tell me?"

Wilde folded his notebook and pushed it into his shirt pocket. "Talk to him yourself. I don't think my notes will survive scrutiny. Let's say he was incoherently cooperative."

"That will work for me, Officer Wilde. Adjust your notes. We're going to get to the bottom of this."

84

ATF

"SO WHAT DO THE FORENSICS SAY?"

"The liquids expelled by the explosion are cleaning supplies with insufficient burn temperatures to melt the engine block. The high heat source is still undetermined."

"Tabloids say it was a crashed UFO. What's your guess?"

"Military grade phosphorus cannister, thermite device, or thirty-watt laser. Any of those or combination of those would disintegrate the vehicle."

"Any reports of a drone in the area?"

"No, sir."

"Are there missing phosphorus or thermite canisters in our inventory?"

"No, sir, but we know the phosphorus canisters have been manufactured in numbers greater than the inventory."

"Are there human remains on scene?"

"No, sir."

"Wow. That's hot. We're lucky it happened in a warehouse area. What do we know?"

"Nothing, officially."

"When you release the statement, scrub all speculation. Eliminate all references to unknown. Replace the phrasing as unidentified. Let the UFO folks speculate."

"Yes, sir."

85

LAUREL CANYON

"WHAT'S THE SOURCE?"

"Knight. Every erasure we've found, so far, originated in his office."

"The entire Dreamcatcher program is erased?"

"The cryogenics unit is a wasteland. The electronic mapping is scrambled. The OGs are gone. We'll have to do some electronic forensics before we can remap ourselves."

"The Skinner project?"

"No issues outside the Soma angle. We feel the missing Kurtwood records are a dead end. The lemming team will have to set a new timetable."

"Personnel losses?"

"We can't locate Agent Dobbins or a New York cleaner crew. We believe Dobbins activated his phosphorus pyro in a New York warehouse district".

"Check each warehouse in the district. Find out why he was there."

Yes, sir."

"Anything else I should know?"

"Yes, about the basic communication grid. We need to work by courier until we come up with something. We can't trust internet traffic."

"Jesus."

"He's not taking our calls."

"That's not funny."

"Sorry, sir. Gallows humor. The franchises are going to drag us to hell."

86

THE WAY SANDEEP SAW IT

SANDEEP SAT SILENT IN THE INTERVIEW ROOM while waiting for his interrogator, but when Donahue entered and introduced himself, he made sure the prosecutor knew he had grievances.

"Sandeep is sitting in jail, a sweaty man, unclean in his personal space, possibly infected with lice from violent men who are caged for God only knows what reason. His wife is no doubt wailing at home over his incarceration. Sandeep's legal firearm is illegally seized, his testimony is questioned, his personal clothing is unraveled, pawed upon, and searched without permission. Unfamiliarity with the English language has proven to be an issue with jailers. Hopabout Cassidy has never been treated this way. Deputy Sandeep will expect he, too, will never have been treated this way."

Donahue set a folder on the table and slid into his seat. He removed a pen from his pocket and tapped it on the table, studying the face of the man sitting across from him.

Sandeep stared back, his defiant expression frozen on his face.

Finally, stare-down complete, Donahue began his interrogation. "I think I have a clear picture of your case, Mr. Sandeep. You're quite the hero, aren't you?"

"Sandeep is only a deputized man and the captain of his cab. He is not a vigilante shooter of thin forbearance. He is not a hero." The words came out argumentatively.

Donahue spoke soothingly. "I want to start with what eyewitnesses have said. You drove the young Miss Asmudi from the airport to her home on Kensington street. Is that right?"

"Sandeep has said so, many times."

"The young lady spoke to you about a house guest. She was suspicious of his behavior?"

"She believed him to be most monstrous."

Donahue removed a sheaf of paper from his folder and crossed through a line on the page with his pen. "Later that night, you had a second fare for the Kensington address. Is that correct?"

"It is so. The young lady's suitor. He had flowers. As he is a man known in his community, I took his concern for her to be well founded."

"You're talking about Mr. Freddy McPheeters?"

"Yes, the woebegone Yankee man. It was he who asked me to wait and witness."

"I see." Donahue chose his words carefully. "Terrific. Yes or no, did Mr. McPheeters bring the Asmudi family to your taxi in an impaired state?"

"Oh, no. Mr. McPheeters was not impaired. It was the three unconscious, smelly, blue-in-the face, gaseous, and limp-bodied Asmudis. Each was most impaired to a degree I believe I have previously mentioned."

"Yes, sir. I misspoke. Thank you for clearing that up. Let's move on. For the sake of brevity, I'd like to skip ahead. Mr. McPheeters takes the Asmudis in ..." Donahue checked paperwork in his folder before continuing. "Mr. McPheeters drives Po Asmudi's car, and the three Asmudis, to the nearby Waffle Den. Correct?"

"That is so."

"You drive your taxi into the garage at the address on Kensington. To do what? Investigate? Shoot a man in ambush?"

"On Sandeep's cab, the flag was up and Sandeep was giving his passengers the protection of his pledge. Having been deputized to proceed to the corral and scout for the presence of the danger man, Sandeep could not ride into the sunset."

"I see. I think that's commendable. Tell me about the truck."

"The truck parked at the gate."

"What kind of truck?"

"A box truck of industrial design."

"There were men in the truck?"

"Two men exit and carry long bags into shadows by entry door."

"Two men?" Donahue put an elbow on the table and leaned his head against his hand. With his other hand, he drew his pen across more typed lines and smiled across the table. "Go on. Do you know what these men were doing in the dark?"

"Sandeep cannot see into the dark. Two voices whispered."

"Could you hear what they said?"

"Sandeep hear, 'mumble, mumble, where are others?' Sandeep hear long zippers zipping, more mumbles, then a voice of excitable youth. This voice say, 'Hey, you should be checking out Swiss Army belt.' A bossy man say, 'Don't play with laundry.' Sandeep is not knowing from mumbles, zipping, laundry, and army belts."

Donahue lifted another sheet of paper from his folder and traced across the page with his pen, as if reading as the pen moved. When the pen stopped moving, he tapped hard once and sat back in his chair. "This is important, sir. Who is the danger man?"

"Danger Man is a man of aliases. He was the house guest of young miss's fearfulness. He carries papers that say he is Van Asmudi. He is the man your jailers say to be Alvin Chipmunk of those who are wanted list. He is the man Freddy McPheebles has been warned against. He is the man called Dobbins who answered the door when men in the dark can't find all of laundry. He is the man Sandeep had to draw upon and shoot down like a dog with rabid foams. What choice would be a betterment for the outcome? When Mr. McFeebbles and the Asmudis pulled into the driveway, Danger Man stepped into the light and his revolver glinted most menacingly."

"The revolver wasn't loaded, Mr. Sandeep."

"Mine was."

"Did you disturb the crime scene before officers arrived?"

"Sandeep would iterate the perspective that the crime scene was disturbing to all of us."

Donahue crossed through lines of type on the top sheaf of paper, then he placed the stack back into the folder. "Just one more issue, sir, then you're free to go. The men in the courtyard. The truck on the street. When did they leave the scene?"

"The men in the courtyard, they scuffle together. One man, he is anger-whispering to the man who knock upon the door. 'No names!'

"Sandeep hears sounds of slapping frenzy and cries of pain. These sounds end with the bossy man telling the youthful, unfocused man to take the laundry to the truck. Sandeep hear a door on truck open and close. A third man also anger-whispers. 'What is problems?' Sandeep sneak along wall like a mongoose stalking cobras and ..."

"Mr. Sandeep. When did the men in the truck leave the scene? Was it before or after you shot the Danger Man?"

"I was approaching just such a declaration. First, boss man have excitable, demanding eruptions. 'Where is more laundry?' he ask. 'I told you, no names,' he growls. 'Leave the damned belt alone,' he say.

"Finally, boss man, he say, 'I don't like messy. Hey, I tell you stop playing with damned belt. We get hell out.' So, they go.

"Next, Asmudis arrive. One car it drive up, one truck it drive away. Danger Man, he approach the car, Sandeep lay him down, dead. All is wailing and grief agitation until explosion. That is the order of events. Sandeep has seen such things in Kashmir. Still, it is shocking all of us."

Donahue stood suddenly and offered Sandeep his hand. "Alvin Chomuk died with a lethal dart in his pocket. I'm satisfied you rid the world of a criminal ready to do harm. However, a warning: There is an ongoing Federal investigation into the explosion. National security is involved. If you're contacted by federal agencies, cooperate. If anyone else asks, I'm deputizing you to remain silent upon risk of deportation or incarceration. Am I clear?"

"Sandeep understands."

"You're free to go. Your wife and Mr. McPheeters are waiting for you. New York thanks you, and the Yankees wish to thank you for protecting their player and organization. I believe they have season tickets for you."

"Bothers." Sandeep scratched his head. "If they can't make my wife happy with Metropitan tickets, tell them Sandeep has enough. They may donate the unwanted tickets to the childless orphans' fund."

87

TODAY'S NEWS

AILEEN MILTON PICKED AT HER BREAKFAST OMELET. Travel weariness was setting in and she recognized the symptoms. Irritability, dead legs, and yearning for a familiar bed.

When Dr. Milton joined her after his trip to the lobby, he waved a copy of the *St. Louis Post Dispatch*. "Look, I found a real newspaper," he said as he sat and evaluated his fancy fruit-laden waffles. "The old trick still works. If you want your food delivered, leave the table."

"Give me the local events section, dear. Maybe we should stretch our legs and stay another night. Are the Cardinals in town?"

Henry thumbed through the paper and pulled out the sports page. "Hmm. What's it been, four days since Freddy McPheeters signed with the Yanks? He's already been traded."

"The bum? Who's surprised. He couldn't hit a ball if you put it on a T. Where's he going?"

The doctor separated the events section and passed it across the table. "He'll be playing for the Angels."

"Mmm." Aileen rolled her eyes. "You should have ordered the omelet. How's your kiddy-candy pile of sugared fruit and whipped cream?"

"Life's too short to avoid kiddy candy with a whipped topping. It's a vacation-mode splurge.

Aileen reached across the table to sample the waffles. "Life just trips merrily along, doesn't it? Hey, did you know Ulysses Grant has a farm in St. Louis?"

"No." Dr. Milton snatched a cheesy piece of omelet. "I thought he was dead."

Aileen unfolded her section of the paper and used it as a barrier between her and her husband. "Too late to rethink your order now. If you reach across my wall, I'll stab you with a fork."

"Don't antagonize a man on a sugar rush, babe. He might not take you to the Cardinal game."

"They're in town?"

"Yes."

"Life is good. I'll trade you some of my omelet for Cardinal tickets." Aileen waited for an answer, but her husband was staring at his plate, trance-like. "Two cents," she said.

"Oh, I was just thinking about Freddy. Let's find out which minor league park he's playing in and set sail to watch a game."

"Really? Why?"

"I want to catch up on the news."

88

THE LAST TIME OTIS SAW CASPI?

SIX HOUSEBOATS, LASHED TOGETHER in the shade of a cove on the banks of the mighty Mississippi River, set the stage for the islanders' first campfire away from home. It was a moment of familiarity for the wanderers, but small comforts are no match for fear of the great unknown.

As the campfire went on, the group grew increasingly displeased with Huana's refusal to reveal the location of their destination. The questions were always answered with the same litany.

"We'll be cold in the winter. We'll eat different fishes. We'll have timber and stone. Hiding will be the first skill taught to the young. Where we're going, there's no path to a competent military."

Huana's lack of clarity was wearing thin. It wasn't long before the mention of light attendance was addressed. Of the two hundred and fifty refugees, fifty-seven rendezvoused for the campfire. Another forty were toiling in the fields of Kansas, waiting to hear the location of their next rendezvous spot. Six unused boats in dry dock accounted for the missing. Much of the tribe stayed in Panama, unwilling to embrace a culture without *Ayahuasca*.

"Oh, no!" a voice called louder than the murmurings at the campfire. "Look around. None of our Shaman have made the trip." A moment of searching the faces around the fire confirmed it.

The tribe wavered between nervously worried and sky-is-falling hopelessness.

A chorus bounced gloom around the campfire like a wave in a stadium. We're going to die in freezing weather. We'll fall ill with new fevers. We're going to starve to death. Our boats will be swallowed in the muddy river."

The unhappy buzz reached a peak, then began to soften into a hum. One at a time, the refugees went quiet as they noticed little Baba standing next to the fire with her arms raised skyward. When the hum turned to silence, a wind gusted through the overhead trees. Rattling leaves mimicked the rise and fall of applause.

When the leaves stilled, Baba put her stamp on the tribe's move into the future. "The short life is a fatal life," she said with certainty. "I'm your Shaman and I prescribe courage. Let's get on with it." Baba drilled down to the basic bottom.

A period of quiet rethinking followed.

Otis, who felt like an outsider in Huana's world, didn't speak at the campfire, and he didn't stay for the conclusion. While watching Caspi from across the fire, he became distracted by a twinkle of blue light on the shore.

From boat to boat, then across the gangplank to muddy soil, Otis walked toward the familiar gleam. A family of nutrena squealed and dashed away from his slogging feet, but he barely noticed. When a warm yellow light burst on and cut through the mangrove curtain, he quickened his pace, maintaining his balance in the slippery mud by pulling himself along with slicing handfuls of saw grass.

Finally, resting against a mossy log, Otis looked behind him and tried to find Caspi in the crowd of a lively campfire. "My ride is here," he whispered. "We'll talk later."

*   *   *

When the *shem* landed, Otis was in the dark, overlooking the same crazy, patternless lights he had observed from Po's rooftop two decades earlier. In spite of the *fweep*, and following gust of wind breezing through the opened cockpit, he waited in his seat until dawn's light exposed a hatch on the roof of the house on Kensington street.

After a dizzying look toward the ground, Otis climbed onto the roof. "Shaman says get on with it."

An hour after rattling the walls and bursting into the closet of a guest bedroom, Otis was sitting in the old Bill Elliott studio with Roberta. They listened to the latest recordings on the blue marble.

With a shaky voice, Otis repeated Baba's words of wisdom to the grieving Roberta. "The short life is a fatal life."

"Yeah, but I want to hear more than the duh of it." Roberta sat in Bill's old chair and set the marble on the desk. "I want to know where this so-called chain is going. I want to know why the marble belongs to me. I want to know where the new marbles are going. I need to talk to my father about it."

Otis looked confused. "The marble belongs to you?"

"It rolled up to my feet, humming like a stressed-out gyroscope, then went silent. Doesn't it know where to go?" Roberta spun the orb like a top. "We are going to make more, aren't we?"

"Yeah, Berti. That's the plan."

Roberta put her palm down on the spinning marble and stared intensely at Otis. "How many marbles? How many chains are going to offshoot from this one? Are things getting too complicated to pretend we have free will?"

Otis looked around the studio, from the broken panel on the wall, to the simulated fireplace, towards Bobby's sculptures dangling from the ceiling, and finally to the corner of the desk where Icarus and the glass angel lay side by side, retired from the story of their past. "There's a lot of stories. There's more to come. Let's wait to see what happens."

"That's weak, man. You have a weak philosophy." Roberta opened the drawer containing the ceramic coil and jiggled the bin above it. "Fresh laughing weed," she said. "Join me?"

"Sure. Pass the tube. I'm taking the day off."

Five minutes later, Otis slid deeper into his seat and drawled, "Wow. You should get the radio show up and running again."

"What would I talk about? How would I ever get a license?"

"Do what Bob did. Broadcast over the top of the big stations. Don't fixate on demolicans and republicrats. Tell stories. Organize your vision for a new Continental Congress. Somebody has to do it. It will drive them crazy trying to trace the source." Otis beamed like he just spoke inspired thoughts.

"Pipe dreams, Otis. It's just pipe dreams."

No more words were spoken in the room until the tube made a couple more passes. Inhaling and exhaling were the only audible competitions for the air conditioner.

After a while, Roberta leaned forward and stood the glass angel upright. She perched the body of Icarus against her wing and smiled.

"I like it," she said. "Isn't that what my father would do?"

89

WORDS FROM TWO FUNERALS

A CEREMONY CELEBRATING THE LONG LIFE of Van Asmudi drew a large crowd of attendees under the shadow of Mount Ararat in Armenia. The weather was perfect; the location ideal.

Hayak spoke a few words. "Is mystery to me. Where will winds blow a single ash from soul of Van Asmudi to rest atop his beloved mountain? Never will we know. Is not so important. Already he is home."

At a smaller gathering in the shaded courtyard of the big house on Kensington, Roberta spoke while laying a tribute next to the bench under the oak tree. "It doesn't feel like we're leaving you behind. It feels like you've run on ahead."

Otis looked at the engraving on the marker and gave Roberta a hug. "In a little while, we'll have the band back together," he said. "I love the gesture."

The tribute, a small box made of polished marble, stood out in the gravel around the bench. On its lid were the words: *Be at Beace, Biller Bee.*

Inside, the box was empty.

EPILOGUE

IN THE YEAR 2045

R ICHARD HOOKER STRUGGLED TO ANSWER THE QUESTION: "What
brings you here?"

"Where am I?" Richard pulled his arm from beneath his pile
of blankets and recoiled in pain when he tried to grip his pillow.

"Careful. I think you broke your wrist. The knee isn't looking
so good either."

Hooker looked around the room. A pot-bellied stove in the
center, its door open, radiated red from its belly. The hot glow
looked inviting. A steaming pot sat atop the old antique. Rustic
walls, made of rough-hewn wooden beams and columns of stone,
gave the room a look of an old cabin. Through the windows, in the
glow of a porch light, he noticed snow was falling.

Turning again to look into the face of the elderly man sitting
at his bedside, he asked again: "Where am I?"

"In the summer, this is the south float camp on the Eleven
Point river. Nobody floats in the winter. Got coffee if you want.
There's nothing else to offer. We gotta take all the food out at end
of season or the raccoons will tear the place up."

"Right." Hooker's face changed expression from confused to enlightened. "Raccoons. I remember. It was those damn raccoons." He started to thrust his right hand toward the man in the chair, but then pulled it back. "Richard Hooker. Nature lover, adventurer, free-lance writer. I'd shake your hand, but you know, broken wrist."

"Folks here call me Oats. Together with my wife, we own the O&C bait shop down by the bridge. We watch after the float camp in the winter. Can you hold a coffee cup with your left hand?"

Hooker braced his elbows against the bed and tried to push himself into a sitting position. When he pushed with his feet, his knee forced him to collapse with a yelp of pain.

"Hang on there. I got his figured out."

Oats leaned over the prone man and slid his arm behind his neck, lifting his head and shoulders while piling a stack of pillows behind his back.

"Good enough?"

"Raccoons," Hooker murmured without answering. "I sat up most of the night, trying to keep the little thieves from raiding my campsite."

"Yep, it's best to hang anything edible from the trees. Hope you like it black. No cream or sugar in the house." Oats poured two cups.

"I know about that. Those thieves kept getting into my Jon-boat and fooling with everything. I had some gear I didn't want to go missing. The little bastards opened my tackle box. I thought if I scared them away a few times, they'd give up and I could get some sleep."

Oats set a cup down on the end table by the bed. "Give it a minute. It's boiling hot. So, it's fishing that brought you here in the middle of winter?"

"No, not really. I do love a fresh-caught trout roasted over a campfire, though." Hooker pursed his lips and looked Oats in the eyes. "It's the mystic nature of the Irish Wilderness. The mysteries. The history. You know, bushwhackers and union raiders. The failed Shangri-La. The allure of curiosity. I've floated this river border a few times. The first bend, after setting in grabs you. The cold spring water, bubbling to the surface, meeting the hot air and making a curtain of cool mist over the water is like a doorway to the beauty. It's like ..." Hooker paused. "Do you think the place is magical?"

"Magical? Like magical, indescribable beauty? For sure. Dangerous, too."

"No … no." Hooker dipped a finger into his coffee and put it to his mouth. "Yep, that's hot. No, I shouldn't say magical. Those hills are hiding real magic."

"Magic? To me, magic is something I don't understand, or a trick that fools the mind."

"I know what I saw."

"Okay, Mr. Hooker, did you come here looking for magic?"

"No, I came here to find who was living in the hills. I've heard voices and laughing on past trips down the river. Voices too high in the rugged stretches for casual campers. Perhaps remnants of the lost Irish living up there? Maybe, still some Indians that took refuge from the culling. I brought spelunking gear to dig into some of those caves."

"You are a romantic adventurer, aren't you?"

"And a realist. When I return, I'm going to set up cameras in every little winding canyon, spring site, and clearing I can hike to. I'm going to set up a base camp and use drones. I know what I saw, and it ain't normal."

"What did you see?"

"You'd laugh at my icicle brain again. I'll wait until I have pictures."

Oats walked to the woodpile by the front door and chose two small pieces to put in the stove. "We're going to be here awhile. Normally, the county would send an ambulance to come get you, but they cut the funding for it when they closed the hospital. It didn't take long for the hospital to go belly-up when insurance rates and red lining left folks around here without a means to pay. The wife had to drive into Doniphan to bring help. There's a fellow named Dunham who bought the radiology truck in the auction. He'll want gas money to get you to Poplar Bluff and whatever you'd want to donate. Probably gonna take some X-rays before he moves you. There's time for the tellin'. I'm not laughin'. What did you see?"

"You are going to laugh. I would. But what I saw … what I saw and heard. I moved away from my campfire and sat on a log nearby the boat. I sat there with some good chunks of rock and waited for the raccoons to come back. When they did, I let out a growl and pitched the stones at them. They scattered in a hurry.

"That worked a couple times. About the third time they came out, I thought they were learning. They crept out slower and disappeared into the brush as soon as I growled. A little later, one big 'coon stood his ground and sat up on his hind legs, staring at me. I growled again and it didn't budge. I hit him square in the chest with a stone and he hissed. He hissed, then walked slowly into the brush, glancing back at me as he went. That scared me a little bit. I thought maybe they were learning I wasn't something to fear.

"After they didn't return for a long while, I began to rethink. Maybe they did learn to stay away, or maybe they were making plans for a different approach.

"The thought hit me: I bet they're all gathered in the brush, watching me. Waiting for me to get in my sleeping bag. I shined my flashlight around the campsite and stiffened up when I heard a rustling noise behind me. I swiveled around and pointed the light right into a pack of maybe ten of them, all about three feet behind the log. When the light hit them, they scattered. The next thing I saw ..." Hooker dropped his eyes and began to rub his swollen wrist.

"Well go on," Oats said with impatience.

"Feet and knees. When the raccoons scattered, I saw feet and knees. Little ones. Naked. I jumped to my feet and raised my flashlight. There in the cold was a little girl — no, not a little girl — a ... a being. A fairy. She was naked as a jaybird, shoulders hunched forward, with both her hands knotted under her chin, smiling. I took another step back and she said, 'I sorry.'

"That's when I stumbled. Off-balance, I stepped into the water and tried to catch myself against the boat. All I managed to do was push the boat into the stream as I toppled, slow motion, into the water. I felt the current grab onto me. I reached a hand to hold onto the gravel, trying to slow my drift., but the boat was full into the current and taking off. It ran right over me as I held on to it with one hand. I managed to keep my grip, even after my head struck a rock and bounced up into a second collision with the bottom of the boat."

Hooker reached up to his temple with his left hand and felt the area of impact.

"It's not much of a bump," Oats said. "Dunham will look at it when he gets here. So that's how you got separated from your boat?"

"Yes. I should have held on to it for dear life. When the boat did a half-spin, I was able to surface again. I miscalculated when I saw the campfire fading away. The current grabbed on like wind to a kite. I panicked. I think I was in shock from seeing what I saw, the clenching cold of water getting through my winter clothes and realizing I was a victim of some self-induced dumb-assery."

"Don't be too hard on yourself, fellah. Being whisked away from the campfire would be my first concern. I'd let go of that runaway puppy too, if I was you. In the bang-bang of events, you had a natural reaction."

Hooker tested his coffee again with his finger and noticed a line of chairs in the shadows. "My clothes?"

"Yep. You was sure bundled up."

"That's why I couldn't get back to shore. The weight of all that, waterlogged, and the heavy hiking boots, like lead. When I washed under a root wad, it was like trying to fight my way through wooden tentacles. If the fairy hadn't glided up in her aluminum canoe ..." Hooker brought his coffee to his lips and sipped. "Ugh. This is instant."

"Ain't you the choosy beggar. What's a fairy doin' with an aluminum canoe? Why didn't she just fly over to you?"

Hooker didn't respond. He pressed his warm coffee cup against his swollen wrist, and said, "I remember now. The wrist was broke when she pulled me up to the top of the root wad. Right through that tangle of roots. She has to be as strong as Hercules. No. Muscles like a howler monkey, she said. Not a fairy. A shaman. She told me she was a shaman just before she put a rope under my arm pits and rolled me back into the water. I couldn't talk. My teeth were chattering like I had a mouth full of jackhammers."

"'You could ride here with me,' she said as she pulled me tight to the stern. 'But, it's a long trip. You'll find the air is kill-dead cold. The water is warmer but it's going to get bumpy on the rocks. Let yourself sleep. Shaman's orders.' With that, she pushed into the current and I drifted off. I don't know what happened to my knee."

"A fairy, roaming naked through the wilderness in the middle of winter. She has a magically appearing canoe, the strength of Hercules, a medical degree, and what else? Pet raccoons? Are you really going to tell that story?"

"I'm not a fool, Mr. Oats. I'll have pictures and video before I do. This isn't like looking for Bigfoot in the entire northern Pacific region. This is finding something in an area of a few thousand acres. I'll get it done."

"Okay, Hooker." Oats took the coffee cup from Hooker's hand and set it on the table. "You're a seasoned spelunker?"

"I'm experienced."

"What do you do if you crawl into some cave, maybe the first human ever to be where you are. What do you do if you find a crystal? A big, rare, beautiful crystal that takes your breath away? Do you chop away and show the world what you found? Do you assess its monetary value and decide to sell it? Do you let it stay? Show respect for proportion in sensibilities? Leave it to thrill another explorer and test his respect for magic?"

"What is it you're getting at? You want to know if I would succumb to temptation, or follow the code?"

"I'll stop with the games. You found something rare, beautiful, and supernaturally magical. I call it Ozark blue magic. It's real. You have to walk away and hold the memory in your heart. You can't be tempted to own it."

"What are you saying?"

"Up in those hills there are a few remnants from the Irish. They've been betrayed by their neighbors, their government, butchered by union soldiers and blood-hungry bushwhackers. They live among remnants of an Indian tribe. They live in peace, now. They're happy, and they are protected by magic. Leave them the hell alone."

"You know this? What do they do up there?"

"Think of it as a lost world. What happens in the lost world stays in the lost world. If the temptation is too much … Let me tell you in the words your fairy told me. 'You'll be true sorry.'"

"I hear you, Oats. But what if? The world could use some magic right now. My fairy didn't impress me as someone dangerous."

"She's not. She's the ying. We call the yang — Evil Eye. She gives one warning. I don't want to know what happens if you ignore it."

Hooker searched Oat's eyes and laughed. You're pulling my leg."

On the other side of the bed, a hand reached across his face and pinched his nose shut. Startled, he recoiled. He slapped at the hand with his injured wrist and yelped in pain. A face leaned into him and he clenched with pain in his knee as he gasped in shock. When he stopped his struggle, he stared into an angry eye with the piercing power of determined malevolence. An eye patch covered the other eye.

"I could start with pulling your leg, Dude. Right off your body. But I would like to work my way up to that." The scary, disfigured face smiled. The creature put a hand to her eye patch and moaned a laugh. "Or, I could show you my evil eye and scramble your little mind. This is my warning. I will find you wherever you slink away to if you decide to challenge my magic."

The fingers let go their grip of Hooker's nose and he turned toward Oats in wide-eyed panic. "What the ..."

What the what?" Oats shrugged like he was confused.

Hooker swung his eyes back to the other side of the bed and no one was there. Turning his attention back to Oats, he asked, "You didn't see that? You didn't see her? Evil Eye?"

"Oh, God no. You caught her attention. I'm sorry. Only you can help yourself now."

"I wasn't going to tell." He swung his head around again and spoke to the wall. "I'm not going to tell. Never."

A light played across the wall and Hooker recoiled again. "What is it?"

"That's Dunham coming down the driveway. I'll introduce you to my wife, Caspi. Get yourself together. You'll be fine."

It took a while. Bruises not seen against blue skin when Hooker was undressed were starting to show. Dunham applied a temporary brace to the knee and wrapped the wrist. Upon being loaded into the makeshift ambulance, Hooker gave effusive praise to "all involved". A promise of a generous donation for Dunham's services was promised.

"I want to write up a story on you, Mr. Dunham. I think you might get some money coming in when people find out what you're doing. I'm glad to stumble on something worth telling the world about."

As the doors closed on the battered man, he winked at Oats. It was a promise for a shared secret, kept.

As the van pulled around the bend, Oats yelled into the cabin. "Okay, Huana, you can come out from under the bed now."

"Dude, I don't know how you talked me into this." She hugged her sister and said, "Come join us at the cave spring this summer. Let me know if Berti ever found a way to get those other marbles to do anything."

ABOUT THE AUTHOR

Paul S. Moore was born in the Missouri Ozarks, raised in St. Louis, and eventually settled in the sand of central Florida. He calls each of these places home.

His inner mix of hillbilly river rat, lowlands daydreamer, sand road hermit, and reader of nineteenth-century history writers form the base of a non-elite education. These roots allow imagination to turn historic events into serendipitous thoughts. Those thoughts organize into stories, and stories become novels.

With the remedial help of a good critique group, and the birth of publishing companies that read a manuscript without asking first, "What are your credentials?", he's found a voice to share those stories.

ALSO IN THIS SERIES

RULES OF THE CAMPFIRE
BOOK ONE FROM STORIES IN GLASS
by Paul S. Moore

If you woke up one day and realized you had memories from more than seventy lives, fluid in every language you'd ever spoken, and recalled all the texts you'd ever read, would you wonder why?

SONGS IN A BOX
BOOK TWO FROM STORIES IN GLASS
by Paul S. Moore

This time, the enemy is human.

Available from Water Dragon Publishing in
hardcover, trade paperback, and digital editions
waterdragonpublishing.com